Gilded Dreams

Gilded Dreams

The Journey to Suffrage

Donna Russo Morin

ISBN 978-0-578-69979-0

Other Works by Donna Russo Morin

GILDED SUMMERS

BIRTH: Once, Upon a New Time Book One

PORTRAIT OF A CONSPIRACY:
Da Vinci's Disciples Book One

THE COMPETITION:
Da Vinci's Disciples Book Two

THE FLAMES OF FLORENCE:
Da Vinci's Disciples Book Three

THE KING'S AGENT

TO SERVE A KING

THE SECRET OF THE GLASS

THE COURTIER OF VERSAILLES

Praise for GILDED DREAMS

"Packed with intrigue, textured world-building, and the fascinating rise of the women's rights movement, GILDED DREAMS is a hit!"
-Heather Webb, USA Today Bestselling Author

"Donna Russo Morin is a great writer who has done her research well and presented a lively and dynamic story. GILDED DREAMS is historical fiction at its highest and all should enjoy the story!!!"
-Crystal Reviews

"This wonderful story is both gripping and emotionally charged throughout. It can be read without having read the first but readers may long to read GILDED SUMMERS as well because of the quality writing in this one. An amazing book."
-Kate Clifford Eminhizer, Manager of Pamunkey Regional Library

"A very intriguing read. The two main characters were very well written... it captured my attention within the first chapters with the sinking of the Titanic that took the lives of Pearl's family. It is apparent that Donna Russo Morin has done her research on the time period and the movement itself... a book worth revisiting. Five Stars!"
-Readers' Favorite

century and how few rights they had at the time. I have long been a fan of this author. She knows how to vibrantly tell a historical story while still staying true to the historical side of things. Her passion for the Newport area shines through in her words. *Gilded Summers* is an insightful glimpse into an age and place where women, even women of power, were merely objects and ornamentation. It is also an inspiring story of two women who chose to buck convention and live lives of their choosing; women who pioneered the way for the women of future generations."

-The True Book Addict

"This is remarkable historical fiction that this reviewer highly recommends. Donna Russo Martin's writing has evolved into something more meaningful, serious but joyfully engaging, and memorable in a creative, new style sure to endear her to readers of all ages! Wonder-full!"

-Crystal Book Reviews

"A wonderful peek at the Gilded Age of Newport, RI, filled with the Astors and Vanderbilts and a bit of mystery."

-Baer Books Blog

For my sons...

For all my descendants to come...

May you understand my fight,

May you always fight the good fight.

Donna Russo Morin

"I long to hear that you have declared an independency. And, by the way, in the new code of laws which I suppose it will be necessary for you to make, I desire you would remember the ladies and be more generous and favorable to them than your ancestors. Do not put such unlimited power into the hands of the husbands. Remember, all men would be tyrants if they could. If particular care and attention is not paid to the ladies, we are determined to foment a rebellion, and will not hold ourselves bound by any laws in which we have no voice or representation."

Abigail Adams, in a letter to her husband, John Adams, written March 31, 1776

The fight for the suffrage rights of women,

the battle to have our voices heard,

began in earnest on July 19, 1848.

It would be a 72-year journey.

This is a tale of the last eight years.

"You bring shame upon us all!" She accused me, her spittle stinging my face. "Get out. Get out of my house this instant!" I knew my pointed finger shook on the end of my outstretched arm. I could not defeat it. I would not lower it. It is the last thing I remember... that and her raised fist.

Ginevra

April 16, 1912

The day started like any other. It would soon become like none other that came before.

I made my way down to breakfast, having stayed in bed too long. My husband had the children in hand, giving me leisure I rarely indulged. The sound of my daughter laughing at him in the other room woke me. Such sounds to be woken by... a child's laughter and the bird song just outside my window, bright as the spring sunshine.

"No, Father, I cannot wear one of your ties to school, silly."

I had lain there, listening, letting the joy they brought me slowly bring me wakefulness. With such happiness filling the house—my heart and mind—I made my way to the kitchen and the small table in the sunny corner of the room.

As was my way, I picked up the *Providence Journal* to read as I ate my corn flakes and sipped my coffee. I had learned English by reading when my papa and I had come to this country from Italy. I would keep reading, keep learning. What I learned with one look at the headline, shattered the joyous morn into tiny shards of bloody glass.

"LINER TITANIC, AFTER CRASH WITH ICEBERG,
FOUNDERS OFF NEW FINLAND. 1200 DROWN"

My coffee cup fell to the floor; I didn't feel the hot sting of liquid on my flesh though I would later bear the scars of it upon my ankles.

I dropped like a stone, somehow on a chair, well-placed by fate.

They had been traveling on that ship. Had they survived?

I read the names, the far-too-long list of them, as fast as I could – those belonging to some I had once watched from the anonymity of my maid's uniform, through spectacles of contempt, and some that had loomed large in my adolescence.

My face grew wet; the hand on my lips trapped the sobs in my throat.

One of the first names was that of John Jacob Astor, of *the* Astors, son of *the* Mrs. Astor, Caroline Schermerhorn Astor who had summered in Newport, whose gown I had once cleaned while the seamstress at The Beeches.

The name of George Widener was familiar as well. They had just started building his cottage down at the very tip of the island, the wealthy tip. Would it ever be built now that he and his son Harry floated like dead fish in the cold Atlantic sea?

The names, the very letters that formed them, blurred in my watery sight… William Dulles, who lived on Narragansett Avenue… the entire Clinch Smith family, whose house sat on the corner of Harrison and Halidon Avenues… Karl Howel Behr and Richard Norris Williams, two tennis champions I had watched play at the Casino, two men I would never watch again.

I kept reading, faster, ever faster.

I cried out. I did not remember the words… if there were words. I did not think or care that it was a wail echoing around the world.

To see their names upon the list was like seeing my own.

At once, she captured my heart and mind, squeezing both with clenched fingers of grief.

On the list of the dead – those who had gone down on the Titanic – were her parents, her brother and his wife… my dearest Pearl's entire family. Gone, all gone.

"Osborn!" My screech, at last released, broke the stillness the morning had brought.

Footfalls of all weights thundered over my head… those of my husband, my children. Yet the sound of them together was not loud enough to bury the savagery of my sobs.

"My darling, what is it?" My husband skidded into the small breakfast nook, falling upon his knees at my feet. The worried care in his blue eyes was not enough to give me the power of speech. I shoved the newspaper with its horrifying headline, creased and ragged where I had crushed it in my fists, into his hands. My shaking finger demanded his eyes fall to the bottom of the list of the dead, the very long list.

"What's wrong, Father?"

Felix came to stand beside me; I could not let him see my face. Angelina squeezed her tiny self between us. My mind spared a fleeting thought for them… at eight and six, how would they be scarred by this tragedy?

Osborn's wrinkled brow and probing eyes now sat on bloodless skin, on a head dropping to his chest. To see my grief upon his face nearly broke me; the heaviness of it pressed down harder upon my shoulders.

Pushing against its weight, I stood. Osborn's hand flashed out, taking my arm, steadying me as I wavered.

"I must go to her, I…" The muddled command I demanded of myself scrambled like eggs with those of my duties, my children, my work.

"Of course you must," Osborn assured me as he so often did, no matter what he might be encouraging me about, it seemed. He was the ease of the turning of a light switch, and not a lamp with only one bulb but a many-tiered chandelier.

"The children, school—"

7

"I will take care of everything."

He put his forehead against mine. That had been our first intimate contact, so many years ago when we had met, the night we stepped out together. I thought he would kiss me. Instead, he gave me this and the sweetness of it had bloomed inside me. We offered it to each other ever since when one or both of us was in need.

"I will phone Anna and Laura as well. They will understand."

"*Sì, sì*, they will," I muttered. My employers – wives, mothers, Italian immigrants, business owners – yes, they would understand.

My hands clenched the fabric covering my body, the silk of my housecoat instead of a dress. I had forgotten what I wore.

Osborn's firm hands fell upon my shoulders, turning me toward the stairs.

"Go, go dress."

I nodded, I went. I moved but couldn't feel my feet upon the floor.

Somehow I dressed, thoughts flashing to the mess of breakfast. Hazel would not come till nine. She never did; we never minded.

I don't think I put on the right hat for the dress I wore – or the shoes, for that matter. My only thought was that I needed shoes I could walk fast and safe in upon the cobbles.

Upon the cobbled streets of Newport, I walked.

We had fled the city on the sea of Narragansett Bay twelve years ago, fled to college at Rhode Island School of Design, and fled the scandal that had been born here, a scandal that nearly felled us. But on that magnificent day eight years ago, as we each held our scrolled and beribboned diplomas in our hands, we knew. We would return to the beauty of this little island, to the place where the "we" of us had been born.

For Pearl, the socialite she had once been – that still hid in a shadowed corner of her soul – insisted she come back, to face those who had treated her... us... so poorly. To stand tall in the face of them.

I had come back for my father and to escape my demons. What Herbert Butterworth had tried to do to me, what I had endured because of it, had to be faced. Only by looking a demon in the eyes could it be defeated.

Yes, we had returned, though neither of us ever imagined we would settle here, marry here, have our children here. But we had. We both wore the medal of victory proudly. I remembered Pearl's words with as much fear as amusement: "The best revenge, dahling, is success."

She had used her old snob accent, as I called it, the one she had rid herself of. My Italian accent had mostly disappeared, save for times when my emotions opened the door to it. My emotions were opened wide and deep at that moment, a jagged hole in the fabric of my soul.

I walked fast and determinedly through the haze of a spring morning on the island, when the cool ocean waters danced with the warming earth, leaving rolling tendrils of elusive white mist to dance itself about us. I did not have to walk far. Osborn and I lived only a few blocks from Pearl and Peter and their daughter, in the Great Common area. We lived north of Bellevue, *the* avenue of the rich who came every summer, who built mansions there and called them "cottages". Pearl could have lived at The Beeches, one of the grandest of all the "cottages", but to do so meant she would have had to endure six weeks of every summer living once more with her mother.

She would never have to endure her mother again, not ever.

I stumbled on the thought, on the stones, on the unreality of it all.

What would I say to her? What could be said? I did not know. I knew only that in our darkest times, merely the presence of the other was enough. I would be that presence for her now, and always.

I stood on the dense dirt walkway streaming past her house on Marlborough Street, no more than two blocks from my own home on Farewell Street. Its lovely white porch wrapped itself around the brown clapboard house, its tower escorted by off-kilter gables, and the decorated eave that hung over the door all blazed with the happiness that had always lived within… happiness that defined this family of three. It might vanish. Happiness could, after all, be conquered by grief.

My breath hitched as I stepped forward, climbed the stairs, and knocked upon the glass-and-wood door. I knocked and knocked again. I stepped back to look up to the shuttered windows, praying for some sign of her.

"Oh, Missus!" The screech wavered, but it was a screech. "Oh, Mrs. Taylor, thank the good Lord you're here!"

Rotund and normally rosy, a pale Sarah rushed from the door, grabbing me by the arm, and tugging me into the foyer. She blubbered in the silent stillness of the house that brought an ache to my gut.

"Sarah, dear Sarah, calm yourself." I took her hands in mine, captured her gaze with mine, and took deep breaths until she followed my lead. Beads of sweat trickled down her pale brow and into her eyes, making a soup with her tears. Sarah had been nanny and governess to Pearl's daughter since her birth seven years ago; she could have borne the family name, so tightly did she belong to it.

"Is anyone else here, Sarah?" She had calmed and I needed desperately to know.

Her head shook wildly. I kept her hands in mine, my breathing slow. I hoped.

"No, no." Sarah continued to shake. Her shaking captured all of her plumpness, made it wobble.

"T-the Mister had already left for work and taken Mary to school when… when…"

Tears fell from her thinning lashes as her lids squeezed and crinkled over her dark eyes, fell and poured around her cheeks.

"When what?" I whispered as I often did to Angelina when she had had a bad dream.

"When the telegram came," she blurted on a quick huffed breath.

"She was alone," I said but not to Sarah. It was the very last thing I hoped to hear.

"She was. She was alone. I was upstairs cleaning the young lady's room when I heard the knock at the door but I just kept cleaning cause I knew the missus would get it, so I…" Sarah sucked in air, her only pause… "just kept cleaning and then I finished and went downstairs, thinking I would go to the kitchen to clean up from breakfast but, when I passed the breakfast room and saw her, I couldn't go anywhere. I couldn't move."

I knew I squeezed Sarah's hands now rather than caressed them; I didn't care.

"What did you see? What was she doing?"

Sarah's chin dropped to her chest and more tears fell to the floor.

"She looked like a ghost but one from winter, so frozen was she. I saw the telegram in her hand. They always bring bad news, always. And then…"

Sarah had climbed the summit to revisit the height of the horror.

"And then she stood up. The telegram fell from her hand as if she had never been holding it. I called to her but it was as if she was deaf. She walked past me and out the door without a word, not a single sound. No coat, no hat, no purse. The sight of her made me shiver."

The chill wormed through the fabric of my coat. Pearl was in shock and she had left the house alone in such a state. I had to find her. I tried to release my hold on Sarah but she would not allow it.

"The telegram just lay there on the floor. I read it, I did, though I know it was poorly done of me. When I saw… as I read…"

Her sobs drowned out anything more she had to say. I put my arms around her as far as they would go and held her as tightly as I could.

Without releasing her, I gave her instructions in someone else's calm voice. "It is a terrible thing, Sarah, terrible. We must do all we can to help our Pearl."

Her quivering head nodded against my shoulder.

"Go and get Mary from school. Tell her nothing, do you mind me? Not a word of this. It is for Pearl and Peter to do so. I will find Pearl."

"Oh, thank you, Missus. Thank you ever so." Sarah pulled away from me – purpose brought her composure. I knew I could leave Pearl's daughter safely in her keeping.

And I knew exactly where to find Pearl.

I took the hill leading from the harbor's edge to the more rarified air on Bellevue Avenue at a very unladylike pace. The pinched looks of passersby marked my passage. I stared them in the eye as I lifted my skirts, revealing my ankles, and the laced boots upon them. Being a scandal in this city was nothing new to me. Being a scandal meant nothing to me, not anymore, especially not then.

Someone had put three black wreaths on the high and rounded arched front doors of The Beeches already. It must have been Mr. Birch; though well into advanced years, his devotion to the family was as strong as ever. Mrs. Briggs still reigned over the servants, but I could not imagine such an emotional gesture from that cold crone.

I slipped around the left side of the mammoth home, the side furthest from the servants' entrance, and scurried along the very edge of the vast lawn that rolled away from the back of the marble stairs and statues. Those statues... their eyes still made me shiver. Before I made it halfway to the trees, I saw her, her blue dress standing out brightly in the center of the moss-colored tree trunks. She stood, just stood there. I ran faster.

My rush brought me within the cave the weeping beeches created, buds just beginning to open on the long trickle of vine-like branches that tumbled from the tops of the trees to the ground. This cave, it had been our refuge through those beautiful and awful years.

I moved to stand beside the ghost Sarah had described, the ghost that wore Pearl's face. Her dark eyes, so like my own, gazed upward... to the tops of the trees, to the heavens... to what I didn't know. Her long dark hair flowed unpinned down her back, a medieval ghost.

I stood beside her in the silence she seemed to need. She knew I was there – how could she not? I left it to her to speak first.

"They're so much taller than they were... back then."

I didn't know how to respond to such words – such thoughts – that owned no belonging to the moment.

Birds twittered gaily all around us, so happy for the growing food that spring brought them. The tips of my fingers tingled with numbness.

"I am an orphan, Ginevra," Pearl spoke her heartbreak flatly, a hollow sound from an abandoned heart.

Without a pause, she stepped upon the long branch that bowed to the ground, the branch that had always been our ladder up into the trees.

We were much older since the last time we had climbed it, older and less nimble. I followed. She wore the same look my father and my relatives had worn at the moment of my mama's death so long ago. I knew what it meant. Pearl might have no knowledge of what she was doing; she could not be alone.

Shock is the strangest form of armor; it could protect the mind when great harm had been done to the body. But it could also shield out reality, allowing us disbelief when we had no right to it. I had to break the shield that surrounded Pearl so thickly.

"You are not an orphan, my darling, I am your family," I said only what she knew already. Pearl patted my hand but still did not meet my eye. I would have to strike deeper.

"Your father loved you with all his heart. That love will belong to you forever." Perhaps it wasn't well done of me, to bring up the first and perhaps deepest love of Pearl's life, to mention that parent who had most understood her, encouraged her no matter how far from the path she strayed, and the man who shielded her from her mother's constant contempt.

A small smile tickled the corners of Pearl's lips. It was not the response I'd hoped for.

"Oh, I know, that I do know."

We were not in a real cave, but I swear her voice seemed to echo.

"I will have it with me forever and I am so very glad he was able to spend so much time with Mary. She will have his love to hold on to as well." Her voice remained like the shoreline on the horizon, straight and the same no matter where one viewed it.

"Has Daisy's family been told?" It was not a question that would break her free but one I should have thought about sooner, for the sake of her sister-in-law's family.

Pearl simply lifted her shoulders and dropped them just as quickly.

Fear came to sit between us on that branch. I could not bear the thought of my dearest friend, one of the most vibrant and vivacious people I'd ever met, become, in truth, no more than a ghost of herself for the rest of her life.

"When did you last speak with your mother?"

Pearl's head snapped around as if slapped. Her eyes bored into me so fast and sharp, I felt their cutting edge nick me. I had hit the mark.

"Not for many, many months. You know that, Ginevra. How dare you ask me that? How dare you ask me that today?"

"I only thought to—"

"Well, do not think, do not think you know what this feels like, what this is. How dare you?" Color returned to her face, the hot color of anger. I preferred it to the white wraith I had first found.

Silence returned but Pearl no longer looked to the sky, she stared at the ground.

"Did you—"

"I never reconciled with my mother, Ginevra, never. I would answer her questions about Mary but we never spoke of anything else, never."

The quiver began in her hands, gripping the branch so tightly her knuckle bones tried to break through her skin. I watched as her trembles moved upward as a vine grows on a trellis.

The face she turned to me was one I recognized, though broken bits indented it like pockmarks.

"I never truly reconciled with her, Ginny, though I should have." Her whole body shook. I inched close enough to wrap an arm around her. Like rain, her tears fell to the ground.

"Yes, I should have. It wasn't her fault, who she was. She was created by her parents, by society… it was too much for her, I think. That's why she did the things she did. She never felt she was enough."

Tears flew from her cheeks as her head shook back and forth.

"I should have told her I had forgiven her. I had, Ginny, I had. I had forgiven her long ago and now… now she will never know. She will never hear…"

Pearl's shield had vanished, vanquished by her truth, the truth buried deep in mind and spirit at last released.

Her head dropped back on her neck, her lips parted, and she set free the scream she had held so tightly within.

Pearl

May 1912

We were to leave for Canada in the morning, or rather to Nova Scotia, to Halifax. It was where all the... the bodies were being taken, those they could find.

It had been nearly two weeks since I lost my family, two weeks of swimming underwater; every movement, every thought, a slow, painful undertaking. I had my darling husband and beautiful daughter, yes, but there was something untethering to lose the whole of the family you were born into. Suddenly, you became a marionette without any strings.

The message had been strangely curt, though I assumed it was because of the vast number of them that had to be sent. *Come here and see if you can find them.* Those weren't the exact words of it but they might as well have been.

We learned more from the newspapers who fed greedily on so much tragedy, filling column after column, page after page, day after day.

It took four ships, ships chartered by the White Star Line, to bring back the bodies of those lost with the sinking of the Titanic. How kind of them; if not for their bungling my family might still be alive. I needed them, though, I needed a target; grief and anger made for a powerful weapon. White Star became the enemy... became my target. Only one ship of the four was a passenger ship. The others were supply ships or cable ships. How appropriate, the bodies became naught but cargo.

The newspapers couldn't seem to agree as to how many bodies were recovered. One had said 316, another claimed it was 337. All seemed to agree, whatever the number, it accounted for only a quarter of those that had perished.

"A quarter, only a quarter," someone mumbled – me. "That means… that means… more than a thousand—"

The newspaper disappeared from my hands. Snatched and crumpled by my husband.

"You don't need to be reading these, my Pearl." That he used the endearment my father had always used became ever dearer to me. He stomped away to toss the crumpled paper in the bin.

Peter tried to hide all this from me, for those whose graves would forever lay at the bottom of the ocean were there because there was little left of them, not enough for any family to identify them… not enough to put any family through looking upon them. Not enough for the greedy crane fingers to grab on to, to haul up. But no one would know who those lost souls were until we identified who they weren't.

I stared up at him, I returned to this place and this time, swimming up from the bottom of the dark ocean where I sank to with every word I read. I nodded. He was right, I knew. I also knew I could not stop and would read them whenever I could.

"You look quite silly, Mother."

I flinched, just slightly. I thought I heard my mother's voice in my daughter's words until Mary giggled.

I leaned down from my place on the settee to wiggle my nose in her face as she sat on the floor and played with her dolls. One of her dolls was a doctor; I had told her so when I gave it to her, another a ballet dancer, and one, like her, a musician. Oh, how beautifully she played the piano.

"And why do I look so silly?" I asked her. I stared at her; her golden, hazel eyes and her dark curls – a true mix of her parents' features – gave me warmth in these spring days where I could find nothing but winter's merciless, unrelenting cold.

"Well," she began and I almost laughed at her matter-of-factness, "your hair is just a mess, it's all…"

Mary waggled her hands above her head like seaweed moving with the tide.

I popped my eyes. "It is? Well, my goodness, and I just fixed it up."

Mary gifted me with her giggles again.

"And just look at your lovely skirt. You've wrinkled it terribly."

I looked down at my lap. Mary was right, it was wrinkled. I could see where my hands had crumpled it in my fists. I had to be more aware. She would be touched by this – how could she not? I wanted to do my best to make that touch as gentle as it could be.

"But… but that is the latest style," I feigned a startled tone. "Aunt Ginny told me so."

Mary collapsed on the floor, her small, high-topped boots thudding upon the floor; she rolled as she giggled. She acted for me.

Children always know so much more than we think they do; they discern truths unspoken. They see all we try to hide. Mary had cried herself to sleep for over a week after we told her. She'd wake in the night calling for her Pop-Pop. How my father loved that silly moniker. Like me, Mary grieved for him most of all.

Her gaze found mine. We both saw our truths glistening there.

I held out my arms. She came into them gladly and for a while I rocked her gently, caring not a whit that she was a seven-year-old. It was what we both needed.

Above our heads, footfalls moved here and there. Now and then a thump thundered. Peter and Sarah finished our packing.

"You are going away tomorrow, Mother."

I didn't know if it was a statement or a question. I simply nodded.

"Will you... will things..?" Mary twirled the ribbon of her drop-waist dress in both hands. She couldn't finish, but I knew.

"Perhaps not right away, but it will help." I held her tighter and as she did me.

The footsteps grew faster, the thuds more.

"Would you play for me, merry Mary?"

We had called her that from when she was still a babe for her giggles, her laughter, that which came long before her first word, were so infectious she made us all merry just listening to them.

Mary kissed my cheek and hopped off my lap. The piano – the Schoenhut with its colorful angels painted on the Fallboard – was still a good size for her. Her Pop-Pop had gifted it to her when she turned six, when she had climbed up the stool of the grand piano at The Beeches and started to peck at the keys, when the pecking started to sound like music. She stunned us all, even Felice who had been among us. Like a third grandfather, he had found her the best piano teacher in Newport, a teacher who told us she was a prodigy. It was a word we would never use again but hers was a talent we would foster, no matter the cost.

She snuck me a mischievous sidelong look, one tinged with the emotion of our embrace, and began playing. I almost laughed though tears were closer. The song Mary played was *My Melancholy Baby*.

It was so early in the morning, the day's light still struggled to pull itself up over the horizon. Mary stood on the porch, still in her nightgown and robe, still with sleep heavy in her eyes. In one hand, she clutched the soft and fuzzy teddy bear, the only toy she ever brought to bed, one that had been born the same year as she. Her other hand sat tightly in Ginevra's.

I knelt to her. "You will be the very best girl for Aunt Ginny, won't you, Mary?"

With the teddy still in the crook of her arm, she knuckled a sleepy eye and nodded. The word precious can be just a word until one has a child.

I took her in my arms, squeezing tightly as if I could make her feel them until I returned.

"Let me come with you."

Over Mary's head, I saw the need in Ginevra's eyes.

"Let me be by your side when…"

Whether she could not finish or would not finish in front of Mary, it didn't matter. I knew.

We would be apart for longer than we ever had, save for our honeymoons which were joyous and rousing fun for us both.

Unlike that time, the stories told afterward would bring no joy. I had no idea what would cling to me when I returned, nor did she. Our fear pooled in the corners of her eyes, as deep and dark as the ocean bottom from where they had raised the bodies.

Through the whole of our adolescence, through the assault upon her and what came after, through the frightening years completely on our own in college, we were always by each other's sides. I would have felt the same need as she were our roles reversed.

I rose, taking her in my arms.

"I need you here more, Ginny. Knowing she is with you will be the best thing you can give me."

I felt her nod against my shoulder.

"Felix and Angelina will keep her merry," Ginevra said with a smile as we separated. "They didn't sleep a wink, knowing she was coming today."

"Come here, my merry Mary. Give your Dada a big hug."

Beside us, Peter launched Mary into his arms. With her head upon his shoulder, he whirled her slowly about.

"She need not go to school if she doesn't want to." I turned back to Ginevra. "Don't push her but I would rather she did."

"Of course. She will go. I bet Felix will take her by the hand and make sure."

I stared at the face I knew almost as well as my own, had seen it change as mine had. There was a home for me there.

"Our children," I whispered.

"We will show them the world is theirs…" Ginevra began, chin aquiver.

"No matter boy or girl, no matter rich or poor," we finished together. It had been our pledge, made upon our engagements, a pledge we would never gainsay.

I kissed Ginevra's cheek and turned for the carriage. There was no delaying the inevitable any longer.

I barely slept on the train, through the very long day-and and-a-half train ride. I knew I should, I knew I would need my strength, but the ghosts were too many and too loud through the whole journey. These relentless specters played me a picture show, each crackling frame a version of what might await me. From nothing to disfigurement and all that lay in between. At times they were nothing but bones, the sea having stripped them of their skin, just as what had happened to so many of them as I had read in the paper.

Perhaps Peter was right, I shouldn't have read so much.

The thought walked the silent, slim corridor down the sleeping car of the train with me as I moved from one end of it to the other.

The worst of them were the ones who weren't there at all. Their existence completely erased by the egotism of men, the greed of corporations, and the anger of Mother Nature.

We were in Dante's nine circles of hell, only they weren't circles, they were a mammoth complex of ice rinks, for curling, whatever that was. But it was the very size and low temperatures of the Mayflower Curling Rink which made it the most best suited to this function… to hold and embalm the hundreds of recovered bodies.

Like a field of misshapen, different-sized mounds, they stretched out before my eyes, to the very horizon… body after body, mound after mound. I no longer felt I existed in a world that was real, but rather a dream world, a nightmare. Nowhere in a sane world should such a sight exist, should I see such a sight. So many people, so little sound; the silence unnerved as much as the landscape.

Only muted sobs, like the gurgle of a distant stream, ebbed and flowed throughout the massive structure. Nurses in blue dresses and long white aprons moved from sob to sob, holding, rocking, consoling. For some came the rush of smelling salts. I thought the whole place smelled like those salts – that smell bit the inside of my nose as the ghosts chewed at my mind.

"I imagine the cries will be the same whether someone is found or not," I thought aloud, expecting no answer, receiving none.

The far corner was closed off by framed draping, silhouettes and shadows wavered behind it. I had no idea what happened in there; I had no wish to know.

A hand clutched my arm.

"Are you sure, my Pearl?"

My gaze traveled from the hand to the face. Peter stared intently at me through a haze of worry.

"You are unsteady on your feet."

"I am?" The notion surprised me. "But… yes, I am sure. We must try, no matter—"

"Pearl!" The wail tore through the silence, bouncing up to the high metal ceiling and back down, ever louder.

The opulently dressed wraith rushed toward me. I tripped against my husband, erratic steps moving backward, not knowing where they would land. His warm, strong hand braced my lower back. I pushed against it. The wraith came closer.

"Oh Pearl."

The wraith was in my arms, the furs covering it tickling my nose. I held it; I knew not what else to do.

"It is Madeleine Astor," Peter leaned down to whisper in my ear. His vision had not been twisted by the same nightmarish fearful distortion as mine.

My arms flinched. I wanted to leave go, to let her fall to the ground. The Astors had shown me little care throughout my life; they, who had deemed themselves worthy above all, had been a harsh judge and jury for as long as I could remember. But then I did remember, it was not this Astor. This Astor was but a nineteen-year-old girl, barely a woman, almost half my age. Some had called her a gold-digger; I believed no man could be dug unless he gave the woman a shovel. No, this poor child had been none of those Astors who had riddled my life with their harshness, their holier-than-thou judgments. She had been a wife for less than a year. This child carried a child in her womb.

I smoothed her dark raven curls even as she muttered into my shoulder.

"He was there, he was standing right there, next to the boat he put me in. I s-sat, I sat down and l-looked up, and he was gone... gone."

A gaze of such devastation turned up to me. The horrors of the moment played in those dark and tear-reddened eyes. I closed my own to it.

"He should have..." She pulled slightly away from me, took me by the shoulders as if I could hear her better that way. I could see only her deathly pale skin, sunken cheeks, and dark circles that turned the aristocratic face into a death mask. "I should have waited for him. I should not have gotten on the boat without him. There was plenty of room for him, for him and more than-than at least a handful of others." She shook me, tossing me forward and back as if we stood on the deck of the ship. My stomach churned. "So many others, I tell you!"

Her screams brought more than one nurse to us, brought my husband's hands to hers as he released the clench they had upon me.

I heard Peter's mumble, "So the stories are true."

I had no time to ponder them, to acknowledge the devastating truth.

"Mrs. Astor, calm yourself," the nurse's voice had a strange lilt to it, an accent perhaps, and yet it only made the sweet calmness of it more so. "If not for yourself, for your wee babe."

Another woman, uniformly dressed, handed Madeleine a glass of water.

"I think it best we help her find her husband as soon as is possible," the first said... to us. Somehow we had become Madeleine Astor's retainers. Peter would have none of it.

"We are not here with Mrs. Astor, we are merely acquaintances." I had never seen my husband's golden skin so blotched. "We are here to find my wife's... entire... family."

There were times I regretted having married a lawyer; this was not one of them.

"Oh. Oh my. I... we... we had no way of knowing. Please let me assist you, let Amelia and me assist you all."

My husband's splotches feathered away; he reached out a hand, "Thank you, Miss..."

Amelia still held the sobbing Madeleine Astor in her arms.

"Ruth will do." The nurse accepted the kindly gesture, returned it. "How many are we... that is, how many members of your wife's family are we looking for?"

To one side of me, the pregnant Madeleine Astor cried in a strange woman's arms. On the other, my husband conversed with another stranger, speaking of me and my family. I stood in the nowhere in between.

"Both her parents," Peter replied softly. "Her brother and his wife."

It was the first time I received the "look." The dark shades came from shock, the withering colors were those of pity. I would soon come to despise such a look.

"We are not supposed to assist," Ruth leaned closer to us, "there are so many looking for so..." she held her tongue, realizing that we... I... were not the best recipients for such an admission. "We are here to help as many as we can."

Peter grunted. Ruth had saved herself well.

"But in light of Mrs. Astor's condition and your wife's great losses, we will make an exception."

I thought that, in reality, it was the Astor name that garnered such special consideration. Perhaps being an Astor retainer was not such a terrible thing to be, after all.

I almost giggled. I trapped it behind a gloved hand. They would think me insane. They would not be wholly wrong.

"Let us start this way." Ruth led us to the corner to our left with an outstretched arm. Madeleine, still in Amelia's arms, followed. "We have found it best to conduct the search in a clockwise rotation on the outskirts, working round toward the center."

"Very sensible," Peter said. He took my arm and wrapped it around his, pulling them tightly against his chest. He anchored me.

"It would be of such help if you had any photographs, then I could—"

"I do, I do have some." From out of the strangeness I found I was a part of this gruesome party, not merely an observer. I reached into my reticule, pulling out a few black-and-white images of my family, some taken at Clarence's wedding just two-and-a-half years ago.

The whiteness of their image would match their skin. It was another thought I'm grateful I did not speak aloud.

"These will be very helpful, Mrs. ..."

We had never given her our name.

"Mrs. Wright," Peter answered for me.

Ruth nodded to me; I think I nodded back. She led us to the first grouping of mounds and a long, narrow aisle with more on each side as far as the eye could see.

What I did next, what I saw next, would find me in the night for the rest of my life, my own screams waking me up, up and pacing the house for many hours, for I would have no wish to sleep and see it all again.

One after the other, the sheets were pulled back. My vision became a blur of bruised and battered faces, of lips and tongues and eyes so swollen they did not look human at all, some with barely any skin at all.

"No, it is not him... it's not him," Madeleine's moans became a litany, the same as the one looping round and round in my head. I should have been looking for them all; I wasn't.

Each time Ruth pulled a sheet back for us, it was Peter who silently shook his head. If he was not my husband, if I did not love him more than I thought I could ever or would ever love a man, I would have after that day, all those hours where he held my arm tightly to him, where he looked for me when the looking became searing pain, when he shook his head for me... and then, when he stopped, turned

27

me to him, and whispered: "My Pearl…"

My eyes went to his first. I saw the truth in them. We had gone round the large space twice, closer in on the second circle of hell. He had been there looking.

I was in New York for Christmas, the last place we had been all together. I remembered my father's smile most as he watched his granddaughter squealing with delight with every present she opened. There, in that place, I could breathe.

"Is it—?"

"I fear you must make the identification, Mrs. Wright. It must come from an immediate family member, if present, in order for us to re… so that you may take them home. I'm sure you can understand."

"Of course," my husband concurred.

"No! No, I don't." Now I wailed. "If my husband says it is… if he thinks…"

"Pearl." His hand upon my shoulders spun me back to him. His voice was harder than I had heard it in many a week. Peter looked down at me. "Pearl, there are legalities here we cannot ignore."

There were times I regretted having married a lawyer – this was one of them.

I no longer breathed. My lungs burned, but I could not help them.

I saw my sister-in-law first, a far sweeter girl than I thought my brother would gravitate toward, would choose to spend his life with. The embalming did not conceal the monstrous bruises that cratered her once pink and blooming skin.

As if they shared the same cosmetics, my brother bore the same marks, more of them. I forgave him in that moment, for falling from the pedestal on which I had put him in my childhood, from which he fell in the growing sophisticated thinking of my adolescence.

"At least you are together, dear brother."

That I spoke to him surprised me as well as those around me. I didn't intend to, I just did. I kept myself at his side. Peter took my hand, gently tugging; he knew what I was about.

I heard a groan as I turned, felt its rumble and its pain deep in my chest. I looked at the third mound, the third to have its sheet pulled back.

One can imagine horror, imagine what we think is the worst, what it will be. So often such visions are far worse than the truth, fear of what may be, expands in the fertile ground of the mind. My imaginings of what I would see did not come close to what I looked upon.

I felt my knees hit the hard floor before I realized I was falling.

"Pearl!" my husband cried out, trying to catch me, missing. I felt his hand on my arm, tugging upward. I shook him off.

I held my wobbling head inches from my father's, my dear, precious father, the man who protected me, shielded me as much as he could. And, at the most crucial moment in my life, who had opened the gate and set me free.

If not for the scar from the wound inflicted on him in the War Between the States, the scar just barely visible on a torn and tattered cheek, one almost completely devoid of skin, I would not have known this most influential man in my life. My mother had always punished him for the scar while I had run my child's fingers upon it.

My finger shook as I reached out, as I touched it once more, as I touched what was left of it, unmindful of the gaping hole in his skin where I could see all his teeth on that side of his face.

Cold, so cold.

The thought nagged and nagged.

"We must get him a blanket." I looked up, I blathered. "My father cannot be so cold. We must warm him."

Peter knelt beside me, wrapping his arms about me.

"Tell her, my darling," he whispered as if to a child. "Tell Ruth who this is."

My head shook and shook, denying my mind's command to stop.

"You must so we can take him home."

Peter plied the key to unlock my madness.

"Yes. Yes, we must take him home." I wanted to lift my father in my arms, to carry him all the way back home. As tears drenched my face, I looked up to Ruth. "He is my father."

Lying in his bed, curled small against him. The warmth of him, the smokiness from his pipe tickling my nose. My giggles, his low grumbly laughs. My short, plump finger, his scar, his closed eyes smiling.

Swirling grayness, swirling room. Low hums, a draining buzz.

"My Pearl." A tender whisper.

I returned.

I found myself sitting in a chair with no idea how or when I had got there. It didn't matter. I had been foolish, still a child not believing what the grown-ups were telling me, not believing he was really dead. I did not know, until that very moment, that such an illogical, impossible hope lived within me. That hope was truly dead, as was my father.

Peter's sigh helped me find him, squatting beside my chair when I had not known he was there. I reached out a hand; he grabbed it fast and hard.

"Would you care for some water, Mrs. Wright, or some crackers, perhaps?" Ruth was there as well. There was no surprise or concern upon the plainness of her face.

"What about her?" I asked instead, ignoring her offerings.

Her gaze slipped from my face to Peter's.

"I believe my wife is asking about her mother," he informed her.

A crease formed between Ruth's brows. "She was not with…" She stopped herself. "Give me a moment, please."

She took herself away, to another corner of the room where

women manned desks.

"Madeleine?" I asked my husband about the woman with just the word.

"She has left, my Pearl." His voice warmed me like his skin upon my hand. "She found her husband and has taken him away."

My brows rose. His news told me that I had been unconscious for longer than I thought. I could only nod. To say I was happy for her, for any of us who found our loved ones, those of us with the financial wherewithal to come here and find them, would insult all the mounds of people and what they had endured, what their families would endure for generations to come.

"Would you come with me, Mr. and Mrs. Wright?" Ruth had returned, silent on her no-heeled, laced-up shoes.

Peter stood, still with my hand in his. "Can you?"

I answered by rising slowly to my feet.

As Ruth led us through yet another circle, she whispered an explanation.

"It would seem that your father and… well, they were found all together. We have tried our best," for the first time I heard her contained emotions struggle for release, "we truly have, to gather dear ones in some logical way. Your father and brother had identification on them that somehow stayed upon their person. Your brother and sister-in-law were found… they were in each other's arms."

Many would find such news ever more dismaying. I found it soothing.

"But there are those, and they are mostly women," Ruth continued, "who were lost when—"

If she said more, we did not hear it.

A male scream like that of dying bear devoured all other sound, save for the crash of what must have been metal things, the shattering of glass, and a heavy thud upon the floor.

"What the hell?" Peter balked.

Every head of those alive in that metal cave swiveled toward the sound, a sound even the dead must have heard.

"Stand clear." We were pushed aside as two men in the white coats of doctors and a smattering of nurses rushed past us, rushed to that peculiar corner of the room shrouded behind the drapes.

"What takes place in there?" My husband asked, boulders of angry fear tumbling in his voice.

Ruth hesitated, but only for a moment. "It is where the embalming takes place."

To know of the shrouded space made the scream all the more puzzling. Ruth tried to move us along to wherever she meant to take us; Peter and I would have none of it. Like everyone else, we waited.

Within a matter of moments, the men carried another, his arms about their shoulders, pinned by their hands, out from behind the curtain.

"My uncle, my own uncle." Tears streamed down the man's face as he keened.

"Oh dear Lord." Ruth crossed herself at the sight, at the words.

"What is it?" I asked.

"Who is that?" Peter demanded.

"It is… it is Frank Newell." Ruth did nothing to keep to her role. No longer a nurse helping others, she was a flesh-and-blood human with a heart that beat and broke for her colleague. "He is an undertaker. One of many who have volunteered their time. He has given hours and hours and now…"

"Now he has been rewarded with the body of his own uncle." The last of my words blurred as I covered my face with my hands. There was no end to the horrors of this tragedy.

I shook my hands away.

"Take us, Ruth, take us to the end of this journey. I do not think I can stand to travel it much longer."

Ruth nodded, stepping quickly as she tried to hide her hands as they wiped the tears from her face.

"You were telling us how others were lost," my husband reminded her, "how some women were lost."

"Oh, yes. Yes, I was." Ruth took a deep breath, straightened her spine back into that of a nurse. "Many women were lost when their lifeboats were overturned by others trying to climb into them, into them and out of the ocean."

She did not soften her words any longer. What would be the point?

"Such women rarely had any identification on them, so we put them in a separate section."

We had obviously reached that circle of hell, for Ruth stopped and gestured us forward. Once more the turning back of sheets began. This time it did not take as long. She was there.

My mother wore no bruises. Her favorite string of diamonds still rimmed her neck. I stood above her, seeing her all too well. She was as frozen in the afterlife as she had been in life. She'd have been pleased with how immaculately she wore death. Looking upon her now, I felt little of the emotional eruption I had disgorged beneath the beeches with Ginevra. I couldn't say why, save, perhaps, for how normal she appeared as opposed to the decimated visage of my father.

It was well I saw her last. I could go out in the chill of the Nova Scotia air... and feel warm.

"Oh yes," I heard myself say. "This is my mother."

They filed past me, leaning over to take my hand, speak mindless words of comfort, and a few to kiss my cheek. Consuelo's kiss was that of the prince upon Sleeping Beauty.

"My darling," I heard myself whisper. I clung to her hand, clung so tightly, I forced her to kneel by my side. "It is so good of you to have come… to be here."

Here was my family home in New York on Fifth Avenue; here was where those invited to my family's funeral came after the services. So many rooms yet full and overflowing – to my eyes, black-shrouded specters hovered from room to room as expensive silver tinkled upon fine china, as glass clinked upon crystal glasses as they were refilled, as low voices hummed, a dark garden filled with bees.

"Where else would I be, dearest Pearl?" I watched as she swallowed her tears down her famously long and swan-like neck, but they kept pooling in her enormous dark eyes, clinging to the thick lashes that rimmed them. I saw those eyes gaze at the woman behind me, the woman who had stood behind me every moment since we had returned. Consuelo must have seen what she hoped to on Ginevra's face, for a bit of color returned to her lustrous skin.

"But to have come all this way, and… and on the sea…" A litany from my lips.

"Do not worry yourself." Her warm arms came around me; my flinching agitation so clear against her steadfast stillness. "I am here and I am safe."

Consuelo understood me, almost as much as Ginevra did; the thought of ocean travel sent me into near disabling paroxysms. My dreams of travel – of seeing the world – had drowned along with my family.

I did my best to thank her with a smile, a pitiful gesture. My eyes darted about to see who watched, a futile exercise as everyone did. But there were two beside us I did not know until I saw their eyes, their mother's eyes. In them, I saw the little children I had met not so long ago.

"Your sons," I whispered and with it, a pale version of a smile that came of its own, genuine accord.

Consuelo rose, reaching a free hand out to the taller of the two boys, boys on the cusp of manhood. "This is John and Ivor. Boys, please make your condolences to Mrs. Pearl Worthington Wright."

As one of her sons was a marchioness who would become a duke upon the death of his wretched father, and the other a lord; by society's rules, I suppose I should have stood and made a curtsey to them. Instead, these two handsome young men bowed before me, taking my hand – that of a stranger – and kissing it in turn.

"Our mother has told us many wonderful things about you, Mrs. Wright. We thank you for being such a good friend to her," said John, the taller and elder, with the composure of a man twice his age. But I supposed, with all they'd been through, they were much older than their fifteen and fourteen years. A philandering father and the public scrutiny and acrimony of two continents at their parents' separation no doubt forced adulthood on them long before it was due. Yet, as I looked at the three of them, especially Consuelo, I saw brighter colors than they had been when last we met. It gave me pleasure, a surprise on such a day.

"We are so very sorry for your loss," Ivor said with the same self-possession as his brother.

My head nodded, feeling as if it was loosely attached to my body. "It is I who am thankful, for your sentiments and the friendship of your wonderful mother." It was the longest sentence I had uttered that day. It was my absolute truth.

"Will you be returning to Newport soon?" Consuelo once more leaned down to me.

Once more, I nodded.

Peter's hands took one of hers. "Will you be stopping there before returning?" He asked.

Consuelo stepped closer to him, rising on tiptoes to kiss his cheek. "We shall. I think the boys would benefit from a summer in the heat and warmth of that peaceful place."

"We shall call upon you there," my husband assured her as he shook the hands of her sons.

"Oh no, we shall call on you. You are to take care of yourselves and worry about nothing – and no one – but yourselves."

My mind puzzled on her last words until I saw who followed behind her in the long line of those waiting to offer their sympathies.

"As I live and breathe." That whisper came from behind me. Ginevra had just seen the indomitable woman herself. The fur-clad woman stood before me, leaned closer still, her abundant bosom crushing against me as she moved her face within inches of mine.

"I, too, have known loss, the sort that you are knowing now, the loss of your father." Alva Erskine Smith Vanderbilt Belmont began where I never expected her to. Even on a mournful day such as this, Mrs. O.H.P. Belmont would not let slip a chance for condemnation and judgments – both of which she frequently aired with great volume – to slip away from her tongue. Not the Alva Vanderbilt I had always known. I thought perhaps this was a different one.

This Mrs. Belmont had indeed lost much… her first husband to the scandal of infidelity and divorce, and her second husband, Oliver Hazard Belmont, only a few years after their marriage.

She had mentioned only my father. It would be ridiculous to doubt that she, and all of the esteemed Four Hundred, the "set," as they were called, knew of the strained relationship between Mother and me, even between me and my brother. I did wonder for a moment how long she'd known. I wondered for only a brief moment. Her knowledge stemmed back to those brutal summers in Newport when, within the armor of adolescence and young adulthood, I defied everything my mother stood for... everything Alva stood for. Just now, it seemed to make little difference.

If there was a proper response to her words, they eluded me.

"When I lost my mother... when I try to tell what her death meant to me..." With each word, a piece of her masks called gentility and decorum crumbled from her face. "I come up against a great blank wall of feeling for which there is no adequate expression. I remember thinking I had lost my best friend."

This authoritarian woman, one I had known only as a terror in my youth, trembled... her lips as she spoke, her hand as she reached it out to take mine. I let her. I welcomed her touch. I realized I had no idea who this Alva Vanderbilt Belmont was. Or who she had somehow become.

"I pray for you, Pearl, as I have every day since, as I will every day that comes."

"T-thank you, Mrs. B-Belmont." My words came off my tongue in the same manner as they scuttled through my mind.

Her dark gaze captured mine, her head nodded ever so slightly, ever so continuously.

"I judged you harshly, both of you." That pinning gaze shifted to Ginevra.

Alva Vanderbilt Belmont had made dumb many people throughout her life, whole ballrooms of them, but rarely with sympathy, never for any purpose but to command or denounce. And never, ever, in contrition.

I no longer heard Ginevra's breathing behind me. I turned for a glimpse of her. On any other day, I would have giggled at the thunderstruck expression on her face.

"But I have learned since then, oh yes, indeed I have." Alva's once

37

trembling lips trembled no more. Her jaw flinched, her chin jutted out at us. "You were right to do what you did, to do what was in your heart to do, to take control of your own life. It is what all women must do. It is…"

We lost her for a moment, but this woman was far too layered for us to even hazard a guess as to where.

"Pearl, Ginevra." Alva returned, but as an Alva we had never seen, never imagined could exist. "I should very much like it if you could join us at our next suffrage meeting in Newport. We are planning a great many things that will move women into the future. Should not women such as you who are our future – who have paved the way into the future already – be there?"

Her words, her very being, came as yet another wave in the tide of shocks that had roiled upon me over the last two months. I was turned to stone.

"Thank you very much, Mrs. Belmont."

I heard Ginevra's voice, though it sounded so far away.

"We will both be there and quite happily."

Of course we would, had we not been following the progress of the suffrage movement since those days in the beech trees when we read and reread *The Women's Journal* after I had seen and heard the passion of the cause with my own eyes and ears and from one of its leaders, Lucy Stone.

"I will send you the address of my suffrage headquarters there," Alva said with a nod of her head, one heavy with the mass of dark hair – her one enviable beauty – piled upon her head.

With a squeeze of her hand on my arm, another soft kiss upon my cheek from Consuelo, they were gone, leaving us all as if in the haunting stillness of a hurricane's eye.

"Egad." Osborn's confounded voice brought sound into the void. "We have fallen into the land of Oz."

Peter chuckled skepticism.

Ginevra spoke for both of us: "It is a land I am happy to go to."

Like a desert stone longing for the coolness of the sea, I fled into my exhaustion while remnants of the day's sun still lent the sky fuzzy light.

I did not wake until it shone brightly once more.

I had no idea how long I had slept. Without opening my eyes, I reached my hand out to the other side of the bed but found nothing but emptiness. The linens were cold; Peter had long since risen.

The door to my room, the one I had slept in as a child, stood open a crack; someone – either my husband or Ginevra – had been checking on me. Through the gap, I heard their voices, the clatter of cutlery… and even laughter. The resilience of children is a thing of wonder.

With reluctance, I shed the numbness of sleep I craved like an addict. I had ignored my Mary for long enough. I had ignored real life long enough.

Washed and dressed, I made my way down, finding them in the formal dining room. Queen Victoria had been gone for eleven years, yet, like the English whom the aristocratic Americans loved to mimic, I wore the scratchy black crepe of mourning. I doubted I would wear it for the dictated year, but I would continue to pay this courtesy to them for as long as I could stand it. When Ginevra had found the time to make so many dresses in the uncomfortable fabric eluded me, but I had more than enough to last me for as long I as could last in them.

As if sending me a bouquet, Ginevra had given me flowers on the one I wore this day. The handcrafted roses had not escaped my eye. Small and delicate, she'd tucked them with creative genius and the perfect air of propriety into the corners of the many layers of draped skirt. I pictured my Ginny up all night all the nights I was away, strips

of fabric in her hands that she twirled and twisted into these flowers…
her worry beads.

"Dear Pearl." Ginevra's chair scratched against the polished mahogany floor as she pushed from it, as she rushed to me. "You must be starving. I can no remember the last time you ate, can you?"

She prattled. Ginevra always prattled with her accent when she was nervous. Her care for me… of me… was exacting its toll upon her.

"I cannot," I replied, taking her hand and allowing her to lead me to the buffet.

It's still morning then, I thought, for only the morning meal was served on the buffet, in this house at least, a house where my mother's rules still presided.

"The bacon does smell delicious." I surprised myself with my own words.

"That's my Pearl," I heard Peter say and found his lovely face on the far side of the table far brighter than it had been in weeks.

There was something final in the burial of yesterday, as the coffins had been closed and sealed, as they had been closed in the ground. Perhaps there was some relief in that something.

"Morning, sleepyhead mother," Mary twittered at me. Peter gave her a feigned frown, which only made all the children laugh.

True attraction – lasting attraction – is that which takes us by surprise when it finds us years after its first flutterings are born. Seeing my husband, how hard he endeavored to bring peace and normality into our lives, I felt again those flutters, struck by how handsome he was, smooth peach-colored skin beneath golden curls, light brown eyes that changed to green at times and still tall and muscular though he had left the rowing team of Brown University upon graduation more than ten years ago. Brown and that rowing team… it was how and where both Ginevra and I had met our husbands.

There were few women at university during our years, the ratio was nearly one hundred to one and there were not that many more now. But the women that were had the good fortune of being overwhelmed by the attention of a horde of male students. Not only did they come from our own college, Rhode Island School of Design, but there were young men from Providence College, Rhode Island College, and the Ivy League Brown University, all of which were so very close by, especially Brown.

Both our husbands studied at Brown, both rowed, and both were nothing like the men we had known during *those* years. The latter made them all the more attractive.

"Here you go, Pearl."

I almost laughed aloud at the plate of food Ginevra handed me, scrambled eggs piled so high the pieces of bacon upon them looked like piled firewood and the four pieces of toast made a star around it all.

My brows rose as my gaze rose from the plate to her face. She had the good grace to blush.

"Perhaps I was a bit too hopeful about your appetite," she said as her shoulders rose towards her ears.

"Perhaps," I replied, kissing her cheek and making for a chair, warmth spreading inside me to see her shoulders fall to where they belonged, to see her sweet smile.

"I was going to come wake you soon, my Pearl." Peter learned over Mary, who squawked, to kiss me.

"Ick," our daughter said simply.

"Did I need to wake sooner? Do I need to be somewhere?" My stricken gaze found the grandfather clock in the corner testifying to the lateness of the morning, nearly eleven. The knot that had taken up permanent residence in my gut twisted; there was so much for me to do and take care of, there was so little I could remember.

Peter smoothed my raised hackles behind Mary's back. "No, you have not forgotten anything. A note was delivered early this morning…"

"A morning that found us all in bed late," Ginevra soothed, "even the children."

"A note? From whom?" I asked.

I saw the skipping looks between the three adults.

"Wilson," Peter at last replied.

"Truly?" I dropped my fork, the eggs upon it scattering, and dropped my head into its now empty cradle. "A note from Herman Wilson. What did it say?"

Those looks traveled around the table again.

"He'll be here in an hour," Peter pronounced the sentencing softly.

My head slipped out of my hand. "Thunderation! Must I deal with this already?"

My anger spilled all over the table, over everyone's food, over everyone's mood, even the children's. For the latter, I was truly sorry. They had endured enough. But my well of fortitude was running dry.

"His note was very polite," Ginevra said, as a teacher would praise a student. I knew it for what it truly was… placating a nearly hysterical adult. "But it did seem urgent, so we agreed to it."

I looked at Peter. *We?* The silent question.

Peter nodded. *Yes, we.* The silent response.

I found the fancifully plastered ceiling now in my sight.

"Please don't cry anymore, Mother."

It's true what they say – the simplest of words can fill or break a heart.

"Oh, my merry Mary." I reached for her, awkwardly lifting her from her chair to mine, tangling legs that at seven already showed the promised length of her father's. "I won't cry," I pledged. *Not today at least. Not in front of you at all, if I can help it.*

"Come on then, everyone." I had never heard my voice so falsely gay. "Let's eat all the food before the bloodsucking lawyer can get here."

My sidelong look found reward in my husband's slacked but silent lips, my ears by the laughter of the others around the table. I heaved a sigh; the clock read five past eleven. We would have fifty-five minutes simply to be.

I had never been more thankful to Ginevra for bringing her Hazel and my Sarah with her when she traveled by train to meet us there in New York. While I preferred to care for Mary on my own while on regular short trips, there was nothing regular about this trip. The two women who had been with us since our children were born, had tucked them into sweaters and taken them to the park.

"Are you sure you want us here?" Ginevra asked from her place on the settee beside me. Our husbands huddled together in the corner, undoubtedly speculating on what the lawyer might have to say. I distracted my mind from the subject by studying the two men, how similar they were. The same could have been said for us, I suppose; sitting side by side, encased in black crepe, our dark hair and eyes, our full lips, we could be taken for sisters. There was a time or two when we had pretended to be. In the deepest part of us, we were.

Like Peter, Osborn Taylor was tall and muscular, fair of hair, though Osborn's was straight and his eyes were a blazing blue. They were both self-made men. Yes, both graduates of the prestigious Brown University, but they had earned their way there with their good grades and good works. My mother had called them both products of the bourgeois. Neither Ginevra nor I had minded. I was struck then, a startling truth occurring to me – I couldn't believe neither one of us had not noticed it before.

Bending at the waist, my shoulder bumping Ginevra's arm, I whispered to her, "Do you think it is by accident that we both married men nothing like Herbert Butterworth, either in looks or demeanor?"

At the sound of that name, Ginevra's back stiffened; she stared pop-eyed at me, but only for a moment. She turned her study to the men, it was a short lesson.

"But we love them," she spoke as if she prayed, "we truly love them."

I nodded, giving her the silence to fill. She continued to stare at them.

"No, I don't think it a accident."

I had upset her; her mastery of the English language faltered a bit whenever turbulent emotions churned within her.

"I didn't intend..." I reached for her; she accepted my hand.

"Of course you didn't, Pearly." It was her name for me, given after I had started calling her Ginny. "Your mind needed something else to worry on. I understand. But I don't think we need to worry. It is true, they are completely different than... than him."

Ginevra would find it harder to speak his name. She had been the one he had tried to rape, not once but twice. I had only killed him.

"We do love them, deeply and truly." Her voice dropped, gained a tinge of a rasp. "But our attraction to them, the first of it, the butterflies in the belly part... yes, I think part of that came from how different they are from him."

I almost felt like laughing again. Perhaps laughter would indeed find its place in my life once more, after all.

With a grin, I slid my back straight against the settee once more. "The butterflies in the belly... silly Ginny."

Ginevra wore the same grin as I; it was something we had

promised each other in college, as more and more men tried to woo us. If they did not give us butterflies in the belly, we would turn them politely away.

Peter crossed the room to squat before us. "I will not even ask what has brought that to your face, I am only glad to see it."

I leaned forward to kiss his cheek.

"Osborn and I have been talking, discussing the possible reasons for Wilson's need for expediency."

Peter had given up his law practice when Mary was born, when we had bought the gallery on the second floor—the enclosed floor—of the Brick Market Building in Newport. He claimed it was to help me, relieve me of some of the duties once Mary had come into our lives. In truth, the law had not made him as happy as he thought it would; it had not lived up to the promise of a young boy's hopes. He had not lost all he'd learned; between his knowledge of the law and Osborn's financial acumen, I was quite certain they'd thought of many reasons for the lawyer to be rushing to our door.

"It could be—"

The knock came as if beckoned by his words.

"We will shortly find out," I said to him as he rose, nodded, and answered the door.

The preening began, as lawyers are wont to do before wealthy people, this time it came with sincere sympathy and I thanked the aging, nearly bald attorney for it.

"I am sorry as well that I had to disturb you so soon." Herman Wilson pulled a thick packet of papers from his creased leather attaché case. "But I felt it prudent that you know the truth of your situation—"

"My situation?" My voice squeaked. I heard it; I did not care. "My situation is that I have lost every member of my immediate family.

45

Surely nothing you could say to me, Mr. Wilson, could be worse than that situation."

Someone had told me – I don't remember who or when – that the time would come when my sadness turned to anger, when grief became rage. If my rudeness to this man who was just doing his job was the first step on that path, I took it gladly.

"And it is for that very reason that I felt it important to come to you so soon." The insipid lawyer had left, now before me sat an old friend of the family. "Your immediate family *is* gone and both of your parents were only children. You have no aunts or uncles or—"

"I believe my wife is well aware of her familial condition." I think Peter walked beside me at the beginning of the path.

"Yes. Yes, of course." The small round man shrank in his chair.

I heard a cluck of pity deep in Ginevra's throat.

"If you please, sir, could you get to the point?" Peter insisted, though kindly. He must have heard the cluck as well.

Mr. Wilson looked way up at my husband. "In truth, Mr. Wright, I thought you would have discerned it, the... uh, the legal implications."

"I studied and practiced corporate law, Mr. Wilson. The legalities of inheritance were but one course I have long forgotten." My husband's self-mockery worked and the man relaxed, a bit.

"Ah, well then." He turned once more to his papers, looking above his half-glasses to find every eye in the room upon him. He put the papers and his case on the table between us, leaning forward with his elbows upon his knees. "You are the sole survivor of your family, Pearl, but as a married woman, you cannot inherit, upon marriage... in the eyes of the law... you are not even a citizen. It will all go to your husband."

In the screaming silence, I felt it wanting me again, courting me like a hopeful lover... the void made of shock and sadness in which I had so often of late disappeared.

"The hell you say!" Osborn spat for us all, broke the spell upon us.

Each of them came to us; Osborn pulled Ginevra from her place beside me so that Peter could take it.

"How could marrying make us invisible? How did we not know?" I heard Ginevra's searing whisper. I wish someone answered her. Osborn pulled her into the crook of his arm as he shook his head.

In his place beside me, Peter turned, took my head and turned it to him. "As with the gallery, all is ours. All is yours, my dear. I will do only as you instruct. I swear it upon my life."

I raised a hand to cup his face. I tried to make my lips form anything but their deep frown; I failed utterly.

Mr. Wilson cleared his throat, asserting his presence upon us once more. "I know you make your home in Newport, but that home and this house… both are now owned by your husband. And The Beeches. As you must know, The Beeches is very costly to run. Yes, there are but a few servants remaining, so many lost to manufacturing. But those remaining must be thought of as well. Some of them, such as Mr. Birch and Mrs. Briggs, have been there the whole of their adult life. I'm sure there are—"

"They know no other life," I mused aloud, "how do we wrench them from it, no matter what they have done in the past?"

The lawyer's brows creased. Ginevra's head bobbed.

He rose from his chair and gathered his attaché case, leaving the packet of paper damnation upon the table. "These are not decisions to be made immediately. I merely thought it prudent that you knew the true picture of the… of things before making *any* decisions. There is enough money to keep things going for a bit of time. Though I must also inform you that your father was beginning the process of selling

The Beeches."

Herman Wilson came to stand before me, but he came as the longtime family friend he was. He reached for my hand and I let him take it.

"But you must take your time. For now, my dear, take care of your grief, take care of yourself. The rest can wait but should be thought upon"

I raised my face to look at him. I hoped he could see the fondness with which I esteemed him. I could not tell it to him. I could not speak. I simply nodded.

We were all on the train when I decided. Mr. Morgan – JP Morgan – had made his luxury car on the New Haven Line available to us for our journey back to our true home; a grand gesture, perhaps, or contrition for buying my father out of his part ownership in the Stonington Line. Mr. Morgan had gobbled railroads as children did candy.

I was not thinking on it, no deep pondering, I did not search my soul. The decision simply came. Its ease told me its strength.

The children napped on the large bedding in a separate room of the suite provided, lulled by the constant motion of the locomotive. The adults sat in the sitting room portion, more than one set of lids drooping as well. Until I stood.

"I have decided." Though the train rocked, I needed nothing to hold to remain steady.

"What's that?" Osborn snorted, sleep had been close for him. I regretted having disturbed it.

"It's Pearl, darling." Ginevra shook his arm. "Pearl has made a decision."

"About what?"

Ginevra and I shared a wives' grin. Oh, men when they had not had enough sleep.

"I don't know. We have to let her tell us."

"Oh." Osborn straightened from his slump, rubbing his hands upon his face. "Yes, Pearl. I'm listening."

The laughter that had once been mine crept ever closer.

"We all are, my Pearl."

I took Peter's hand, held it while I spoke. There was no point in hesitation.

"I have decided to sell the Fifth Avenue house and most of its contents and—"

"Not the artworks?" Peter sounded as insulted as he was afraid.

"No, not the art, dearest," I assured him. We would keep most of it, especially the three by Mary Cassatt, of course. A few would fetch us quite a sum in the gallery. "Not all of it. The proceeds from the sale of the home as well as its furnishings will be used to maintain The Beeches."

They were all awake now, wide awake but as quiet as the sleeping children. I gave them the time they so obviously needed.

"Do you…," I was not surprised that Ginevra spoke first. "Will you… live there?"

I understood the vastness of her wonder. I had fled that place with her – the "cottage" and everything it stood for – after the terrible thing that had happened to us both there, had fled it long ago. Why would I keep it?

"Heavens, no." I shivered at the thought. "No, I could not live there, not ever. But it was a place that my father had come to love dearly. I will keep it for as long as I can. For him."

I turned to Peter, my husband sitting so rigidly in his chair. "I promise you, Peter, together we will decide when that time has run out. I will not let it disturb the quality of our life or put Mary's education in jeopardy."

Peter nodded with a sigh and a close of his eyes; I could almost see his muscles unclenching.

"Yes, the New York property should take care of things for some time to come." Whether I said that to them or myself I don't know. I knew only that with the words, the cap of finality sat upon my head and it fitted me well.

I took myself to the buffet; I deserved a glass of champagne. But while I poured, I watched them.

I saw the glances that passed between them like they doled out cards in a game of bridge. They understood but I could not tell if they supported my decision. It was of little consequence to me whether they did or not.

Ginevra

"Whatever you need of me, Pearl," I said words I had been saying for two months. They didn't need saying except that she needed to hear them. She and Peter and Mary were the members of my family that had become my first concern, second only to my own, but even over the responsibilities of my work.

I was so thankful for them – the Tirocchi sisters, my employers – for their understanding. Immigrant Italian sisters who not only owned one of the only female-owned fashion houses in the country but one of the most successful. For the moment, they could spare my hands on needle and fabric and they allowed me to send my designs to them by post. It was not an arrangement they would accept for too much longer, I didn't think; work on the fall line would soon be a demanding task.

Pearl gave me a pale smile. She seemed to be getting better. Our return to Newport, her return to her own home and her own bed, helped her healing, I think. That's what homes do.

"Thank you, Ginny," she said as she helped me with my tailored jacket. I had reached for my shawl but then changed my mind. The beginnings of summer had come to New England, but there, in Newport, the surrounding sea kept the fresh air a tad cooler. "It is not that I… that I fear them." She shrugged. "I fear myself."

"From what?"

Her eyes, so like mine, rolled. "From losing my temper. Especially with Mrs. Briggs."

"Oh, well. Don't think I'll stop you from having at that witch.

51

She's had it coming for years."

I hooked my arm with hers, left it there as we walked along Farewell Street, heading south past the docks. There is never anywhere quite as "summer is near" as by the ocean, in the nip of the brine in the nose, in the clanging bells and flapping sails in the ear.

"They're coming," Pearl said simply as we strolled, as we passed more people – alone, in pairs, in groups – than we had just a few weeks ago.

"They are. It's that time."

Like the geese who pointed the way, the warm weather brought them back… the yachts and the sailboats and the rich who owned them. The quiet streets and walkways of our city, one of the oldest in the land I had learned when Pearl had made me study history, so peaceful in winter, would be teeming with people by the end of the month, nearly impassable by the height of summer. Neither of us ever complained; if not for this habit of the rich, if not that they had turned Newport into their summer playground, the amazing woman on my arm would not be there. I could not imagine life without her and if I did, it was a sad tale I spun.

Such thoughts brought me to a strange place.

"Pearl, about the house…" Though I had lived there, at The Beeches, for nearly ten years, it never felt like home. I never felt at home, away from the small village in Foggia, Italy where brash arguments burst abruptly, where twice as much love dowsed them immediately, until I married. "About *your* property, your wealth. Shouldn't we—"

"I did nothing to earn that wealth."

My stomping foot ended her words, our movement.

"I—" She tried. She failed.

"Don't! I will no let you."

Pearl bit her lip, eyes frowning at mine, her chin dipping.

I closed my eyes, thought hard. She had to hear my words in American.

"You earned every penny." I took a step closer to her. "What you suffered from your mother… from 'him' that hurt us both." Another step closer. My nails stung my palms.

I always thought her the smarter of the two of us. But not just then; then, we were the same. Pearl hadn't moved through it all.

"Can you not see this as the truth?"

Pearl's head tilted to the side as the sigh escaped her lips. She nodded even so.

"You are ready to talk then, yes? Seriously? Sensibly?"

Pearl took the last step left between us, anchored gaze still in place.

"I am," she said. I believed her.

Fear, frustration, confusion were the mountain of worry that had been growing within me since that moment with Pearl's attorney. Holding that fear in so long brought it out with a whip. "So, we married and we disappeared?"

Pearl shrugged, huffed a breath. "So it would seem."

I had done what was needed to become a naturalized citizen of these United States; I thought it as good as a citizen. I had done it before I married, while I was still in college. To learn it made no difference was a lesson I found hard to understand.

"It is… *assurda*."

"Absolutely," Pearl agreed

Both of us, throughout different periods of our lives, had been forced to be silent in many ways. We had shaken off the shackles of silence long ago.

"Actually, I would call it madness," Pearl's thinned lips whitened.

"What do we do?"

We moved forward in stops and goes, yet still, our breath came faster.

"You would think, with all we have read…" Pearl began to walk again as her words trailed away.

She stopped; black eyes pierced mine again.

"We will go to Alva Vanderbilt Belmont's suffrage meeting, that's what we're going to do," Pearl declared.

I felt my familiar half-smile form on my lips. "And we will read more."

Her smile came a little closer.

City workers polished and preened Bellevue Avenue, *the* avenue. What was that expression… rolling out the red carpet? Yes, that was it. Instead, they scrubbed, literally scrubbed with long-handled wire brushes, the white cobbles of the avenue till they sparkled beneath the sun. It would not be long before the carriages and automobiles would be bumping over them.

Pearl pulled me up at the outside of the grand gates to The Beeches. So still and silently did she stand and study it, I thought she might change her mind.

"Do you remember when you watched me from there," she pointed to one of the two large stone columns that held the gate, "when you hid in the bushes to watch us parade?"

"I *knew* you knew I was there!"

Pearl gave me a dose of sidelong skepticism. "Of course I knew you were there, silly."

She fell into silence once more; this time I understood better.

"You have made your decision, Pearl, and it's a good one. You do not need to question it." I did my best for her, as she would for me.

"Right you are and right I am." She came to life, pulling me away from the gate, around to the carriage path. "Let us enter by the servants' door. That should start things off well."

I giggled behind my free hand; the true Pearl was making her way back.

We stepped beneath the grating over the delivery circle and the servants' entrance; the ashy vine of wisteria twirling through it preened with their plump buds. I reached a hand out to open the door, when Pearl's arm wrapped around mine stopped me, when a finger upon her lips stilled me.

It was laughter we heard, an odd quiet sort of laughter, but laughter it was.

"I heard tell the Mister gave his daughter one of the first bicycles."

Pearl and I both squinted, both shook our heads. It was a young male voice we heard, and not one we recognized.

"Oh, that infernal contraption."

"Birch," we chorused softly with the same roll of our eyes. And yet, as he began to tell the tale in earnest, one I had been a part of, a softness came to his voice, even when describing Mrs. Worthington's temper and distaste for it all. In that softness, I realized what went on… the older servants, those who had served in this house for a lifetime, shared their memories of the family with the newer, younger staff. A lump formed in my throat; after someone's death, we seemed more capable of forgetting the bad, only remembering the good.

"Come, come now," I hurried Pearl. If a lump formed in my throat, I couldn't imagine what she must be feeling. She could not be weak or let any weakness show if she did feel it.

"Hello, the house!"

The authority in Pearl's voice startled me, so quickly did she change faces these days, as we stepped into the small foyer. The glass door leading to the kitchen and laundry areas stood open. There was no possibility they could not have heard her.

A chair scraped, footsteps thundered, and a large head popped out from around the hallway's corner.

"Who dare—?"

Mr. Birch loomed large, the guardian of a castle without a king. Eyes sunken in dark circles were now carried in baggage far fleshier than I had ever seen. His drooped, thin lips trembled at the sight of the house's new mistress.

Miss Pearl." His bulbous head dropped as low as his voice.

She went to him. She released her arm from mine and went to him, rising on tip-toes to put her arms around him. His arms rose – faltered in his unknowing, in the unfamiliar ground – then flashed around her, gripping her as he would a ballast in a storm.

It was a sight I thought I would never see; it was a sight that tightened prickly strings about my heart.

"Come, come now." Pearl pulled away after moments uncounted, wiping the tears from her face with her hand until the butler offered her his handkerchief. She took it, plying it with the gentleness in which he had offered it. "We have much to discuss."

One hand motioned him back into the servants' dining room. Her head twitched for me to follow.

This was Pearl's anguish, an obstacle in her path to healing, and yet I feared them, seeing them. The few times I had passed them – the four remaining from my time as a servant with them – they had ignored me. I gladly walked invisibly past them. If I took those steps, the curtain of anonymity would rise. I took them.

"Mph," Mrs. Briggs, the housekeeper – the head of household staff – snuffled her dismissive response at the sight of me.

"Good day to you, Mrs. Briggs." I smiled the words at her.

I had changed so much since we had left this cottage; we were only nineteen when we left but now Pearl and I were thirty-four, married with children, accomplished and ambitious. She would only hate me more for it, for all of it.

To my eyes, she had changed little. The bun of hair at the back of her neck was still pulled so tight it stretched her skin, slit her eyes. If she were a dog, she would have growled. I wondered if, in her eyes, we were still the fallen socialite and the servant who thought herself better than they. I never thought myself better, I only wanted better.

"Please, will you all take a seat?" Pearl herded the servants together. Their number, now less than half of what it was, what it had been in the heyday of Newport's rich and indulgent.

There were two young men dressed as footmen and two young women in the uniform of maids. I saw no lady's maid, those who would be dressed without apron or cap, and no valets in tails. The other four in the room I knew all too well. Besides Mr. Birch and Mrs. Briggs, I barely recognized Bruce Grayson, the groundskeeper; he had become so old so quickly. And the dashing Chef Pasquel had lost his dash.

They all sat while Pearl remained standing. I stood beside her.

"Well," Pearl began, not the best beginning. Her throat bobbed and bobbed again. She started again. "We have suffered a great loss, have we not?"

I marveled at her strength; I had lost my mother more than twenty years ago and still could barely speak of it.

In sympathetic silence, the servants nodded.

"Hah!"

I almost knocked my knuckles against my head. Surely I could not have heard that, heard a barked guffaw, not from Pearl. I must have, for all the eyes in the room stared at her, eyes bulging, jaws dropping.

Pearl shook her head. "My father would have hated all this."

A manly snicker. "Indeed, he would have, Miss Pearl." Mr. Birch shocked us all as well.

"But he is not here to chide us, so on we must go." Pearl dabbed her eyes again. "I'm sure you've all been wondering what will become of The Beeches, what will become of you. Of course you have." She answered for them. It was easy for her to; the fear was plastered all over their stiff bodies, their tight fists, and their pinched faces.

"I can tell you all that I will not be selling this home. I will not be selling, but—"

"Will you be coming to live here then, Miss?" This from one of the young men. "With your family?"

It was a question of hope, hope about to be dashed.

Pearl simply shook her head.

"Why ever not?" A snap from the most snappish woman either of us had ever known.

Pearl flicked me her annoyance with a glance; I returned it. Would Mrs. Briggs never learn any manners?

"Not that I owe you any explanation, as you now work for me." If the housekeeper had been standing, Pearl's words would have put her falling back into her chair. "I cannot live here because I cannot live among ghosts."

No one said a word, not even Mrs. Briggs. Naked truth unexpected is by far the truest, and often the most painful.

"But still you won't be selling?" Mr. Birch sounded as baffled as the rest looked.

"No. No, I shan't. My father came to love this house and I hope to keep it as long as I can, for him."

"You'll keep it only to let it stand empty?" Mrs. Briggs spat again. Pearl ignored her.

Pearl stepped over to the two footmen. "Boys," she began. To our eyes, they were mere boys. "I fear we have no daily need for footmen or valets. Should there be a cause for the need, say a special event I may hold here in this house, you will be the first I call upon. Though I'm sure handsome men such as yourselves will find new employment soon enough."

"And wha' 'bout us?" This from one of the young girls, one so new to this land, she still carried her cockney accent.

"This is a large house and it will grow dirty, even with no one living here." The two girls looked hopeful for a moment. "But I do not think it will require daily cleaning. I can offer you three days of work a week. And, like the boys, if an event is planned here, there will be more hours to make the house ready."

They grumbled.

"It is your decision," Pearl assured them.

"What are these events you speak of?" Mr. Birch asked.

"My husband and I have talked about entertaining here, perhaps having Mary's birthday parties here. It does offer a great deal more space for guests than our home does."

Mr. Birch nodded repeatedly. She had won his approval.

Pearl moved to Chef Pasquale, still in his high, tube-like white hat – his toque blanche, as he had pompously corrected me long ago in those days when I was an uneducated, immigrant servant – and pristine white, double-breasted short jacket. "Unfortunately, Chef, I fear I cannot afford to keep you and I know you would not accept only hit-or-miss work."

The French chef answered her with a glare of contempt. "No, I will not."

He rose and without another word left the room.

"Ah, that *is* how one gets a sterling recommendation," Pearl spat at his back.

The man faltered a step, but didn't turn back, didn't stop. Pearl gave me a shrug as she shrugged him off. This island city brimmed with fine chefs; she would have no trouble finding one when she needed one.

"And what of us?" Mrs. Briggs asked for the three remaining.

"Much to my surprise, Mrs. Briggs, I will have you stay on."

Oh, she enjoyed that one, I thought of Pearl.

"You will see to the two days of cleaning with these young women or others if they no longer find the arrangement to their liking. And you will be cooking for Mr. Birch and Mr. Grayson. They will both be remaining as well."

"Cook?" the hag squawked.

"Yes, as in prepare food for them and yourself."

The two women battled with a stare. If Mrs. Briggs thought Pearl still a girl, that stare corrected her.

"But I must tell you and Mr. Birch." Pearl turned. "This won't affect you, Mr. Grayson, as you've always been here year-round." She faced the butler and the housekeeper. "I can only afford to keep this home by selling the one in New York. If you decide to stay in my employ, you will no longer be going back and forth as my f... as my parents did. You will remain in Newport year-round."

The two aging servants now stared at each other.

"I know you consider your home to be in New York but that home will no longer be mine to give you. If you do wish to go back to the city, I'm sure you could find other arrangements."

Pearl did not say other work; at their ages, they were far too old to find employment. They were a dying breed in more ways than one.

"There is one thing more I must tell you before you make your decision."

I felt my brows bunch together; to my ears, she had said everything I thought she came to say. But Pearl was Pearl after all.

She cleared her throat. It held words not willing to be freed.

"As I have heard is being done in England at many a great manor house, I am contemplating the notion of opening the house to visitors."

"Visitors?"

To my surprise, I spoke aloud the same word as Mr. Birch and Mrs. Briggs.

"Do you mean to allow strangers to sleep in—?"

"No. Oh no, Mr. Birch," Pearl hurriedly assured him with her words and a waving, wiping hand. She was afraid, as I was, at the reddening, trembling sight of him that his heart might fail with the onslaught of so much unsettling news. "No one will ever sleep here, save perhaps my own family."

The man leaned back once more in his chair, dabbing his head with another handkerchief. I wondered how many he carried. I wondered what Pearl truly meant.

"No, what they are doing in England is allowing the curious and the travelers to tour the house… for a fee."

So many words, so many voices; they pummeled poor Pearl. She didn't flinch, she didn't falter. She was my Pearl, the girl who had lied in court, the woman who could wield a brush with such talent, who dared to wield it.

Pearl opened her small purse and pulled out her calling card, and, with a gentle move, laid it upon the table.

"I offer to make this easy… for all of you." She jutted her chin at the card. "There is where you can send me word as to whether you'll be staying or not. You may leave of your own accord and with excellent recommendations. I am quite sure I can find others who will take your salaries, those based on when there *was* a family in residence, though your duties will be drastically reduced." She looked pointedly at Mrs. Briggs. "Drastically reduced."

Pearl spun on her heel, took my arm once more, and pulled me away.

"Come, Ginny. I believe my work is done here… for now."

"Indeed it is," I assured her, not even trying to keep the smile from my face. "Indeed it is."

I waited until we were too far away for any prying ears to hear; though short, it nagged like a pebble in my shoe.

"Did you mean it, Pearl? Would you really open the house to outsiders?" I did my very best to sound curious rather than disapproving.

Pearl made me wait for the answer; once more, the pebble nagged. If I did not love her so much, I would have kicked her. We were almost to the end of Bellevue Avenue where it met Memorial Boulevard before she answered.

"Not yet, no." She had slipped back in her grief. It was there in the woeful version of her voice. "But it may become a possibility. I will keep it for him as long as I can, no matter what I must do."

The loss of my mother at such a young age traumatized me and turned me into a rather shy, reserved child. Knowing Pearl, having her in my life, sharing all we had shared, changed me entirely.

I pulled Pearl into my arms, hugging her tightly, judging looks be damned. I held her till I felt her tightness – of muscle, of mind – ease and loosen.

We separated and she used Mr. Birch's handkerchief again before taking my arm once more.

Pearl stepped forward, but I turned her to the right.

"Would you mind, Pearl, if we stopped in to see my papa before heading home? I haven't seen him since our return, and I—"

"Of course we can." Pearl made the turn on to Memorial with me. "Of course you need to see him."

We made our way toward the Great Common, a place that, in

Italy, would be called the town square. We didn't need to but we chose to walk through the Parade, on one of the three intersecting circles within the triangle of the green. I would always choose to walk near the Liberty Tree. Though it was not the original one, not the one planted in 1766 when something called the Stamping Act was lifted. I didn't know that much about the Revolution's history, but I knew this tree symbolized freedom and I had fought hard for mine. Spring burst in there, in the bird song, in the bright tree buds, and the blooming daffodils. From there, it was a short walk to my father's studio on Broadway.

The biting freshness of newly cut wood, the swirling nodes of sawdust dancing merrily in the air, my aging father's soft voice playing the background music... one step in and I traveled back to my childhood.

"Papa?" I could hear him but not see him amid the teeming work taking place in every corner of the small, packed woodworking studio. There were beautiful tables of oak, breakfronts with my father's signature fine carvings, and, of course, violins and violas.

I called out for him again as Pearl stepped to one bench where a young man planed a large round table, unusual for its non-traditional shape.

This place, this dream of my father's that had come true, was much like I knew such places were in Italy, studios where the *maestro* schooled his apprentices, teaching them his craft, designing for them to create. Yes, Papa was aging, hands growing more gnarled by the passing time, crooked by years of overuse. Never did I feel so grateful for his long life, especially after these past weeks.

"*Sei tu, figlia?*"

From far behind the many workbenches, his low, crackling voice reached out.

His English had broadened by leaps and bounds in the almost twenty years since we had come to these American shores, yet Papa's tongue moved more naturally upon Italian.

"*Sí*, Papa. It's me." I followed the sound through the maze of men, machines, and wood to find my father huddled over a desk covered in illustrated strewn papers; a collage of beauty to my eyes.

My heart burst with joy as my eyes found his. How we can take those regularly in our lives for granted until we are reminded just how quickly they can be taken from us.

I walked around the desk to kiss him atop his head, one with nothing but bits of hair left on it.

Deep eyes full of surprise beneath bushy gray brows questioned.

"I just thought to stop in and say hello, Papa," I answered. "We are on our way back home from The Beeches."

"We?"

I nodded. "Me and Pearl."

"Pearl, she is-a here?" His gnarled hands pushed against his desk, his long, creaking legs against the floor, and he stood, though not nearly as tall and straight as he once had. Time had seemed to have frozen him in the bent posture of when he worked, when he designed. The light I had sparked in his eyes dimmed. "Where?"

I pointed out to the workshop.

I hadn't seen Papa move so quickly in years. His age and unease of movement, his wife's illness, had kept them from traveling to New York for the services. He had not seen Pearl in many months, not since the before of her life.

I followed in his wake, watched his head swivel to and fro, searching, stopping all when he found her. I did not know what was on his face but I saw the invitation in his raised, open arms. With bittersweetness blurring her features, Pearl accepted it, walked into those arms.

Papa closed them about her so tightly as if, in the firmness, he could absorb her pain.

"*Mi dispiace molto*," he whispered into her head crooked between his chin and his shoulder. "So sorry, *cara mia*."

I could not see Pearl but I could see how her hands upon his back fisted the cloth of his shirt.

"I can no be your papa, re… re…" he struggled.

"Replace," I whispered.

"*Sí,* replace. I can no replace your papa, but when-a you need a papa, I be your papa. Let-a me be you papa."

How I wish Mr. Birch had given me one of his handkerchiefs. I stepped around my father; I had to see her. Pearl did not move from his embrace or the one made by his beautiful words.

"*Sí, piccolina?*"

I don't think he would have let her go until she nodded her head he held against him.

Papa released her with a kiss upon her forehead.

Pearl dabbed her face with Mr. Birch's handkerchief.

"How are you? Are you feeling well?" She asked of him.

"Well, *sí.*"

"And Mrs. Costa?"

I flinched, as I always did as I heard the woman I knew as Mrs. O'Brennan, the sullen woman, a widow, who had once been Chef Pasquale's assistant, called by my mother's name. I did not begrudge either of them for the love they had found in each other, in fact, I was grateful for it. In the dead of the winters when only four of us remained as caretakers of The Beeches, Clara had taught me to cook, had taught my Papa how to speak English, and had shown his heart how to love again.

My father put out a hand, waggled it from palm to back and back to palm again in answer. "So so," would be the most fitting translation.

It grieved us all that Clara's lungs troubled her.

"I'm sure you're taking the best of care of her," Pearl assured him.

"I do best," Papa said.

The three of us stood in a triangle, but we were not alone – death, grief, and time's unstoppable march stood with us.

"Are these tables becoming popular?" Pearl broke the cloud upon us stepping back to the round table with the finely carved legs.

"*Si,*" Papa said, nodding.

"I may just order one." Pearl rubbed her hand over the smooth top. "They are so very intimate, don't you think, Ginny?"

"I do."

"You no order," Papa said. "I make one, just-a for you."

I think he touched her heart yet again. Pearl knew enough about Italians to know how to respond.

"You are so kind. I would be honored." To turn any gift away from an Italian was to insult the giver himself. Besides, I think she really wanted one.

"We have to go, Papa. The children will be home from school soon." I gave my father one last hug, as did Pearl, and we made our way to the door. As I opened it and stepped through it, Pearl turned back.

"*Addio…* Papa," she said to him.

With a crooked smile, he nodded. "*Arrivederci, cara figli.*"

Pearl's arm curled with mine again and we walked home in silence, our family, living and dead, walked with us.

Ginevra

June 1912

So many of the island's people so often complained about it, about its many steps, but I never minded the journey from Newport to Providence. It was often not the easiest; the short steamboat ride from the pier in Newport over to Wickford on the mainland of Rhode Island could be brutal in the harshness of winter. Then it was on to a train for a short ride from the Wickford pier to the Wickford Junction Railroad Station and then, at last, the final leg of the trip from Wickford into Providence by yet another train.

There were times when the nearly one-hour journey was the favorite of my day. I had no one to take care of, worry about, save myself. In truth, I often did my best design work while bobbing or bumping along. For that, and so much more, I would always be grateful to the Tirocchi sisters.

Half sisters, Anna and Laura, born fifteen years apart, owned and operated one of the most successful dress shops in the state, in the country for that matter, one of the few owned and operated solely by women. After the disaster that had been my first position after graduation, I had been thrilled and so very hopeful to be working for women, and Italian immigrants like myself for that matter.

Before becoming a seamstress and then a designer for the Tirocchi label, or A & L Tirocchi Gowns, as was the official name of their establishment, I had worked for – suffered under – one Mr. Jackson Neigle. A brash, egotistical, tyrannical, and stingy man but I endured it all in the gratitude of employment. It was only when he had stolen my designs, claimed them as his own, and warned me against revealing his treachery, did I walk from his shop, never to return again. When I slammed that door, I thought I had slammed the door on all my dreams, until I met Anna and Laura.

I walked the last leg of the journey to their elaborate Victorian home – and the location of their business – on another street named Broadway, this one in the heart of Federal Hill, the center of Italian immigrants and culture within the capital city of Providence. I walked in that day as I had done on my very first… with wonder and a true sense of belonging.

Fashion, everywhere the eye fell, fashion greeted it. There were dressmakers – in truth, no more than seamstresses – by the hundreds, working from their homes in and around the city. The very threads sold by J & P Coats and those in Fruit of the Loom undergarments were manufactured in this very city, one that could boast itself as the primary manufacturer of worsted textiles in the country. But there was no place, no garments, as grand as those produced by A & L Tirocchi Gowns. They had, after all, worked in Rome for one of the dressmakers to Queen Margherita of Italy.

"*Buongiorno,* Ginevra."

I looked up the staircase that hugged the right wall and led to the second-floor rooms and the landing above.

"*Buongiorno,* Anna," I called back with a wave.

"I am happy to see you back."

"I'm happy to be back, Anna." We hugged when I reached her.

"You are well… your friend?" Her dark eyes squinted as if by doing so she could see inside me.

"As well as can be," I wouldn't lie to her.

Imposing and assertive, with a bosom to make any Italian man bite his finger in admiration, Anna was the stronger force in the business than her half-sister Laura, who had just married Dr. Louis J.

Cella Jr, whose offices were in this building as well. Anna had not married; at the age of thirty-nine, it was unlikely she ever would. She was married to her work and each gown and dress were her children. As one of the lead designers, I worked closely with Anna, listening and learning everything I could.

"I am so thankful for your understanding of my time away." I did not speak such words of gratitude merely to gush upon my employer but to offer the truth in my heart.

Anna waggled my words away with a plump hand. "*Sciocchezza*! As much as this work means to us, it is nothing without family. She is like your family, *sì*?"

"She is," I nodded.

"Well then." Anna threw both hands up in the air and that was the end of it. "Get to your pencil, Ginevra. Already they come asking what your suits will be for fall."

I hid my smile, one the humility my father taught me would not approve of. The House of Tirocchi was famed for its gowns, all kinds of gowns, perhaps the most elaborate gowns I had ever seen in person, especially the bridal gowns. But since my promotion seven years ago from seamstress to designer, my style of daywear, especially my suits, were becoming just as popular, just as sought after. I hoped, though I did not design many, that my gowns would one day be considered among the grand ones of the house as well.

"Humility be damned," I muttered.

"Eh, what's that you say?" Anna asked as we walked in opposite directions from each other.

"Oh, just, um, how glad I am to be back today." I did my best.

Anna merely smiled and trudged her way down the stairs to the showroom in front of the sewing rooms.

Hours sped past, the sunlight in my little space – no more than a closet with a window – shifted and danced. My neck and back creaked as I uncurled them from over my tilted table. I had completed three suits, each with a jacket, skirt, shirt, and the appropriate undergarments. I spread the sketches out on the table before me, kneading my sore neck while feeling rather pleased with myself. The sketched faded from my thoughts when I heard my name mentioned in the showroom below.

I slipped out and then down the stairs, hugging the last post of the railing as if it were big enough to hide me.

Mrs. Ashbel Wall, Lucy, one of Tirocchi House's most dedicated – and wealthy – clients flipped her way through a design book with gloved hands. She had stopped on one, stared at it, as the sisters sweet-talked her.

"Well, ahn't these something." It seemed that those who lived on the East Side of Providence spoke with the same haughtiness as the rich in Newport. Her words brought me that flutter, the fluttering wings of both satisfaction and pride.

"Ginevra's work is so very distinctive, no? You would look splendid in that."

Though I had yet to see her, I recognized Laura's voice immediately. Her never-balanced balancing of work and family life found her in the showroom more often than anywhere else.

"It is perfect for your lovely figure," Anna assured the woman.

I slipped off my perch and tiptoed down the hall, to enter the room behind the showroom, to peek through the curtains that separated the two. I had to know which of my designs they were looking at. I saw it and my jaw tightened. It was one of my Oriental gowns. I had hoped it merged the growing obsession with Orientalism, with its full, kimono-like draping, with the softer, more fluid silhouettes coming out of Paris.

"You will be the belle of the ball in that, most certainly," Laura continued to flatter.

"Hmmm." Mrs. Wall's study of the design had not been broken by the sisters' coaxing.

"A bell, indeed." Mrs. Wall flipped the page of the design book; a flap that flattened me. "But one that would ring much louder than I prefer."

Obviously, she thought her sky-high hats and fur-trimmed everything were not a loud, large bell.

I felt my deep sigh as well as heard it. As popular as my suits were becoming, no one had yet to order one of my gowns, gowns of the haute couture I dreamed off long before I knew what to call it.

I took myself to the back room and sat at the table where all the employees ate lunch. I ate nothing but my bitter disappointment.

They found me there, the sisters, after Mrs. Wall left.

Laura smacked a kiss upon my cheek. "I'm happy to see you, Ginevra."

I nodded like a child denied a toy.

Anna would have none of my self-pity.

"You are just ahead of your time, *cara*. But your time will come."

I could only keep nodding, this time with a pretend smile. Time had never been a good friend of mine.

Pearl

It was my church as much as Trinity Church was, the historic Episcopalian church we attended every Sunday, always trying to sit in the pew with the engraved silver plaque that read: *In this pew George Washington worshipped when visiting Newport.* What American would not want to sit in that pew? I loved the church's tall, thin, striking spire, one so visible from the bay that sailors used it as a guide when navigating their way into port.

But this church, the one I visited daily, the one where I was free to be the artist I had always longed to be, was the Wright Gallery; indeed, the *right* gallery, owned and operated by my husband and me.

I stopped at the door on the second floor of the Brick Market Building. As it closed softly behind me, an aberrant notion knuckled its way into my mind—one that had taunted me ever since speaking with Herman Wilson, Esq. Legally, I had no ownership in an establishment that *I* established, that *I* paid for with my family's money, that *I* filled with paintings, my own and those of others I curated. There are thoughts in every life that fill the gullet with dread so deep and twisting it made one feel sick. Such had this reality of my legal state – that I had none – done; I had choked on that dread every day since the revelation of my truth.

"Yes, this is one of my wife's pieces." Peter's dear voice – bubbling with pride – spat at that dread.

More patrons strolled about the gallery, ornaments on the tree of my hopes and dreams. I had filled the gallery with as many local artists as I could, as deserved to be hung on these walls. But what brought the people in were those few works—small in size, mammoth in influence and stature—that I had managed to acquire for rather healthy sums. Georges Seurat's *La Tour Eiffel* not only exhibited the epitome of Pointillism, but it also reminded me of our honeymoon in Paris, when we danced beneath the tower itself. Though it was small at nine inches by five inches, I had, nonetheless, given it a place of honor in the center of the main wall beneath the best lighting.

Beside it was a work by a deceased painter, a genius to my eyes. I had no clue as to why it was only after his death that his works were starting to gain attention, thanks in large part to his sister-in-law whose husband had died young as well. But I was quite thrilled at the moderate price I had paid for it and found it difficult to think of parting with it. It spoke to me so loudly, with such a distinct voice.

I often stared at *The Sower*, a small depiction of a subject that the artist had depicted more than once. His contrasting hues of yellow and purple, his heavy application of paint that made the sun look as if one could reach out and touch it, be burned by it, that made the river look like it flowed, found me studying this artist's work as often as I could. Every time one of Vincent van Gogh's works was featured in a periodical, I cut it out and tacked it on my studio walls. Their vivid colors and gut pounding emotion was the tapestry within which I worked.

I had started to see his influence in my own work, along with that of Pablo Picasso. That I attempted to marry Post-Impressionism with Cubism was far greater a challenge than I had anticipated but I would not be deterred.

"It's a rather curious technique," I heard the woman who spoke with my husband say as if she had somehow heard my thoughts.

"Right you are." Peter's charming exuberance filled the gallery. "And that is what makes it not only unique but masterful. For who but a master would attempt such a style?"

73

At that moment, his gaze found me. I could have mouthed the words, 'I love you'. There was no need. He gave me the slightest of winks and turned back to our customers. I slipped behind the left wall of the gallery to sidle to the back and my studio there.

My husband's words had started the wheels of my mind… why *did* I attempt to merge two styles so dissimilar? Perhaps it was how I defined my life. As one of my feet was planted in one world, the other stood firmly in another. It was all right there, on every canvas I had covered with my paints, in contrasting hues of light and dark, soft and bold strokes competing with each other… the question of who I am, what I am.   I knew my truth but I would forever paint the question I had to answer, no matter who it had hurt.

I put a new, blank canvas up on my easel, arranged my paints and brushes in the manner I always preferred… and sat there. I sat, wallowed, without picking up a brush, without deciding on a topic, or colors, or form. I had no idea how long I sat there. My brush and my muse had failed me since that day in April. In that failure, dark emptiness filled me. Too often my mind, the brush in my hand, attempted to fill the canvas with images. But any forms undulated as if in the water still, bloated and bruised and missing skin. Yet I could not banish the blankness, fill it with something other than that darkness. I had learned that year that darkness ate the light, light did not dispel darkness.

"Are you ready to head home, my Pearl?" Peter stuck his head around the corner of the studio. I had been sitting there for a very long while.

He came to me, perched before the blank canvas that screamed its frustration at me.

"They bought it, you know," he said as he stared at the damnable sight with me. "That couple you saw when you came in… they bought your piece."

"Well, that is something, I suppose."

Peter did not look surprised not to hear words of joy, words that should have been mine. Nor did I seem able to move my gaze, until Peter turned me, until he pulled me to my feet, lifted me up and to him. His sandalwood scent filled my senses. I retreated into him as I did so often, though retreat of any sort was anathema to me. Or had it been before?

"It will come back, my Pearl. I do not doubt it."

How I was so blessed to have found this man, to have him in my life, after the things I had done, would always remain a mystery to me.

"My soul is empty," I muttered into his chest where my head rested. "And it is the soul that feeds the artist."

He kissed my cheek, lips lingering near my ear. "Then you must find something to fill your soul back up."

Pearl

September 1912

"I think we should read this one next," I said to Ginevra as we sank into the cushions of my sofa and our children played on the floor at our feet. We all huddled close to the fire. Though the end of September could be like a summer day here in Newport, that day a drenching rain washed all its warmth away.

"What book is that?" Ginevra asked, arriving with armfuls of newspapers.

It had become the way of us since we learned the truth of our legal standing as married women – since we learned we had none – to read and discuss anything and everything we could find on the suffrage movement, on what was being done to change our non-existent status. Whether at one of our homes or beneath our trees, hours would pass as we immersed ourselves, educated ourselves as we should have done long before, as every woman should do.

"It's called, *A Woman of Genius*, and it's written—"

"Oh, it's about me, then." Ginevra snickered, as did her daughter, Angelina. Though but six years old, she listened. Parents often forget just how well children listen when we least want them to.

"It's written by Mary Austin," I continued with but a sidelong look of feigned petulance at the interruption. "It is a novel, but the subject matter is quite appropriate." I turned the book over and read the description: "*A novel of a woman's success despite her social constraints. A Woman of Genius draws its inspiration directly from the author's own life and experiences as a talented woman – in the novel, an actress – whose pursuit of a career places her in conflict with the values of a small, Midwestern town.*"

Ginevra snickered no more. "Did you get two copies?"

"I did." I handed her the second copy with a bit of an I-told-you-so flip of it.

I began to scan more pages as she finished reading the book's description: "*Olivia McGee's decision to leave a dull husband to pursue a career, and her rise to fame, are portrayed against the background of an inhibiting social order.*"

"That sounds a bit too familiar," Ginevra responded to what she read, read with such acumen, astounding as when I met her she couldn't read English at all.

She dropped the book in her lap. "As we are speaking of husbands, I truly do not understand why ours felt it so necessary to travel to Boston. What is so exciting about watching a bunch of men hitting a little ball into a little hole?"

I chuckled. Sometime over the summer, laughter and smiles had found me again, bloomed again, though their brilliance did not sparkle quite as glowingly as they had before, as they might never do again. But chuckle I did just then. Through Ginevra's immigrant eyes, no matter how high their vision had risen, life always seemed reduced to its basic truths, as if she could see them better than the rest of us.

"They are there, at the U.S. Open, Ginny, because it is the major golf tournament in our country," I explained as best I could without allowing the chuckle to grow at her expense. "And our men felt it important because of a young man named... um... Francis Ouimet. Yes, that's him. He's a poor young man from the Boston area and an amateur at the game. The son of immigrants, in fact. But it appears he could beat out the rich hoi-polloi."

"Really?"

My face stretched by my wide smile; I adored to see that glint of fascinated discovery in her eyes. I had seen it day after day as she and

I had traversed our teenaged years together. It was strangely comforting to see it still could appear, that my dear friend still relished learning as she had in the past.

"Really." I nodded. "Now he is a man you can understand."

"I understand his determination," she admitted. "When you are poor and from another country, you have to fight harder."

I could not argue with that.

"Speaking of fighters." Ginevra drew her bundle of papers on to her lap. "You will not believe what Alva has written in her latest column."

Our Alva Vanderbilt Belmont had been writing a column in the Chicago Sunday Tribune since the spring, using the space as a platform to articulate and inculcate her suffrage and women's rights philosophies upon those who read them.

"Listen to this." It was Ginevra's turn to read and I watched as the three children – one boy and two girls – slowed and quieted their play. I was glad for it. *"The world is arranged for the comfort and pleasure of men. Women and children are the victims of that arrangement. For example, predatory men feel free to engage in extramarital s-e-x…"* Neither of us wanted our children – the oldest, Ginevra's son at eight – to hear everything, though, at eight, Felix could figure out the word, *"and then infect their wives with venereal disease while employers force female wage earners to work in unhealthy conditions, thus making it impossible for women to fulfill their maternal responsibilities to bear and rear healthy children. While men have willingly given women responsibility for preserving the sanctity of the home and rearing children, they have neglected to give them the means to do so. Only through the vote could women protect their families from such threats."*

I wanted to applaud, yes, applaud Alva Vanderbilt, applaud her audacity. "She does not mince her words, does she?"

"What's a venable disease?" Felix asked, his dark eyes – so like his mother's – widened with curiosity.

"It's a rash that dirty people can give to other people." Ginevra stretched the truth as she answered her son without correcting his pronunciation of the word. His father would teach him about the real word when the time was right.

"That's why you must never argue when your mama tells you it's time to bathe." I just had to use the moment for all it was worth, for all our children.

Ginevra hid her smile behind her hand, her laughter behind a cough. "I think it powerful. I'm glad she writes so true."

"As am I," I agreed, "but she is taking blows for it."

"Only from the rich."

I nodded. "The rich and powerful." I put the book still in my hands on the small table before us, which the children were now using as a fort. "It is rather ironic that while she criticizes wealthy women for not assuming more leadership in the fight for the vote, those below her... of a lower income... criticize her as merely a socialite looking for more attention."

"At least the party itself does not. They have no problem using her status to further the cause."

"Or her money." I turned to my lifelong friend. "We must use whatever weapons we can to fix this. You believe that, too, don't you?"

Ginevra hesitated. I knew where her hesitation came from. As an immigrant, her position was even more precarious than mine. We had learned that, were her husband to die, the government would send her back to Italy, a home she hadn't been to in almost twenty years – and without her children.

"Yes, whatever we must do, whatever weapons we must use."

Her hand found mine across the cushions and gave it a hard squeeze. We were both firmly in this fight.

Ginevra

November 1912

We went that day, as we promised each other we would.

It was one of those sparkling late fall days, where dead leaves of vibrant colors swirled in circles, dancing in the wind beneath a pure blue sky even as the sun's perch became lower with each day that passed.

Neither Pearl nor I was surprised that Alva held the meeting at the Meetinghouse of the Society of Friends on Marlborough Street, just blocks away from both our houses. With our continued reading about the fight for suffrage, we'd learn that Quaker women, though they lived simple lives and were devout, had enjoyed an equal footing within their close-knit society since the religious society was formed in the 16th century. That equality put the rest of the world to shame.

From every direction, across the large spread of meadow that surrounded the meetinghouse, women flocked toward the door of the very square-shaped, very plain shingle building. Always in twos or threes – none alone as far as I could see – agile women fairly skipped along, while bent women helped each other along, some dressed in fur-trimmed coats, others in threadbare ones, yet they streamed together with the same aim.

"Pearl? Pearl Worthington, is that you?"

Together we turned, together we stopped, and together we recognized the woman rushing toward us, the large pile of straw-like, strawberry-blonde hair beneath a gauzy hat threatening to escape its pins. "Oh, and it is Ginevra too!"

"Mabel?" Pearl called back.

I clucked my tongue as I finally put a name to the familiar face; Pearl remembered faces better than I. It was Mabel Tucker flying to us. We had met Mabel in our first year at the Rhode Island School of Design, had become fast friends, but we had all lost touch after graduation, Mabel going one way, Pearl and I another.

"Oomph," Pearl croaked as plumper version of the Mabel we had known threw herself into her arms. "How lovely to see you!"

"Oh and you, Pearl… and you, Ginevra!"

It was my arms she thrust herself into and I couldn't help but laugh. She had always been so bright, so full of life. While not the classic beauty that was my Pearl, she drew a great deal of attention with the abundance of that hair, an abundance rivaled only by that of her bosom. The three of us had gotten up to some mischief in those days, as college students did within the freedom of the campus and the spark of learning.

"I'm so delighted to see you too, Mabel," I told her truthfully.

"And surprised," Pearl chimed in. "We thought you were still at home, in Virginia."

"Oh I was, I was."

I had forgotten how breathy and sweet her voice was.

"I had thought never to leave home again after college. But you will never guess where my husband, whom I met in Virginia, comes from?"

"Where?" Pearl and I asked.

"Portsmouth!" Mabel declared. "We've been living at his family's estate since we married almost eleven years ago."

"And you never came to find us?" Pearl chided.

We three became stuck stones as the stream of women rushed past us.

"I had every intention to," Mabel assured us, "but the children started coming and, well, with the five of them I have little time to myself."

"Five!" Pearl and I squeaked. I looked at Mabel with more respect.

When we had known her, she was that flighty girl, full of fun but not as serious about her studies as many of us. But any woman who gave birth to and raised five children deserved more of my respect. The question of the straw-like condition of her hair had been answered – if I had five children, I thought, I'd be bald.

Mabel laughed her tinkling laugh and shrugged her round shoulders bashfully.

"Did you come here alone?" I asked; there were no women who seemed to be waiting for her, none that I could see.

"I did," Mabel said, pouting. "My group of lady friends was too fearful to join me."

"Fearful?" This from Pearl. "Of attending a suffrage meeting?"

"Yes, that, and of Alva Vanderbilt Belmont!"

We all laughed then and together splashed back into the stream and continued toward the door, prattling on about husbands, married names, children, and such.

"Will wonders never cease," Pearl whispered as our feet hit the first of the three small wooden stairs leading to the main gabled door of the meeting house. In its frame stood the woman herself; Alva nodded and greeted each woman who passed through the door, who passed by her, women she wouldn't have looked twice at twenty years ago. Or if she had looked, it would have been in disapproval.

"There you two are," Alva enthused. "I was so hoping you would come, and here you are!"

Both Pearl and I looked behind to see who Alva gushed at… until she pulled Pearl into her arms. She gushed at us. Who was this woman?

"Doing better, are you?' Alva pushed back from Pearl to squint at her. "You look better, but it will take time."

"Thank you, Mrs. B—"

"Alva, please," the woman demanded. "The time has long come. You are grown women and we are united in a common cause. Ceremony, be damned."

"Thank you, A… Alva," Pearl tripped upon her name. We had been calling her that in private for some time but to do so to her face was something quite different.

"Ginevra Costa Taylor," she took my hand, shook it till my teeth rattled, "you are a shining example of all that the suffrage party stands for, that we aspire to, to rise despite our disadvantages, to rise above them."

Who was this woman? I almost couldn't speak. Thankfully, Pearl's elbow in my side helped me find my tongue.

"What a beautiful compliment," I said with my best American accent. "Thank you."

"And who is this with you?" Alva rose on tiptoes to see past my shoulder. Her eyes became circles at the woman she saw.

"Well, if it isn't Mabel Tucker Washburn, as I live and breathe."

I doubted if there was anyone Alva didn't know or know about.

"I must say, I am rather surprised to see you here." That was the Alva I understood; she greeted our friend with a sting. "Your mother is whole-heartedly and quite stupidly against suffrage."

I dropped my chin, hid my grin. Some things might never change.

"Oh, she is, Mrs. Belmont," Mabel effused. Alva did not invite Mabel to call her Alva. "And I pray you won't reveal my attendance here to her."

For a moment, the powerful woman who had organized this meeting stared at Mabel with steely black eyes as if she didn't quite swallow Mabel's words. Alva fluttered a dismissive hand.

"You can count on me, dearie. Anything I can do that is against the antis is my pleasure."

"The antis?" I whispered to Pearl. But Alva, as always, heard.

"It is what we call the women *against* suffrage," she spat. "The women who have organized to fight against our cause. The anti-suffragettes."

I looked up to see if the sun had gone behind a cloud. It hadn't. That was not where my shiver came from.

"There are enough of them that they have formed organizations?" I had to ask. My disbelief demanded it.

"Damnable ignoramuses," Alva snorted. "There are far more than you would think. In some states, there are far more against than in favor of suffrage. There are far too many antis... period. As if we do not have enough to fight against, we must fight our own gender as well."

Alva's gaze curdled even as she forced a smile upon her lips, as she waved us into the meetinghouse. "Quickly now, go take a seat. Toward the front, if you please."

It was not a suggestion, no matter the polite sound of the words. We did as we were told, walking towards the front on the wide-planked floors under the high-beamed ceiling and took three seats in the sixth row of plain benches.

We had to wait only a few minutes before the large room and all its chairs were filled with women, even the balcony overflowed with them, a tapestry of every color cloth that women were in that life, in that time. The presence of so many was both calming and exhilarating. Alva closed the door and stormed to the podium.

"As we have many new members among us today, I would like to have them introduce themselves. Ginevra, please start us off."

If I could have shrunken to the size of an ant and scurried off, I would have. Pearl's poke and Alva's stare denied me the escape.

"Good-a..." *Damn, speak American,* "Good day, ladies. I am

Ginevra Costa Taylor."

That was better. Yet, even as I spoke well, as I said my name, my husband's name, the name of my two children, that I was an Italian immigrant with a degree from Rhode Island School of Design and worked as a fashion designer for the Tirocchi sisters, the other truths of me ran through my head. I fought the grin these thoughts brought out even as they dared me to say them... *and my dearest friend here is Pearl Worthington Wright – she killed a man who was trying to rape me. I lied and said I did it to save her. She lied in court, under oath, to save me from hanging. Then we ran away from our families and ran off to college together.*

Oh yes, that would endear us to this group.

I looked down, Pearl up. Our mirrored smiles told me our thoughts were mirrored as well.

I was surprised at how few of us were "new" and most of the new women were our age or younger. Husbands and children; the core of our lives and yet...

"How many of you..." Alva's voice became a blasting foghorn heard so often in Newport, a call for attention and a warning. "How many of you have felt inhibited by the realization that men have traditionally used their patriarchal power to silence and distort women's voices?"

Every hand rose, ours included.

"We do not say the truth of our souls." Alva banged a tight fist upon the podium. "We say things men have taught us to say, have told us what is becoming and fitting for us to say."

All she had suffered in her life infected her voice with bitterness. "I have returned from my time with the suffragettes of England. I have returned invigorated by what I saw and heard. I have returned with the resolute belief that American women are simply not doing enough, we are not fighting enough for our rights."

Alva paused, a furrow forming upon her brow, a cloud crossing over the shine of her zeal.

"One of the great regrets of my life is that, while I had a close relationship with my sons while they were children, when they reached a certain age, I could play no role in their political education or philosophies. I could not offer a wider perspective through my eyes, my life, for it was a life deemed inferior and unworthy to offer any notions, simply because of my gender."

Pearl reached over and uncurled my tight fists where they rested in my lap. The realization that Alva had thrust upon me cut me to the bone. My dear Felix and I were so close... would I truly "lose" him when he came of age because I was his mother and not his father? I shook my head against it.

"And I assure you, this lack of voice hurts most those who are in greatest need of it," Alva continued. "What of the overworked, underpaid woman, the mother toiling for hungry children, the drunkard's wife, the woman of the scarlet letter, the wife replaced by one younger and fairer?" With the last, she slipped herself dead center in the cause. "They have no voice to fight against these injustices, they are weaponless. The duty now facing us is to improve the conditions under which women work and to help them obtain an adequate price for their labor. We, dear ladies..." Again that fist, again it banged. "We must give them their voice, we must give them the vote so they may improve their lot."

We were suddenly in a Baptist church with a rousing preacher giving the sermon. The rallying cries of the women filled the room, their voices cried out for the justice, for the need to be heard, that Alva incited we fight for. I heard my own among them. Only with Alva's flapping down hands did we quiet.

"I have called you all here today with an immediate goal... to go out and multiply. No, not to birth more children, but to inform and convert as many women to our cause as possible!" Her thunderous voice shook the rafters, shook that vein of blood that ran through every woman there who knew lack, invisibility, and even harm from not possessing a voice.

"Who's with me?" Alva cried.

"I am!" came the loud, determined answer as many voices rose as one, including mine and Pearl's.

Looking back, I realized not every voice joined in the chorus that day.

When the long meeting adjourned, Alva encouraged us to sign up for one of the many activities necessary to further the suffrage cause. Painting signs, working on a newsletter, recruiting other women to join the fight. This last appealed to Pearl mostly because she knew so many people on the island and people of different standings in society. I wrote my name beneath hers on this paper.

"It was so wonderful to see you, ladies." Mabel made her goodbyes as we chose our chores. "I'm sure I will see you at the next meeting."

"It was a lovely reunion," Pearl agreed. "What have you decided to help with? It'll be just like old times, the three of us getting up to mischief."

"But this time it will be for a good cause," I laughed, remembering some of our antics.

"Oh... um... I-I haven't decided yet," Mabel struggled, looking away, looking on as all the other women signed up for something. "My family, my children, well, they just take so much of my time."

"I bet they do," I agreed heartily. I could not imagine it.

"Perfectly understandable." Pearl supported our friend as well. "But you must come and call upon us." Pearl handed Mabel a card from her reticule, as did I. "Bring your family. I'm sure our husbands and children would be delighted to meet each other."

"Or we could come to you," I offered. "With so many of you, it might be easier if we did."

"That would be lovely," Mabel replied. Kissing us quickly, she hurried off.

"It was so nice to see her," Pearl said as we finished adding our names, as we made our way from the building.

"It was. Seeing her has brought me some fond mem—oh!" I stopped, squinting into the distance to see if I could still see Mabel. "She did not give us her card."

"Oh dear," Pearl tutted. "But with so many children, I'm surprised she can remember her own name."

I laughed. "We must remember to get it at the next meeting."

Our families dined together that night, as we so often did. The children ate at the breakfast table in the cozy room off the kitchen while we grown-ups dined at the large table in the formal dining room, with its shining mahogany furniture and glittering but small crystal chandelier. Though intimate, Pearl had still brushed it with the lightest strokes of opulence and elegance.

It was a very good thing our husbands enjoyed each other's company. It would have made things rather difficult if they didn't for I doubt if even the love of a good man could have kept Pearl and me apart. The men had known each other in college; they had become fast friends when they married us.

Pearl laughed too much that night; I said too little.

She urged me with bulging eyes; I denied her with pinched lips.

"All right, you two." Osborn dropped his cutlery – cutlery so fine my mother would have cooed every time she had held a piece, that her daughter ate with such beautiful pieces if she had ever been alive to hold a piece – far too loudly upon the table. My eyes rolled behind closed lids; he knew me, knew both of us, far too well. "I have no wish to spend the rest of this fine meal waiting and wondering what you're reluctant to tell us."

With the hint of a smile on his lips, Peter chimed in, "I'm willing to wager it has something to do with the meeting you went to this afternoon."

"Oh, you are just the smartest," Pearl chirped at her husband, a twittering bird's high, sweet tweeting.

"Pearl, please," Peter disarmed her, not only with his words but with a scathing stare, the sort that seemed to belong particularly to married couples. "Do you think such wheedling is not obvious after more than a decade of marriage?"

"Oh, all right then." Pearl dropped her cutlery, her voice, and her façade. "It does have to do with the meeting we attended this afternoon."

"It was a very informative meeting," I offered. She had begun, but I would help.

"And if we are speaking truths…" Pearl tossed her linen napkin upon the table and plunked her elbows upon it as well. Wherever her mother was in the beyond, she was most certainly squawking in horror. It is in great part due to the loss of my family that I went. What I… what we… learned from our attorney as to our rights, or the lack thereof, frightened us both."

"As well it should," Osborn said softly. My husband knew what becoming a naturalized citizen of these United States had meant to me. To learn it had all crumbled because I married him troubled him greatly, though none of the blame was his to carry.

I reached across the table to give his hand a quick squeeze. As I drew it back, I gave them the heart of the truth. "We are joining them, the suffragettes."

Peter squinted and frowned at his wife. "And you thought I would be angry about this? Surely, you know me better, my Pearl."

Pearl's gaze slipped to me then back to Peter. "No, dearest, I never thought you would, I swear to you. But... but we have volunteered for a particular activity, among many, that Alva thinks—"

"Oh, so it's Alva now, is it?" Peter did laugh then as Osborn chuckled softly.

I could not contain myself. "She asked us to call her that, even me." The squeak in my voice at the end of my words came from the before Ginevra, the servant Ginevra.

"My, my, my," Osborn marveled, "perhaps she is truly for equality in all matters."

"I believe she is," I assured him.

"Exactly what is it that you'll be doing?" Peter asked. He would not be thrown off-topic by the frivolity of a woman's first name.

"We are to be part of the recruitment squad," Pearl informed him with an upward tilt of her chin.

"And exactly what does that mean?" Peter was no longer a practicing attorney, but he was an attorney.

"We will be going house to house, among our friends and neighbors, to speak with the women—"

"To inform them," I jumped in.

"Yes, to inform them about the need for suffrage."

"And to get them to join the suffrage party."

There it was; it was all out there on the dining room table, served with just a sprinkle of persuasion. Pearl and I waited. I don't know if she was breathing – I wasn't.

Our husbands took their time. Like mirror images, they each sat back in their chairs, each crossed their arms over their chests. Were men taught this posture as boys?

"Will it put you in any danger, darling?" Osborn asked of me. I could have flung myself across the table to kiss him. I almost did. That his first concern was for my safety and not in disapproval made me love him more, something I didn't think possible.

"It will not. We will only go to those homes within our neighborhood, among families like us." I didn't say the words, but the implied class distinction – financial distinction – was there, though to belong to a different class from the one I was when I arrived at these shores still felt to me like a pair of shoes that didn't fit quite right.

"We have sold paintings to some of those families, some of your paintings, Pearl." Peter had nodded while I assured them of our safety, then turned his mind to the more practical. "We may lose some customers."

"If *those* customers would be lost, then good riddance to them," Pearl said, spitting the words with contempt. She took a good, long swig of her wine. "Besides, it could turn out quite the opposite. As that man said…" Pearl snapped her fingers once, twice, three times; her mind scurried. "Oh, that man with the circus, he said—"

"Barnum, P. T. Barnum," Osborn helped.

"That's him! Thank you, Osborn. He said that bad press is better than no press at all. It seems to be working for him. Perhaps this will work for us as well."

She tried so hard to shine a light upon the clouds that could roll in with our activity.

"Perhaps…" My mind rushed about. "Perhaps we could tell the ladies who are friendly and approve of our cause about the gallery. I'm sure we'll be talking to many nice people, perhaps even friends of Pearl's from her childhood. We may gain some customers for your gallery rather than lose any."

Pearl gave me a look, the kind that lived only between two people who had saved each other time and time again.

Peter nodded, though I still saw no smile on his lips or in his eyes. "It's possible," he conceded. "We shall have to see how this falls out."

"Wonderful!" Pearl jumped up then and round the table to hug his shoulders. "Then you'll be so pleased to hear we start tomorrow."

"Unh," Peter groaned as his eyes looked heavenward.

Osborn laughed at his suffering.

Pearl

"These are very powerful, aren't they?"

Ginevra and I set out at nine o'clock the next morning, time enough for children to be in school and husbands to be at work. We wore our most sensible outfits, suits of Ginevra's making, with little of the extra flair that made her designs so distinctive from others. We often wore these same suits to church. They spoke of fineness but not opulence, solemnity but not dreariness. And we both carried as many pamphlets as we could, those Alva had given us at the meeting.

"They are, yes." Ginevra agreed as she read them, as we walked.

I had read and reread them many times. I'm not sure who wrote them, but they knew what they were about, they knew the power of words... words formed to forge the pen that is indeed mightier than the sword.

The first line, a small headline, read, *Votes for Women!* But the words that demanded one's attention were on the next line, in larger type, *The Woman's Reason*, with another word below it: *Because.* This word was repeated in bold, capital letters seven times and after each instance, it answered the question as to why women wanted and deserved the vote, everything from the fact that women must obey laws just as men do without a word as to their formation, to the truth that there were now eight million women earning a wage in our country, to the blazing assertion that women are citizens of a nation with a government OF the people, BY the people, and FOR the people, AND WOMEN ARE PEOPLE.

This last hit hard, both for the power of the words, and the astonishing fact that they needed to be said. Imagine, having to fight for the right of existence. But that was the sad truth of it. I had tacked one to the wall in Mary's bedroom.

We came to the end of Colonial Street, a turn of a corner and a short walk from Ginevra's house. As she had predicted the night before, I did know the woman of the house from my childhood.

Hattie's family had always lived on the fringes of Newport's society, close enough that invitations did find them now and again, not so close that they were considered part of the "set". Each time they had been grateful for whatever crumb was tossed their way. I hoped Hattie still felt the same now that she was married and with three children of her own.

"Pearl Worthington, at my very door," Hattie answered quickly after our knock. She offered a greeting, one that could be construed caustically, yet came with a smile. "It's lovely to see you outside of church."

"It is, isn't it," I said with all the warmth I could muster. Had we found friend or foe? Her grin around a cutting tongue tasted both sweet and bitter upon mine. "May I introduce my friend, Ginevra Taylor?"

Ginevra quickly thrust her hand out. Hattie took it and shook it. "Of course, who in Newport does not know Ginevra?" Once more, words that sliced were offered without a knife. There could be no doubt they referred to the fact that everyone in Newport still believed Ginevra had killed a man, even if he had deserved it. I would wear that cloak of guilt my entire life.

"It is a pleasure to meet you," Ginevra said with soft kindness; how she found it in the face of this reception would always be a mystery to me.

"What brings you to my door, ladies?" Hattie still smiled – I still worried.

"Well, Hattie, I remember what a smart girl you are and I thought you might like to hear a bit about a group of women and our efforts to obtain the vote." She *had* been smart, always, mentioning this was a truth as well as a compliment. As I spoke, Ginevra handed her one of the pamphlets. As Hattie's bright, blue eyes scanned the paper, I continued, "We feel it has come time—"

"*You* have joined the suffragettes?" Her eyes flew from the paper to my face.

"I have, as has Ginevra."

Hattie leaned out the doorway and looked up and down the mostly quiet street. As she pulled back in, that smile of hers grew as wide as the street her gaze scoured. She pushed her door all the way open. "Oh, please do come in. I have been wondering about it all myself. But if Pearl Worthington Wright is for it, there must be something to it."

As I followed her into her home, Ginevra gave me a small pinch on the back of my arm. My name had opened the first door, had opened the first mind.

The next woman had let us into her home, though neither one of us knew her. The small home stood just behind the White Horse Tavern, a tavern in which Thomas Jefferson had quenched his thirst, a tavern that had stood in Newport since the 17th century. The typical crowd of patrons could be rustic and raucous, but there was always fun to be had within the tavern's walls. More than once the four of us had donned our least opulent threads and immersed ourselves in the bawdy reverie and more than a few bottles of Narragansett Beer.

Cora Scoon responded to our introductions, our reason for the visit, with a silent nod of her head and a soft, "Do come in."

Though the square, gambrel-roofed home appeared small, it did not suffer in either opulence or cleanliness. Finely crafted furniture filled every spotless room, pearls within oysters. Ginevra and I both hesitated to sit, to disturb the elegance of Cora's home until she invited us to do so.

"May I offer you something?" Cora asked as her hands invited us to sit upon the brocade settee.

"No, thank you, Cora," I replied. "We don't want to take up too much of your time."

Time she mostly spent cleaning, I had no doubt.

Ginevra handed her a pamphlet and, as Cora studied it in her cocoon-like quiet, I hoped to engage her further.

"What you read gives many reasons why women deserve the vote as a right, but there's a great deal more to it, as I have learned first-hand."

I continued, telling her of my family's death, for which she offered heartfelt condolences without surprise. She must have heard, as most in this small community had, as most of the world had. The shock of my loss of legal rights to my family's property and wealth, all women's loss of citizenship upon marriage, I did not have to feign; it still confounded and disturbed. As I revealed my story, Cora's soft green eyes lifted from the paper, grew wide and unblinking upon my face. It moved only when Ginevra told her personal story, the threat she now knew she lived under, and the need for the vote.

Ginevra's tale came to an end and we found ourselves tightly held within Cora's silence. She studied us as one would a da Vinci masterpiece. My knee began to bob. Ginevra clasped and unclasped her gloved hands.

"My husband is a good man," Cora finally spoke; a beginning that troubled. "But he is a firm man. I must…" Cora looked away and out the two windows of her lovely sitting room, "I must ask permission to leave the house for anything other than errands."

And there it was, the most prevalent obstacle we would encounter from so many women who wanted suffrage, but needed "permission" to fight for it… the highest obstacle we must hurdle. Between my father and my Peter, I did not have experience with men such as this, good men, as Cora had said, but controlling men. It had been my mother who had built the borders of my life. I had no words – no weapons – against a foe I had never truly encountered.

Ginevra leaned forward, elbows on knees, gaze pinned to Cora's face.

"Do you have daughters, Cora?" she asked with a softness to match Cora's own.

Cora nodded. "Two," she said simply, and, for the first time, we saw that she could smile.

"When you talk with your husband, when you ask him for permission to join us…"

I could have applauded my friend; I would have advised Cora to call her husband a fopdoodle and that she would do what she wished to do. Listening to Ginevra coddle this woman, I knew such an attitude would find us defeated more often than not.

"…Ask him to think of your daughters. Ask him to picture them in Pearl's situation, having no legal right to anything her father had worked so hard for." Ginevra leaned closer still. "I'm betting your husband is a hardworking man."

Cora nodded with enthusiasm and another glimpse of her small smile. Her husband was her master, the master of this household, but love filled this house grander than its marvelous furniture.

"Ask him how he would feel if he spent his life working hard for a good life for your family, enough to build some saved wealth," Ginevra sat back with a snap, "then ask him how he would feel if it was all lost because his children are female."

Ginevra had caused my own heart to pump faster, for the blood to run hot in my veins. I could see such heat brush red upon Cora's face. She began to nod.

"I will talk to him," she said simply.

Ginevra stood and I followed suit. "That is all we ask, for now." She held out her hand to Cora, standing now as well. "When you are ready for more information, please feel free to come to either of our homes." She handed Cora her card, as did I.

"And bring your husband," I suggested on a whim. "I'm sure he would benefit from speaking with our husbands, strong men both firmly in support of our suffrage."

"Thank you, ladies," Cora said as she walked us to our door. "I woke up this morning with a feeling today would be different somehow. I would never have guessed the truth would come in such a form."

It was the most words she had said throughout our visit and they put on display the keenness of her mind.

"We are hoping all our tomorrows will be different. Good day to you, Cora." Ginevra closed our visit with the woman with rousing words and gentle manners.

As we continued up the street, I put an arm around my sister.

"Have I ever told you how brilliant you are?" I asked her.

"Not nearly often enough."

We giggled our way to the next house on our list.

"How dare you!"

We were greeted by a screech at the next door. It was a grand door of a grand house on Coddington Street, opened by a grandly dressed woman, but a woman who could yell as grandly as any drunken sailor in the bawdy taverns near the docks.

"Do you dare to eliminate the purpose of womanhood? Do you

mean for us to forget our duties to our children, to our husbands? Will you emasculate our husbands?"

Her screeching joined that of the seagulls overhead as if she called them to her. Doors and windows opened along the street to hear it better after hearing the first notes of its squeaky shrieks.

"Oh, I am not surprised, not surprised at all, that *you* two," she continued, her lip curling as her gaze racked us, "would be such women, would try to bring our nation to ruin with your capriciousness. You will suffer that which you deserve, oh yes indeed you will."

Was she actually threatening us?

"You are nothing but—"

"One moment, please, madam." She had gone too far for me. Though Ginevra tried to hold me back, it was a futile attempt. "I will not allow you to speak to us in such an insulting manner, we are undeserving of it, of your vitriol. You simply need say no thank—"

She rushed away from my words, from us, and yet she left her door wide open. Ginevra and I looked at each other with the same gaze of pure stupefaction. I glanced over my shoulder. There seemed to be many more "strollers" than there had been but five minutes before.

"Should we…" Ginevra began, just as the woman came rushing back.

"Here!" she bellowed. "You need to read this. We will stop at nothing to stop the vote, to rid our society of the likes of you, a curse on the family unit, an insult to womanhood itself! You disgust me, you hussies!"

She threw a pamphlet at us as she spat at our feet and slammed the door in our face.

Our legs were knee-deep in stone.

Ginevra moved first, bending to pick up the paper at our feet.

"*The Case Against Woman Suffrage,*" she read, though I could see clearly the large, bold headline. "*It is by the prom... promu...*"

I leaned and looked. "Promulgation."

"*It is by the prom-u-la-gation,*" she continued to read, her Italian roots inserting an extra vowel, "*of sound morals in the community, and more especially by the training and instruction of the young, that woman performs her part toward the preservation of a free government.* It is a quote by a man named Daniel Webster. Who is he?"

"He..." I heard the growl in my voice. I didn't care. In fact, I raised my voice so that the gawkers in the street could hear me as well. "He was a good man, actually, a man of government, who died...*almost a hundred years ago!*" It felt so good to yell, to tell the world just how outdated such thinking was.

I wrapped my arm with Ginevra's, held my head high as we left the stoop of this misguided woman's home, as we walked past all those who had enjoyed the tableau.

"You may all return to your homes," I called out to them, "the show has come to an end."

"Hush," Ginevra tried, squeezing my arm.

"It was a terrible show, wasn't it?" I asked the crowd. "Poorly delivered and even more poorly written. But what can one expect from the small-minded?"

I tipped my finely-hatted head at them as we walked away.

"Have I told how devilish you are?" Ginevra asked as we turned a corner and left them.

"Not nearly often enough." I laughed but held her tighter when I noticed how pale her tawny skin had become. "That was fun, wasn't it?" I tried to joke her fear away.

Ginevra shook her head like a clock's pendulum, going back and forth with no thought or control.

"Alva told us. But I didn't believe her," she finally confessed.

"And now?"

"Now… I am a believer. A frightened believer."

Ginevra

March 1913

"We are on the tips of slagging tongues again." I did not often disturb Pearl at her studio; I knew what focus an artist needed to create the things their minds saw. I had spent my childhood watching my father turn blocks of wood into the most beautiful violins. When I designed, I "saw" my fashion and then drew it on paper. Art is born in the mind, made real when we do the creating. "Why do you laugh? It is not a funny thing."

"No. Of course it isn't, dear," Pearl snickered. "But the expression is 'wagging' tongues, not 'slagging.' Slagging is—"

"Wagging, slagging, whatever." I waved away my wrong word away as I did her silliness. "The point is we are being talked about... again." I knew our work, our support of suffrage, and our activities to move the cause forward would possibly not be met kindly by everyone. I also knew I could not go back to being the Ginevra of *those* days, days when I sat in a prison, when my name was on every tongue in Newport. I knew I could not return to that pain.

Pearl's snickers died away; her mouth became a straight line across her lovely face. Seeing her like that made me feel a little better, but just a little.

"How do you know?" she asked. "And what are they saying?"

"Clara told me. I just came from my papa's studio." Sometimes I wondered if Clara enjoyed giving me bad news about myself. Sometimes I wondered if I was still a child who never wanted her father to be with anyone but her mother. "She said she heard someone say something like that murderess is up to trouble again with that fallen socialite friend of hers."

As soon as I said it, I knew I shouldn't have. Darkness fell over her face like a veil.

"Oh Pearl, I—"

"I should tell the truth. I really should." Pearl dropped the brush thick with paint on to her palette, rubbed her knuckles across her forehead. "I—"

"No! Never. You promised." She had... promised never to tell the truth. What did it matter? We both survived, both saved from any punishment. "I did no tell you to dug up the past, only to... to... well, I just needed to whine. That's all, Pearly. I swear."

Pearl grinned. She looked like she would snicker at me again. Instead, she stood and wrapped her arms around me.

"It's dig up the past, Ginny dear, not dug."

"Dig, dug, whatever." It was my turn to giggle.

"Whatever indeed." Pearl giggled with me, but then didn't. "The past is buried and no one will dig it up, whatever we do. And whatever we do, those who gossip will always like to gossip about us. Who cares?"

I didn't answer. I didn't want her to know how much I cared.

"You are not yourself tonight, *tesoro*. Is something troubling you?" Osborn snuggled close to me on the settee where I had retreated after putting the children to bed. It always made me smile when he called me that, *tesoro*... his treasure. I had tried to teach him more Italian but I had laughed too much and too loudly at his accent on my native language. The haughtiness of a New Englander's speech couldn't roll enough to speak the curling Italian words.

"It's true." I never lied to my husband. There was just one lie between us and it would stay that way.

I told him what Clara had told me.

Osborn pulled me closer to him, those blue eyes that always dazzled me narrowed and darkened. "That old biddy. She just likes to taunt you. She knows she will always have third place in your father's heart."

Yes, those blue eyes of his were dazzling, and they saw a great deal.

He turned me to him, his forehead kissing mine. "Don't let stupid words from stupid people stop you, dearest. What you and Pearl are doing is something that should be done."

I moved our kiss from our foreheads to our lips. There are times when just one person loving you, loving you truly, is all one needs.

Pearl

September 1913

"Goodness gracious, Pearl. Are you really going to exhibit that?"

Peter's eyes looked as if I might need to push them back into his head. They protruded from his head almost as far as the breasts of the female nude painting I had just finished. My breasts, my body, rendered as if looked at in a cracked mirror, curves within jagged, sharp-edged tiles of reflection.

I had never painted a nude before, but after Peter and I attended The International Exhibition of Modern Art, one some called the Armory Show as it was held in makeshift galleries in the 69th Regiment Armory on Lexington Avenue, last February, I knew I at least had to attempt one. In the course of doing it, I found myself expanding, not only as an artist but as a person. There is so much power in doing what we ought not.

Peter stepped closer to it, squinted eyes followed each stroke. "Never stop challenging yourself, my Pearl," he finally said, stepping back from the work to get the distance impression. "But whatever compelled you to take on this particular challenge?"

"Don't you remember the furor, the outrage, at the Armory show? I wanted to paint that shock... something that would elicit it." I shrugged, tipping my head this way and that as I studied my work.

We had attended the opening night of the show, we and 4,000 others who had received a coveted invitation. Almost all the painters who had earned wall space were American artists. In the end, it was as if they hadn't existed, so dominated were they by the works of

Cézanne, Picasso, Matisse, Gauguin, and the late Van Gogh.

So many of those attending were shocked and disturbed. The work was so unique, so unlike anything they had seen before, they had no notion how to process what they saw.

The same was not true for me. I had felt a jolt, a jolt of change, of evolution, of revolution. As my soul was already that of a revolutionary – a suffragette – it spoke to me so loudly I could not get the sound of what I saw out of my head, my mind. When we break one restraint, one that keeps the life we desire – that we deserve – from us, breaking the next chain gets easier, and the next, till we become the true masters of our destiny.

"Art will never be the same," I told Peter – a fact I knew to be true in the deepest depths of me. In so many ways, we were living in an era not unlike the Renaissance. "The very definition of art, that there is a definition, is becoming outdated. And I long to be a part of it."

I rose from my stool to stand beside him in front of my work.

"Do you understand me, dearest?"

Peter's arm snaked around my waist, its muscles pulled me close to him.

"I have always understood you, my Pearl." He pulled me in close, kissing the tip of my nose, a tiny angel's kiss. He often gave me his love in just such a kiss. "The real question is, will it sell? Will there be a market for such works?"

I laughed joyfully even as his brows rose almost to his hairline. "I can tell you this, when word of it gets out, there will be many more who come to the gallery." Once more, my shoulders rose to my ears. "*This* may not sell, but if more come, we may sell more of the others."

"A hook to pull in those who have never come before." Peter nodded thoughtfully as he mused aloud.

"Exactly." I rose on tiptoes to kiss his cheek.

We stood that way for a few silent, studious minutes.

"You were wrong, darling," I told him with love. "The real question, the only question, is this... does the artist create only that which would please others, make them money? Or is an artist's true calling to create what our soul tells us we must?"

My husband stared down at me, his gaze a glowing one. "Yours is a beautiful soul, my Pearl. I will not do or say anything to dim its brilliant light."

Ginevra

May 1914

"There is another!" Pearl stormed into my house without a knock. She never knocked. I never minded.

"Another what?" I asked as I shuffled and tended to my children scurrying at my feet. They were growing so quickly. At ages ten and eight they were still young enough to be babies in my eyes, but they were old enough to start getting up to real mischief, those years that test the patience of every parent.

"Another nasty article about Alva and the Congressional Union for Woman Suffrage." Pearl scrunched the paper under her arm as she picked up Angelina with a grunt. "Shush now, your mama and I have to talk. Will you sit quietly if I let you play with my locket?"

Her words silenced even me. Pearl had long ago learned the difference between the importance of things and the true importance of what mattered in this life. That locket was the one exception.

Peter had had it made for her… after. It held four pictures, not those of her husband or her daughter, but that of her father, brother, sister-in-law, and yes, even her mother. The last was a form of penance. Though not a Catholic, Pearl would do penance for that unreconciled relationship for the whole of her life.

Angelina nodded eagerly, her still childish, plump fist pumping open and closed until Pearl drew the chain over her head and placed the glinting item in my daughter's hand. One whining voice was silenced. I sighed.

I took Felix by the hand. He was much harder to quiet, much

more physical in his naughtiness. On rainy Saturdays such as this, his wholly masculine need for exertion was denied and I the one punished for it.

I sat him at the breakfast table, grabbed every wooden spoon in the kitchen, which I confessed was a great many – Italian cooks do love their wooden spoons.

"There," I declared as I clunked them upon the table. "Show me how you might make something out of these… if you can."

I laid down a gauntlet before a budding man; harassed I may have been, stupid I was not.

Pearl laughed as I joined her in the sitting room with a clear view of Felix and the spoons. "That's a bit unfair, isn't it?"

I did my best to put all the fallen strands of my hair back into some semblance of neatness; the only answer I gave her came by way of tight, curled lips and a narrowed stare. She had the decency to hide her amusement.

In the true, blessed silence that took over my home, Pearl and I read the article.

"*Nothing more than a widowed socialite looking for attention…*"

"*A bull of a woman looking to unseat the true place of man…*"

"*Mrs. O. H. P. Belmont thinks she can buy women their votes…*"

We took turns reading out the most damaging, the most insulting of lines in yet another article intended to insult Alva and the entire suffrage party as well.

"*They talked suffrage and 'Down with man', and danced the Boston dip and two-step. Those were happy days for suffrage! But they were all over now, and the songs of the suffragettes have given way to the songs of the Beauty Barkers. It is soap, not votes for women, it is down with corns, not with man, today.*"

"*Mrs. Belmont, at heart, means well. Whatever she does is for the good of the cause. But in her recent experiments, she is using bad judgment, in the opinion of the prominent women associated with her."*

Pearl read this last portion. Though I read well, I still read English slower than Pearl.

"It is all nonsense and… and… oh, fush to bungtown!"

"Pearl!" I admonished, glancing at my son still at work with the spoons, at my daughter twirling my locket. We both hated such darkly colorful language, but I suppose there were times when such words were the only words to be used.

Pearl turned to me in a huff. "You cannot tell me you don't agree?"

"Of course I agree," I responded as if to a child. "But these words will not stop her. She has no care what these rags say of her. When has anyone ever been able to stop Alva Erskine Smith Vanderbilt Belmont?"

My words amused her, she could not hide it. "But that does not mean…"

Her words trailed off as her eyes returned to the article, as they read some of the last words of it.

"Look!" Pearl's finger pointed to a post-script beneath the illiterate, irrational author's name. We read it together.

"Mrs. Belmont plans to leave New York for Newport this month where she intends to spend the summer and further establish a suffrage headquarters in the summer resort."

Our gaze met across the paper. The children, the spoons, and all fading into the news.

Alva was returning.

It was no surprise to any of us that the first meeting upon Alva's return took place in the Colony House… the Meeting House had become too small. We had done our jobs well and so many of the women Pearl and I had talked to, so many women others had talked to, had joined the cause. It did my once-a-servant soul good to see so many "common" women among the crowd, and in this historic building of such importance. It was a place for all, no matter the size of their purse.

Here, at one time the capital building of the state, the Declaration of Independence had been ratified and proclaimed from the balcony by the mayor. British troops had once used the building for a barracks, and the French for a hospital. And here the French General Rochambeau paid tribute to General George Washington during a dinner of celebration.

As I looked down upon Washington Square from the building's many windows, I reflected on how the beauty of the building matched its historical significance. I found the symmetry of the building's face so pleasing to my designer's eyes... how the balcony above the door matched its curve, and that two round windows above the balcony kept company with the large clock between them. The distinctive, almost delicate gazebo-like portion at the very top conjured images of soldiers on sentry duty.

Every woman who had stepped in that day – who hung on every word Alva delivered to us, buzzing like bees on the first truly warm day of spring – left even more enthusiastic, ever more prepared for battle. George Washington would have been proud, I think.

"She has bought a building on Bellevue, 128 Bellevue. It will be an actual headquarters! Right here in our city!"

"There is to be a conference, a large one, at Marble House, no less!"

Pearl and I talked over each other after dinner that evening, wanting to tell our husbands every little thing, every glorious thing. They sat in quiet endurance as we rambled on. I wanted more than their endurance.

"Julia Ward Howe will be there."

Osborn put down his pipe. Peter sat forward in his chair.

"Yes," Pearl chimed in; she knew what I was about. "The very woman who wrote the Battle Hymn of the Republic."

"Well, that is something," Osborn admitted, almost begrudgingly.

It made me wonder if our men, so supportive, did not truly understand the depth of what was taking place or how far we would go to see it through.

"And there will be…" Pearl began but stopped to swallow and swallow again, though she had long since finished eating. "There will be a Titanic survivor in attendance."

Neither man said a word; what could any of us say.

"Her name's Margaret Brown," Pearl continued, though she didn't seem to be speaking to any of us. "Alva said she'll be staying at a cottage next to the Muenchinger-King Hotel."

Peter took her hand that lay so still on the settee beside his.

"Perhaps you may get a chance to speak with her," he cooed to her softly. "Perhaps it would be good for you to do so."

"Perhaps," was Pearl's entire answer.

"Anna Howard Shaw will be speaking, the president of the National American Woman Suffrage Association." I knew they would not know her name, but her position, one of great national importance, that they did understand.

"Alva has formed us into a certified association, the Political Equality Association." Pearl's face shone with wonder as she spoke those words. Our distance from New York, our inability to leave our busy lives behind, and take part in what the national organizations were doing was a pebble in our shoe. With Alva's new group, we were at last relieved of its sting.

"PEA will be recruiting members from all of the New England

states," I informed the men with my nose in the air. But they brought it down quickly.

"PEA?" Peter snickered. Osborn did his best not to but failed.

I looked heavenward for strength; men always stayed boys.

"Children." Pearl clapped her hands together as she did to get our real children under control, dropping her voice to a tone that promised determination and dire consequences. "This is a serious subject. We expect you to take it seriously."

She spoke for us both without question. She knew I would have no objection. I rarely did when she spoke for us.

Pearl

July 1914

We lay in each other's arms, in the after of a sweet joining, in the moist nakedness of us.

I would wonder, in the days ahead, if it was the announcement that day of Europe at war that had driven us so ferociously into each other that night or our never-failing need. No sweet words came from our lips to the pillows that cradled our heads that night, no expressions of love that were the favored fruit we ate upon in the after.

"I admit my ignorance, dearest," I confessed, listening to the slowing beat of his heart as my ear rested upon his chest. I felt no need to defend my ignorance as any sign of deficient intellect for Peter had always claimed he admired my brain as much as my body. My brain had been too full of daily life and suffrage for much else of late. "Explain it to me, would you? But simply, you have exhausted my body and scrambled my brain far too wonderfully for overly complex notions."

Peter chuckled, a low, sensual, lascivious sound; I almost stopped him to have him again. But what I had asked he had obsessed over these past few months. He told me, simply.

It began with arguments between powerful cousins, an assassination, secret treaties, and broken alliances, until one country declared war on another, then one more on yet another, and yet again, until one country rained violence upon another, until so much of the world aimed their weapons at each other.

"I fear greatly for my homeland, my Pearl," he pulled me into the darkness of his fear with his words. "For all that England has fought with the French throughout history, it will go to France's rescue. I just know it will."

Yes, Peter had been born in London; yes, he had come to this country at such a young age that only the lightest brushstroke of an accent painted upon his words. And yet it would always be the place of his birth. His voice rang the bells of loyalty, of honor, of the loud clanging of alarm.

I chewed upon his tale, even the bitter seeds of his fear.

"Do you think... will we, the States, get involved?"

I shouldn't have asked for I hated his answer.

"I certainly hope so."

Pearl

August 1914

We walked slowly along Bellevue Avenue that morning, the air bursting with the scents of summer, of the plump and round, blue and pink hydrangeas, of the star-shaped orange tigers and the pink and white lilies, of the warming, briny sea. But there was something more in it as well, something that made my skin tingle and the little hairs on the back of my neck stick out.

"I will never forget our bicycle ride," I mused aloud. That something in the air made us remember the momentous instances of our lives that took place on this avenue, the so many of them, for I felt, as surely as Ginevra must as well, that such an instance was upon us once more.

Ginevra laughed a brighter laugh than I had heard from her in a long while.

"We are so different from those girls and their silly dreams..." she paused. "But they weren't silly, were they? Our dreams. We have made much of them come true, yes?"

"Yes, yes we have," I said. We had made most of our dreams come true; perhaps it was why we believed we could make the dream of suffrage come true as well. We walked taller.

We turned in at the carriage entrance to the grounds of The Beeches. We had left early for this very reason, to go to our trees before moving on to the conference, to remember the dreams those young, naïve, but sweetly innocent girls spoke of, to acknowledge – if only to ourselves – how far we have come.

We could not climb as they did, nor as high, not upon our tree, but we had in our life.

For a while we let the birds sing to us, the squirrels and chipmunks to scurry about below us without infringing our noise upon them. We sat and reveled in hope rewarded, in new dreams being born.

"Alva makes it sound so easy, doesn't she?" Ginevra asked the question that whirled in my own thoughts.

I nodded, snatching one of the beeches' long, fuzzy leaves to peel as I used to do. "She does."

"But it won't be." Ginevra turned her eyes to the pure blue summer sky. "I do no think it will be at all."

"Nor do I," I sighed heavily, feeling my back curl downward against the weight.

Silence came to us again, but not for long, there was too much to fill stillness in those days.

"We must change men's minds as well as women's," I spoke my ponderings. "And now the world is at war. It will be all men care about."

"Will America go to the war, do you think?" In the grip of her fear, Ginevra again became that uneducated, naïve, frightened young girl I had met nearly twenty years ago.

"President Wilson is firmly against it."

"For now."

I nodded. She was not that naïve after all. "For now."

"Are you still angry at your mother?"

The question almost knocked me off our branch perch. I could not follow her mind to where it came. It didn't matter. It was a good question... for this place at this time. It was in this tree that I had, as a girl in my teens, first learned of my mother's infidelity, when my anger for a cold and demanding mother had turned to the disgust at an indecent person.

"I think…" I began slowly, for it was not a question I had not thought about, "I think there comes a time when we become old enough to see that our parents are not some sort of gods, that they are human with human faults and frailties. I know how she was raised, how desperate she was for attention." I looked my friend dead in the eyes and said something I had never said, not to another living soul. "And I know my father was incapable of giving her all she needed. Did she ask too much?" My shoulders rose to my ears. "Possibly. Could he have tried a little harder? I think that is possible as well."

As I spoke, I watched as Ginevra's eyes grew moist, not for me, but for them.

She took my hand. "I am proud of you."

It was the last thing I expected to hear.

"You no longer look at them, at her, with anger. Not as a child but as an adult looking at other adults."

She was right, of course. It is a bridge that we all must, in time, cross.

"I have."

"And it has brought you peace."

"Of a sort." I squeezed the hand still in mine. "It has also taught me how to be a better wife, a better mother. And is that not what every parent wants, for their children to have a better life than they had?"

Ginevra nodded. "It is. It is what made my papa bring us here, to this country."

"Then we could say that, in their own way, my parents did the same for me. We have both lost now." My words turned her stare upon me.

A sigh. A stare now turned to so long ago and yet like a dagger still. "*Sì*, we have."

"It breaks bits of you."

Like her, I watched as, in the distance, the glint of the sea, a single sail, a single sailor passed through our small portal of a view through the trees.

"It does… and makes you wonder, question."

I felt the crack in her; I felt it through our clasped hands.

"So," I sighed now, "what do we do?" I asked a question I knew the answer to, that I knew there existed no true answer.

"Eh," Ginevra shrugged as if I'd asked her what she thought of a plain piece of bread. "We do as Alva insists we do, suggests we do… we fight on. They would want us to."

For the most part, she was right, it was what they would want us to do, most of them.

"We fight on," I agreed.

We swung our clasped hands like children as our lips tilted upward.

In that uplifted spirit, we climbed down from our tree, followed the path back to Bellevue, and headed south toward Marble House once more.

"Get off our street!"

The scream shattered the sweet somnolence of the avenue, filled it with caustic, angry venom.

"What was that?" Ginevra asked, head twitching this way and that like a pigeon.

"Whore!"

"Homewreckers!"

"*Dio mio*, they yell at us." One of Ginevra's shaking hands clamped over her mouth, the other pointed to Wayside, one of the smaller cottages owned by the Dyer family, direct descendants of Roger Williams, Rhode Island's founder, one of *the* families.

I squinted. I knuckled my eyes. Neither did any good. What I saw, I saw. Two women, younger than us but women I knew, women on

119

the lower steps of the social ladder but still upon its ladder. They hung from an upper window and hurled slander at us like rocks.

"Such hatred," Ginevra hissed.

There was a hand gesture I had never used, though I had seen it used before, down on Thames, where the fishermen and farmers set up their stalls, in Providence near our college were drunkards fell out of taverns. Yes, I had seen it but never used it.

I used it.

Ginevra gasped.

I circled her arm in mine, stuck my chin in the air as well as my finger, and kept walking.

"And a good day to you, ladies," I yelled like one of those fishmongers. "We have someplace to be! Ta!"

A giggle came from behind Ginevra's other hand still covering her mouth; it sounded like applause.

The closer we came to Marble House, the thicker the stream of women – and even quite a few men – became. We had just passed Chateau-Sur-Mer, the home of the Wetmores, one of the founding families of this cottage colony, the former home of two of my dearest friends throughout our childhood summers.

"*Dio mio*," I heard Ginevra gasp. "So many."

'So many' was an understatement. There were not hundreds as Alva had hoped for… but thousands. Some arrived on foot, others in automobiles rumbling down Bellevue Avenue in a cloud of floating chiffon. So many came and from every direction.

Ginevra and I jumped into the stream, one forced to narrow as only one gate of the iron fence around the mansion was open, only one woman stood at it to greet every person who passed through it. Brilliant in the white we all wore, as she had encouraged attendees to wear in all the many newspaper interviews she had given about the event, Alva smiled and chatted and—

"Is she… collecting money?" Ginevra's incredulity echoed my own.

There had been so many traumas and shocks in the lives we had lived and, though not anywhere near as cruel and scarring as most, the sight did indeed jolt us to our core. Alva exacted money from every woman who entered. Ginevra and I scrambled in our drawstring purses to see what money we had on hand, praying we had enough and would not be turned away.

"Put your money away, ladies." Alva pushed our hands with their Morgan Silver Dollars back toward us. "My dahlings of our PEA do not have to pay. But you will be put to work." She squinted those demanding eyes of hers at us. "I assume you have no problem with that."

"Of course not."

"Not at all."

As if either one of us had the gall to naysay an Alva demand. Though I think at heart we were both longing to be seen as "working members" of this suffrage conference.

"But, if I may ask…" When one is around Alva, one had to speak as she did. "What are you charging for?"

"Why, to raise money," Alva barked. "This fight may be long. It's been long already, and it will take money to drive it. I am charging one dollar for those who have come to hear our lectures and five dollars to hear the lectures and take a tour of Marble House. All of it, every penny, will go into the coffers of suffrage parties, our own and that of the National American Women Suffrage Association."

Ginevra gasped again and my hard elbow found her ribs.

My head shook with both surprise and admiration. Alva never failed to surprise.

"You are ingenious, Alva," I spoke pure truth. "Though I confess, I never imagined you would allow strangers to walk upon Marble House's floors."

That she had done so had set a precedent in America that would polish the tarnish off the act should I do the same at The Beeches.

Alva's somewhat bulbous nose crinkled. "Oh dearie, just between us, it does rankle a bit. I've always felt that it was best not to open Marble House to public view as I do use it as my private residence. I departed from my rule simply because I believed the step might increase interest in our crusade. And look!"

Alva turned with the opening of her arms as if drawing back a curtain to reveal the horde of women and men scurrying upon every speck of gravel-strewn drive, every blade of grass.

"You are a force to be reckoned with, Alva," Ginevra said with such strength, with no hesitation to call this woman who had always frightened her by her first name. I knew that we were both already changed by this day.

Alva cackled. "Don't I know it, dearie. Now get to the Teahouse and help distribute refreshments."

We hurried ourselves off, tingling to throw ourselves into the powerful spirit of the moment. But we hurried in silence, gazes too full to allow words into our mouths. Thousands of people all in white, so sharp against the backdrop of the deep blue Atlantic Ocean that edged the estate and the Cliff Walk, mingled upon the slow sloping lawn. The huge tents that had been erected where the speeches would take place fluttered in the soft, cooling breeze off the ocean. I knew I would soon paint this memory.

And then there was our recognition of faces, both known and renowned. There were the society women, the likes of Mamie Fish, Tessie Oelrichs, and Gloria Morgan Vanderbilt – Alva's cousin by marriage – as well as the women who represented the most ardent soldiers in our battle.

From the many newspaper articles and interviews by and about them, Ginevra and I recognized Alice Stokes Paul. Though only in her twenties, she was one of the leaders of the suffrage cause. And there was the elderly Julia Ward Howe in her lace cap and shawl.

It was my turn to gasp at the sight of Dr. Anna Howard Shaw. Short and indomitable-looking, she had been born in England but Massachusetts had been her home since the age of four. She had attended college not once, but three times, obtaining degrees in both theology and medicine. If George Washington, Thomas Jefferson, John Adams, and the like were the founding fathers, Dr. Shaw was inarguably one of the founding mothers of what we hoped would become a new form of our nation.

I stood frozen until Ginevra pulled me along.

"Come," she insisted, "we must do as Alva wants."

I hadn't heard her that submissive since we were young. I laughed at her, though lovingly so, as I waved at Consuelo across the vast lawn. The Duchess of Marlborough had been a powerful draw for the event, not only as Alva's daughter but as a member of the English nobility and a suffragette who fought just as hard in England as we did here in the States. There would be plenty of time for a visit with her later.

In the distinctive red-and-black-lacquered Chinese teahouse Alva had built only the year before, we served tea and lemonade to the crowd of women, using china Alva had commissioned to be made just for the event. Thick, with beautiful design lines, the cream porcelain bore blue cursive on both the cup and the saucer, words that demanded, 'Votes for Women.'

"I don't know how, Ginevra," I said through the side of my mouth as the other side smiled at the women I served, "but I'm going to find a way to take one of these cups and saucers home."

"Well, if you do figure out how, take a set for me," Ginevra giggled back.

"And one for me," Sarah Eddy laughed.

"Me too!" Maud Howe Elliot chimed in.

The four of us worked in tandem. Like us, these two women were quickly becoming – purely by our actions alone – leaders within the PEA organization.

There we stayed until the lectures began. But once started, I did not give a whit what Alva's commands had been, I would not miss hearing these powerful women speak. We made it under the tent just as Dr. Shaw took the podium.

"When I arrived in Newport, I thought of the last time I was in your city. More than twenty years ago, I came here with Susan B Anthony, and we came for exactly the same purpose as that for which we are here today. Boys have been born since that time and have become voters, and the women are still trying to persuade American men to believe in the fundamental principles of democracy. I never quite feel as if it was a fair field to argue this question with men, because in doing it you have to assume that a man who professes to believe in a Republican form of government does not believe in a Republican form of government, for the only thing that woman's enfranchisement means at all is that a government which claims to be a Republic should be a Republic and not an aristocracy.

"A gentleman opposed to our enfranchisement once said to me, women have never produced anything of any value to the world. I told him the chief product of the women had been the men and left it to him to decide whether the product was of any value."

"Amen," I whispered as so many of the women twittered. I no longer knew the where of where I was, only the what of it.

"Now one of two things is true: either a Republic is a desirable form of government, or else it is not. If it is, then we should have it, if it is not then we ought not to pretend that we have it. We ought at least be true to our ideals. If woman's suffrage is wrong, it is a great wrong; if it is right, it is a profound and fundamental principle, and we all know, if we know what a Republic is, that it is the fundamental principle upon which a Republic must rise. Let us see where we are as a people; how we act here and what we think we are. It is better to be true to what you believe, though that be wrong, than to be false to what you believe, even if that belief is correct!"

Dr. Shaw had not finished her speech, but the audience didn't care. They rose to their feet like the waves crashing against the rocks beside us, an explosion of pluming white, our applause so thunderous, she would not be able to be heard again for many minutes. When the heart of an issue is touched upon, when words burn flames in our blood, we are but flesh made vessels at their mercy.

Speech after speech fired our blood, filled us with the rightness and righteousness of what we were doing, what we demanded. Just before the speeches were suspended for lunch and for those who had paid to tour Marble House, Alva took to the podium. It was as if she spoke directly to Ginevra and I, for what she spoke about we had both encountered.

"Many of you have heard me speak that a woman's right to vote is not just for those of us here who do not have to worry as to how we will pay for food for our children, yet that is a right every woman should possess, equal pay for equal labor. A woman voting will ensure they are paid that rightful wage." Alva paused, eyes narrowing, jaw clenching. "But it is equally important for the married woman. *She* must be granted the rights to her own property. And *she* deserves to have custody rights over her children!

"But remember this, each and every one of you." Her outstretched finger slashed across the thousands of faces, "when a woman joins the suffrage movement, she... no, you, need to accept the fact that you have become a public person and you will deal with public disapproval. But I will take such disapproval any day of the week over a rag being shoved down my throat so that my voice cannot be heard!"

Once more the attendees jumped to their feet. Once more the applause frightened the birds from the trees, the gulls from the ocean's edge.

I reached down and took Ginevra's hand. We had suffered much together. There was little that could frighten us away from this fight.

"I must get back to mother," Consuelo pecked our cheeks as she made to leave us, as our lovely visit came to an end, having found her as the crowd milled about after the speeches. "Is this not the grandest event?" Hers was a smile of such unaffected joy her youthful beauty bloomed once more, a flower almost withered by her tribulations, yet resurrected with her purpose and freedom. The warmth of it upon us remained even as she took herself away.

"Howdy-do, ladies."

We swung round at a voice both brash and warm. In a hat so large it could serve as a parasol, with a bosom that entered any room long before the rest of her did, stood Mrs. Margaret Tobin Brown.

"Mrs. Brown," I greeted her effusively.

"Stuff and nonsense, call me Maggie. Everyone does."

The most famous survivor of the Titanic sinking shook our hands in turn as we introduced ourselves. My teeth rattled along with her enthusiasm.

Why her and not my father?

It was an unbidden, unkind thought; one I had had before. Yet purpose brimmed in every ounce of this woman. Perhaps God had found her purpose more worthy of saving. From the moment I learned that she would be attending, a fellow passenger on a journey that had orphaned me, I had read much about this woman who stood before us, smiling wide with little care that it displayed her two crooked front teeth. No, she was not a "beauty", but warmth and friendship blazed from her eyes like the first stars in a moonless sky.

Born into poverty by her Irish immigrant parents, Margaret Tobin had known only scarcity, even after marrying miner James Brown – their first home had been no more than a rustic cabin. It was only after J.J., as her husband came to be known, invented a new mining mechanism, after he dug for gold rather than silver, unlike most miners, did wealth find them, find her.

And oh, what she had done with it.

At the Carnegie Institute in New York, Margaret had studied languages and literature, and though she still sounded like the girl who grew up poor in Missouri, she could speak three languages. From the moment her husband had brought them riches, she had turned all her abundant energies to philanthropy of all sorts, and suffrage.

"I know who you are, Pearl, indeed I do." Maggie had taken my hand after Ginevra's and she did not let it go. "I can imagine what you must be thinking and I don't blame you for any of it."

Had she read my mind or just my face?

"I... I have heard of your bravery." I would not speak ill of this woman, not to her face or anyone else's. "Your actions were admirable."

Maggie let go of my hand and flapped it before my face.

"I did only what I could. I wish I could have done more." Her dark eyes looked at the ocean but I saw not a glint of fear. "I met them, you know. I met your parents, your family."

I saw nothing but her face, her eyes, eyes that had looked upon my family long after my own had had their last sight of them. I don't know why she surprised me so. Everything written about her warned how well she could astonish people.

"That father of yours was a real sweetheart." The softness of her smile told me she had in truth come to know my father's truth. She did not mention my mother; it seemed the most polite way to talk of my deceased mother was to not talk of her at all. "He'd be right proud to see you here, to know you were fighting the good fight."

Her mannish face swam in my tears. "Thank you, Mrs.... Maggie." It was the best I could do, the only way I could accept the gift she had just given me.

Margaret Brown leaned closer to me. "Money can't make a man or woman... it isn't who you are, nor what you have, but *what* you are that counts."

Sherevealed her truth to us with ease.

"I'll see ya around, ladies."

And with that, she was gone. Ginevra and I could but stand in the powerful current of her wake and wait for it to pass.

Ginevra

September 1915

Our numbers had risen as had our hemlines, a true tapestry of crinoline to cotton. Alva had brought us together, the cause kept us there.

"I want all who can afford to do so to subscribe immediately," Alva instructed as Doris Smith, who had been introduced as her assistant, began passing out copies of *The Suffragist*, a weekly newspaper first produced by the Congressional Union for Woman Suffrage, now an affiliate of the NAWSA.

On the cover of the eight pages dedicated to our cause lay a beautiful illustration. Lady Liberty herself had climbed off her perch where I last saw her so many years ago when Papa and I had made it to the shore of New York City still alive, though barely. Here she stood before the capitol building in Washington D.C., arms reaching out beseechingly but still with dignity, the perfect symbol for our desire.

Like *The Una,* a newspaper once published in our state, in Providence, *The Suffragist* was wholly dedicated to the enfranchisement of women. Both newspapers were owned and operated solely by women, *The Una* had been the very first in this entire nation to fly that flag proudly.

"Those who can afford it, you will be asked—"

Pearl snickered beside me. "Asked, indeed," she murmured.

"You will be asked to give your copy to those who can't once you've finished reading it."

"Perhaps we could deliver our copies to the PEA offices," Mabel

Washburn, who sat beside us, once more called out. "That way, anyone who can't afford their own copy may simply go to the office and pick up a used copy for free."

Alva smacked her palm upon the table she stood before, the makeshift podium. "A mahvelous idea, Mabel. And here I thought you were just here for show."

Only Alva Vanderbilt Belmont could praise and insult in one sentence with such ease.

"Take no offense," I heard Pearl whisper to Mabel, who gave a curt nod of her head as if she understood. My gaze lingered upon Mabel's face, her tightly fisted hands, and the vein upon her forehead pulsing faster than the second hand on a clock; these told me a different story… she understood, but understanding did not take away the sting.

The dry, scratchy sound of paper being held and flipped filled the room.

"That's quite enough now," Alva demanded, and the sound disappeared as if every paper had turned to ashes. "There is a most important item on our agenda today, an item of action."

If she had used that word first, she would not have needed to ask for quiet. Action. We all longed for it. Many of us had felt let down after the conference over a year ago, as we read of our more strident sisters in England, as if we ran but stayed in the same place.

"As of now, eleven states, or territories as is the case of some, have granted women the right to vote without the need for a federal amendment to be passed."

Her words brought out many a hooted huzzah, while Pearl and I whispered and tapped our fingers… "Wyoming, Colorado, Utah, Idaho, Washington state, California, Arizona, Kansas, Oregon, Montana, Nevada…"

Pearl and I could recite them by memory and in the order in which these states had seen sense.

"Yes, eleven," Pearl agreed quietly with Alva's count. I giggled at the very idea that she would tell the woman she was mistaken, were her number wrong.

"But it is not enough, not nearly enough," Alva continued. "It will not be enough until all forty-eight states and territories are granted the right through federal law. But it is, in part, the state-by-state, territory-by-territory battles that we must win first. To that end, NAWSA is organizing yet another march for next month, a month before the Senate Committee on Suffrage once more votes on the Susan B. Anthony amendment."

I couldn't remember, and Pearl didn't either, how many times the amendment had been voted on or how many times it had failed to pass. The number was the same and we had no wish to dwell upon it.

"I will be there with our sisters in New York as will the nearly 40,000 other women who have pledged to march."

No doubt Pearl saw the shock of the enormity of that number in my popped eyes, as I did in hers. There had never been a march that large, not ever.

"Why did she not ask if any of us wished to march?" I slithered the words at Pearl from barely separated lips.

"I know many of you might have wished to be a part of that event..."

I straightened up as if pinched by my aunt in church when I was a child and failed to listen to a sermon in Latin I could not understand.

"But I have a greater mission for you."

She held us captive and she knew it. We waited without breathing.

"I want you to mirror that march, right here in Newport. I want you to take to the streets as other women in other states are doing. We want our voices heard from sea to shining sea!"

The applause followed as Alva knew it would, as it should. This was the action we were all prepared for, longed for.

"Oh my," I heard Mabel whisper as if in wonder, but once more a puckered brow accessorized her frown.

"Yes, yes," Alva applauded with us. Until she used her hands, palms down and pushing towards the ground, to bring our feet back upon the earth. "There will be a march in Providence as well, run by the Rhode Island Equal Suffrage Association, but I want one right here in Newport, right here where I brought this cause to our city on the sea.

"As I will be in New York, what is needed – what I need – most importantly, is for one or more of you to take charge of the event here."

"We will!" The words flew from a woman's mouth like a captive bird finally let loose.

The response was almost immediate. Heads, including mine, swiveled this way and that to see who had called out so quickly and with so much assurance. I found all eyes but my own looking at me… no, at the woman beside me.

"We will!" Pearl cried out once more, this time she grabbed and raised my hand along with hers.

"We? We who? Who we?" I clenched her arm as the words hissed out of my clenched teeth.

Alva smiled one of her smiles, a pleased one but darkly so.

"Pearl Worthington Wright and Ginevra Costa Taylor," Alva said, far too pleasantly. "I could not be happier than to leave you two in charge."

"What have you done?" I slithered my snappish words out through lips spread stiffly and teeth stacked.

Pearl looked at me, her face bore a smile, one much like Alva's. "I have done what needs to be done."

***

Two days later, a message boy brought me the note.

Meet me. One o'clock. P.

The place was not mentioned. It didn't need to be.

She was already there when I arrived. I had set out with great stomping strides, each one a word of scolding I had been saving for her when next I saw her.

Pearl had made sure I could not say them on our walk home from the meeting that day, the day when she spoke for me but shouldn't have, bringing others into our usual group of two, telling me she feared we would be harassed again and sought safety in numbers. She had not fooled me.

Oh, she would be charming and amusing and as persuasive as I knew she could be. I also knew I would forgive her. But she would receive a few lashes of my tongue first.

"You had no right."

I did not climb the tree to sit beside her. I couldn't wait that long. Two days of fuming annoyance demanded I spoke my stored words as soon as I saw her. And so I did.

"Get up here, silly."

Already the persuasion began. I climbed to our new perch, the new, lower perch for the older us.

"It will be—" Pearl tried to begin as soon as I sat beside her.

"Why?" I silenced her before her coaxing could continue. "I would hear why before you say one-a more word."

"Oh, dear." Pearl heard the accent squirm into my voice. She looked at me, really looked at me, not at what she only wanted to see. "Well…" she began, taking a deep breath. "We had been reading and reading about the women in England and what they were doing there, the radical actions they had been taking for more than a year. I knew

133

we both wanted to take such steps ourselves. To bring action into our actions."

"Will you have us putting bombs in mail bins, too?" It was nasty of me; I felt nasty at the time.

Persuasive Pearl departed. The Pearl with me now was my sister, an older sister annoyed at the younger one, if only by two days. Her chin dropped as a sneer made her beautiful lips ugly, as her large eyes narrowed to slits.

"Do not be so pedantic, Ginevra, it does not suit you."

I was unsure of what pedantic meant, but her face and her tone told me enough.

"I am no pe... you should have spoke to me first! Do you know how much time and work this will take? We must prepare our children for the start of school. I am so busy at work, as you should be. I have heard Peter say more than once what a busy time this is at the gallery. Osborn will no be pleased should I spend so much time at the PEA office. He will worry... I will worry. I—"

"I thought you'd be pleased."

"I should have been asked! I should have decided for myself!"

Birds fluttered off the branches around us. Chipmunks and squirrels scurried into hiding.

Yet I suddenly felt lighter as if I could have climbed as high as we did as young girls in this tree, as I had felt as a child when I made my confession at church each week.

We sat in the wake of my spent anger, till the silence made me itchy. With resentment relieved, my heart took over, feeling the hurt I imagined she felt.

I took her hand. "I know we have come to make such decisions for each other. You did not do anything you have no done in the past."

A hint of a grin dared to pluck at the corners of her lips.

"But this is so... so big." I did not have the words I wished.

"There is too much to this decision. We should have made it together."

The grin scurried away before it came fully out. Pearl had the grace to hang her head between her bent shoulders.

"I did not think that…" Only her gaze rose. "I did not think."

I huffed a sigh, at her actions, at my own.

"Well, that is the first smart thing you have said since." Relieved of my anger, I could forget it. "Now, tell me how we will do this thing, do it well or feel Alva's wrath, and in less than a month."

Pearl began to talk, to lecture, to rant, to tick things off almost all her fingers. I suddenly understood why she had waited two days before seeing me, talking to me. She had been hard at work.

Already she had a group of volunteers together, already they had their chores laid out for them. Where we would start and end, what we would wear and how.

I stopped her with a glare, brows high, one crookedly so.

"What?" she asked it.

"Well, it seems as if you do not need me at all." I may have been a woman in my late thirties but I sounded like a child. I had swung from anger and resentment to petulance before the sun had barely moved in the sky. "If all is ar-rang-ged, what do you need me for?"

Pearl turned to me as much as she could on the branch that held us. "I need you to get those still in service, Ginny."

"*Uffa!* Me? You think servants will listen to me, the one who dreamed she could be more? One who they see to have spat on their life… on-a their way of life?"

"Exactly!" Pearl barked. "You dreamed and then made those dreams come true. They may scorn you to your face, but believe me, they do not do so behind it."

"How do you—"

"They *will* listen to you, Ginny. They will follow your lead if you have but the courage to lead them."

She did not let me finish my question, hear her answer. There was a reason for that, too. Perhaps there was a reason I had dared to dream above my lot in this life other than to make my dreams come true. Showing others, giving them the gift that I had given myself, was a purpose that would have made my mother ever more proud of me; it was a hope I had always tried to live my life by.

I stared up to the sky as if Heaven was truly "up there," as if she was.

"Fine," I said in a way I had heard the rich women answer their husbands when they agreed but with a price. "But you shall tell our husbands, both of them."

For the first time since I came to her beneath the tree that day, I saw true worry crinkle her brow.

"Oh, dear," she said again.

This time, I laughed.

"Are you surprised by Mabel?" I asked as we strolled home together. I had forgiven her; we were the regular "we" again.

"Which part of her?" Pearl asked with a laugh.

There were flashes of the old Pearl in the new now and again, but I would never tell her unless the old showed up too often.

"Well, did she no tell us her husband… um…?"

"Jackson."

"*Sì*, Jackson." I would try to remember better. "He is wealthy, no?"

"Well…" Pearl thought her answer out. "She did say he owned one of the old coal mines in Portsmouth but we know they're closing down. Like the others, the owners are turning them into farms."

"Still, he must a made a pretty penny before," I thought aloud but Pearl followed my thoughts, nodding. "But she wore the same dress at the last meeting as she wore before."

"Only a fashion designer would remember," Pearl chided me. "I didn't—"

We jumped out of the way as the trolley bell clanged behind us, close behind us.

"I didn't remember what she wore at the last meeting," Pearl finished her thought. "Perhaps she didn't either. Five children and all."

I couldn't argue with that and didn't. "Let us ask them to dinner again. I'm curious about them."

Pearl laughed at me. "You've been spending too much time with our Alva."

I tried not to laugh. I failed.

At the PEA office on Bellevue, we read the nasty article in *The New York Times* just three days before the march. It wasn't really an article, but a damning warning, *"If women get the vote, they will play havoc for themselves and society. Granted the suffrage, they would demand all the rights that implies. It is not possible to think of women as soldiers and sailors, police patrolmen, or firemen. Heavens, think of the chaos!"*

"Do you think it will deter many of our marchers?" Pearl stared at the nasty words smudged upon the paper.

With the work of Pearl and her band of volunteers, as well as my efforts with those still in service – who did listen with respect, though I would never tell Pearl just how respectful they were – we had recruited nearly 2,000 women from Newport and surrounding areas like Portsmouth and Narragansett. More and more women dreamed with us.

"Perhaps a few, but no more than a few." I did not want her downhearted and yet we had to be realistic. "If Osborn's bank did not get *The Times*, we would not have seen this. I 'spect there are few who will ever see this."

Pearl's sigh carried her relief. "A very good point, Ginny." With a glance about the small space filled with women at work, she crumbled the paper I had brought and threw it on the small fire, just large enough to chase away the chill of an October morning. "Now, are all the sashes made, do we know?"

What a feat it had been to have our thousands of sashes made to be identical with those they would wear in New York; upon purple cloth bordered in green, letters of gold embroidery demanding, "Votes for Women." We would wear these sashes over our all-white attire. The white outfit had been adopted to signify our purity, even as we fought for enfranchisement. The gold signified respect to the state of Kansas where Susan B. Anthony and Elizabeth Cady Stanton had begun this fight so many years ago. Britain women had replaced the gold with green to signify hope and when they did, the three colors became the official hues of the suffrage parties around the world.

"They are," I assured her.

Pearl had put me in charge of this particular chore as many of the servants I had recruited were seamstresses and then there were those I knew from my work at the Tirocchi House, who were more than happy to help.

"I know the signs are ready. Peter has seen to that."

Our husbands would march with us. When Pearl told them what we planned to do, as I had demanded she do, they had both gifted us with not only their support but their participation. We had heard there would be men among all the parades taking place. Though small in number, the presence was loud.

"I do like this one." I picked up one of the many signs stacked against the wall and held it up, the muscles of my arm seemed hardened, stronger than they had ever been. This sign, specifically intended to appeal to men, men who held the power to grant us this right, read, *"We talk with you, we eat with you, we dance with you, we marry you, why can't we vote with you?"*

"I prefer this one," Pearl snickered as she picked up another, which read: *"VOTES FOR WOMEN: Convicts, Lunatics & Women… all have no votes!"*

"It is a bit extreme, no?"

"The more extreme the better, I say," Pearl insisted loudly, loud enough for the busy women in the office to hear; they cheered and chuckled without an instant's pause in their work.

These women were energized, we had energized them. All we could hope for now was no rain and no antis.

We stood under a brilliant blue sky at the very end of Bellevue Avenue, where the carriages used to make their turn around for afternoon parades. It was the most appropriate place to begin this parade. While the wide circle was in front of Rough Point – the "cottage" built and owned by Frederick Vanderbilt, Alva's brother-in-law from her first marriage – Alva's cottage, Marble House, was the next we would pass as we made our way down the length of Bellevue.

With her "Votes for Women" flag held high and with the American flag equally high in my hands, we would lead this procession we had arranged.

"We've done it," I heard Pearl whisper. "We've really done it."

I do not think she spoke to me but had no care if I heard. She spoke to herself, to the women who had fought this fight before us, who inspired us to do this, and to Alva and the other leaders of the suffrage movement gathering in New York as we did here in Newport.

"Yes, dearest Pearl, we did." I could not stop myself from jumping in the pool of her joy. I looked to the heavens, I looked to my mother and prayed she saw me that day, almost more than any other that had come before.

I looked into a cloudless sky, as we had hoped, not a rain cloud – or any cloud, for that matter – could be seen.

Whether antis awaited us along our route… that remained to be seen.

"There are so many of us," I sounded like a child marveling at her first sight of all the stars in the sky. From behind us, the line of women and men ran down the southernmost tip of our island, around the bend, and along the edge of Bailey's Beach. It was a garland of people bound together by strings of purpose and justice.

I felt the flutter of a kiss upon the back of my neck and giggled.

"I have never been more proud to stand beside you." My darling Osborn's sparkling blue eyes were so full of me. "To stand with you, to call myself yours."

I would not let the threatening tears of joy he brought me to fall upon my face, but allowed my lips their freedom to spread wide upon my face, if only for a moment, a moment in which I put my forehead to his.

We had been instructed, and more than once, that we should wear no smiles for what we did was not frivolous or jovial. What we did, we did to change our world.

The bell atop Trinity Church began to clang. As it gonged for the twelfth time, I looked at Pearl, she at me, and once more we took steps unknown together.

My legs shook, knees feeling weak. If one is lucky, there are moments in life that you know, not when looking back but when looking from within them, that what you do is a great thing, a powerful thing. I was so very lucky that day.

We did not walk long until we saw the lines of people formed on both sides of the avenue. There, on Bellevue Avenue, where the elite of Newport society had built their cottages, we were bathed in words of encouragement. Servants cheered their fellows as they passed. The wealthy who were still in residence long after the season had past encouraged us most politely, the soft thuds of applause by gloved hands.

From Bellevue, we would turn east on Bath Street then north again on to Spring Street, which would take us all the way to the Great Common and the band of musicians we had arranged to carry us into the square.

Would our reception be the same all along that route?

"We begin with glory and we shall end with it." Pearl pondered as I did. But where I worried, she stomped forward in battle.

Ours would be a nearly three-mile walk, far shorter than the one in New York, and still it would take us close to two hours to complete, at the least. More importantly, we would pass Newporters of every rank, station, and purse. The route took us from the enormous cottages, through a commercial district, then through neighborhoods of "regular" people. We would pass before eyes that saw life through many different lenses.

Quiet reverence brought us to the end of Bellevue, just a few feet from the Casino, the center of Newport's socialites' social life. We made the turn on to Bath Street, a street crowded with businesses and selling stalls owned and operated by men.

Words showered us once more, but now they were words that cut to the quick, thrown like sharp stones at the men in our ranks.

"Where are your skirts?" a fat-bellied man with a rough-looking beard covering his round face bellowed.

Pearl turned. I knew she looked at Peter. It would be hard for him, to hear these words, to suffer the slings and arrows of men aimed at men. He was far too righteous. Holding his tongue would be a struggle. But then, were he not such a man, he would not have been a match for Pearl.

"Nothing to say, henpeck?" Another man joined the slinging of epithets.

"He has much to say," I heard Pearl whisper though her lips did not move, "but not to the likes of you."

Our turn on to Spring Street found both our steps faltering… the crowd was so thick on both sides of the street, we could not see the fences and their decoration of fall chrysanthemums that lined it.

I looked over my shoulder and saw a river of snow; we had not lost any of our marchers in their blazing white clothes. But the harder test was upon us.

At first, we heard quiet applause.

"Thank you!"

Pearl and I both turned. A woman in threadbare clothes stood with a child in her arm and three others at her feet. We saw no man with her. From the look of her and her children, so thin and pallid, there might be no man in her life, or worse, a bad one. Pearl and I both walked taller, for her and all those like her.

I saw the sign first, felt my teeth grind, then Pearl saw it.

"Zounderkites," she denounced them under her breath.

They *were* idiots, at least the few antis that were there, the few that made themselves known.

Go Home Socilests! That first placard bobbed up and down in the hands of a woman, well-dressed yet unable to think – or spell – for herself.

Further down, another: *Learn How to Behave like a Lady.*

The flabby woman who held this sign spat at us as we passed her.

"Now there's a real lady," Pearl softly joked. Her face showed not a speck of amusement.

"Fire! Fire!"

A scream burst out behind us. Not one of hate or solidarity, but true fear. We stopped, turned. Two women stamped out the burning hem of another woman's gown. Just a few feet away from them stood a policeman, one of the many the city had offered us for our safety. This man smiled as he blew the last puff of cigarette smoke from his mouth, though I could not see the roll-up in either of his hands

To hurt another is an ugly urge, a craving that poisoned both the one who would hurt and the one that would be hurt. I had known this ugliness before; I had used its power upon a man, the man Pearl had killed to save me. Never since then, not until that moment, had I felt such ugliness within me, as I glared at the smug face of that policeman.

We continued our march.

We entered the uneven triangle of the Great Common. A loud, encouraging greeting rose up and lifted us off our tired feet, drowned out any that would slam us to the ground. In my hope to inspire, I became inspired, an outcome of this day I would never have predicted, or how deeply it would warm my heart.

As the large brass band took up their instruments, I felt the blasting notes of the horns deep in my warmed soul. My hands chose to lift, to raise the flag it held as high in the air as my arms would reach.

I looked at Pearl. Her head had fallen back upon her neck as tears fell from her eyes, spilling into her mouth spread wide and joyously. I reached for her and she for me.

We would not know what difference our actions had made that day any time soon. It didn't matter, not a whit. We had done it, blazed through a trail of both beauty and ugliness, of gratitude and venom. If we had changed one mind, if we had made others think, in my mind, we had done our job.

Together we raised our hands high. Together we sang the words so perfect for the moment… words of our country, *our liberty, our freedom… Let Freedom Ring!*

Pearl

October 1915

"Mother, Father!" Mary's changing voice broke as she called to us, as she pulled us out of our death-like slumber, yesterday's exhaustion barely eased though we remained in our beds.

Peter bolted up and out and I fast on his heels, nearly tripping on the long hem of my nightgown as we fairly slid down the stairs, bare feet scraping on the treads.

We could see only our child's form as she stood in the open front door, the bright glow of a sunny morning turned her into a silhouette.

Peter grabbed her, lifted her, and brought her face on a level with his.

"Are you all right? Are you hurt?"

Mary shook her head, pushed down upon the arms that held her until her feet once more touched the floor.

"No, Father, but-but look!" She demanded as she pointed a finger out the door and into the light.

As a family, we stepped out upon our porch, heedless of the intimate attire we wore. It mattered little once we beheld the sight our daughter revealed.

Great dark holes of earth littered the small front garden where once beautiful plants had been, plants that now lay withered in the street. Pieces of wood lay upon the ground, turning our fence into a row of missing teeth.

Mary stepped off the porch, turned, and in silence pointed at our house.

We rushed out to her. We turned.

"Dear Lord," I heard my voice waver yet didn't know I spoke.

"Damn them!" Peter cried out. "Damn you all to hell!" He spat the words at the street, as if those who had smattered our house with rotted food, eggs, and even small, dead animals still stood in the street from where they hurled them.

I did not even think to chastise him for his language.

I grabbed my daughter by her shoulders, those now almost as high as my own. "Run to Ginevra's, see if it is the same."

On legs grown so long in just the last year, legs that her father had given her, Mary ran. She returned in but a few minutes, panting too heavily to speak. Her nodding head gave us the answer.

I looked at Peter and he at me, our thoughts collided.

"The gallery," we said together as we rushed into the house to dress.

The three of us ran – it would have taken longer for Peter to fire up our automobile. The Runabout sat beside our house, mostly unused, saved for when Peter felt like tinkering with it. We had no time to find out if it would even start.

We ran up the stairs of the Brick Market, ghostly quiet so early on a Sunday morning, to find a tall policeman standing outside the glass door with the words *Wright Gallery* that I had painted upon it.

"Slow down, slow down nigh, al' is well," the tall man's brogue matched the blazing red of his hair.

"Did anyone come here during the night?"

"Is there any damage?"

My words and Peter's tumbled over each other.

"Ah aye, they came, sir. But oi frightened dem aff, yer bet oi did." He punctuated each word with a smack of his truncheon upon a large hand. "Thar's been naw damage. We got a tip an' were waitin' for

145

dem."

Though such a different accent, this peacekeeper's drawl reminded me of Ginevra's heavy accent when first we met. How strange it is, the places where we find consolation.

"Thank you, dear Lord." My relief opened a window and my exhaustion flew in it, hung on me again, heavier than before. I had been working so hard, painting so many images of the revolution that was upon us in the new technique I had adopted, works that were dearer to me than any I had created before.

"So, they've been arrested?" Peter asked, ever more practical than I.

"They 'ave. An' ah've been on watch ever since, in case they 'ad lads."

I abruptly became as fully awake as I was before. "How long have you been standing here, sir?"

"Ack, aboyt foive 'ours. Not so long."

"Five hours?" I repeated. "You poor man. However can we thank you?"

"Naw t'anks needed, mistress. It's me duty an' privilege," the policeman smiled, charming us with deep dimples in his round, freckled face.

"Nonetheless," Peter said as he pulled his wallet from his inside jacket pocket, pulling out every bill within it and handing it to the man. "Take this, Officer..."

"O'Leary, sir. Colm O'Leary," the large man told us even as he tried to push Peter's hand and the money in it back to my husband.

Peter would have none of it. He stepped closer to Officer O'Leary, took his hand, and shoved the wad of bills in it, closing the policeman's fingers upon them.

"Take your mates out for an ale," Peter insisted further. "Or, if you have a wife, take her out for a fine meal."

To this last, Officer O'Leary tipped his head and pocketed the bills.

"Nigh dat sounds gran', it does. She'll be roi 'appy aboyt dat." Colm O'Leary turned sparkling blue eyes upon me. "She's plum tuckered oyt, yer see. She went on a long walk yesterday."

My mouth flopped open like a broken shutter as O'Leary's lips spread into a wide, mischievous grin.

With manly affection, Peter slapped a hand upon the policeman's shoulder. "Take yourself home, sir. I'll be staying for the day."

The policeman looked Peter up and down, at his tall build, at his lean, muscular form.

"Roi yer are," O'Leary said cheerfully as he made for the stairs. "Yer call if yer nade us?"

"We will, officer," Peter assured him.

"An' yer..." he pointed his club at me, "keep up de gran' work. Me struggle an' strife is longin' ter cast a ballot. Freedom is waaat broot us 'ere, loike so many others. Isn't dat so?"

"It is, sir. Indeed it is."

We watched the large man take the stairs like a ballet dancer. He had given us not only peace of mind but a bit of our laughter back as well.

"That man seemed awfully kind," Mary said from between us, all but forgotten. "But I couldn't understand a single word he said."

Between our cackles, Peter and I leaned down to kiss one of Mary's cheeks.

Ginevra

We spent most of Sunday cleaning up our street and our yard, making our children run back and forth between our place and Pearl's, passing missives of strength, of certainty of what we had done. The three of them seemed to have a fine time with it.

The short days of October found us there till almost sunset and I longed for my bed, knowing I had to rise early to make my way to Providence in the morning.

"We are not firing you, Ginevra," Anna said as if somehow that made it all better.

As soon as I entered through the grand door of the Tirocchi Fashion House they had been waiting, ushering me quickly to the design room – strangely empty of other designers – and my drawing table.

Have all the others been given the day off? I wondered at first. No, they had been shushed away; at least the sisters gave me that bit of dignity.

"No, oh no," Laura agreed. "We would never do that. But… but…" Laura hung her head, dark eyes unable or unwilling to meet my own.

"But everyone knows about the marches," Anna finished her sister's thought with a matter-of-factness Laura couldn't manage. "And everyone knows of your involvement, your leadership of the march in Newport."

I knew my face, knew it would fail to keep what was inside of me what was mine, so I did not bother to keep the thoughts that gave birth to my expression.

"I am so very surprised," I spoke my truth. "You are both so progressive. What you have done, daring to own this business, start it by yourselves, run it by yourselves, with no man involved. You have marched as surely as I have, if in a different way."

Anna pulled a chair up beside me, the one she had planted me in. "It is not that we are against suffrage. *Dio mio*, every time I pay my taxes, I feel like I am tossing my money in the trash. What-a good does it do me?"

"*Esattamente!*" I barked, though I did not mean to. "Do you not want that money to give you a voice? Do you not want a say as to what is done with it?"

I had never preached as Alva and Dr. Shaw did, not even as Pearl did, not until that moment.

"When you die, Anna," I used words as sharp as our sewing needles, "your part of this business will not – cannot – go to your sister, but to her husband. It is as the law of the land demands." The sisters looked at me as if my face belonged to someone else. "It is true. It has just happened to my dear friend, Pearl."

I didn't need to say more of what had happened, everyone knew of Pearl's loss, especially as she had always been such a good customer of the Tirocchi's. I didn't have to defend my words, either; they would never question my honesty.

Anna leaned closer to me. "Between us, I tell you, I admire what you did. And I will be first in line to thank you if—"

"When," I corrected.

Anna nodded. "When… we women get to cast a vote. But you know our customers, Ginevra, you know they are not as modern as we are."

"They are the prim-a and proper," Laura chimed in as best she could.

149

"*Sì*, they are," Anna continued. "So we moost-a, I am afraid, take you name off your designs. They will bear our general label only."

They would not give me the credit I was due any longer but thought that not giving it to another would somehow make me feel better about it. It did not. As with my first place of employment, I had become invisible.

"And you cannot talk to the customers. Oh no," Laura's meekness sounded like the grating of metal on jagged cobbled streets.

"And..." Anna squirmed in her chair; for the first time in our acquaintance, she spoke to me without looking at me. "And I do fear that if your activities continue to reach our customers' ears, we will have no choice..."

Her accent grew thick like an old oak. She hesitated, dangling on the hook of her words. I knew what she would say; I would make her say it. "No choice but what?"

"We would have to let you go, Ginevra."

I sat in a bubble of silence as if I had had cotton in my ears for so long. The sisters began to stare at me with unblinking eyes. But still, my mind churned and churned like the ocean when I had seen it during a great storm hurtling over my island city. The waters would still and in the storm's wake came calm. In the wake of my storm, I knew what I had to do, what I must do.

Standing, I reached below my drawing table, hauling out my large case of pencils and sketching paper that had been there since I first began work for the sisters. I closed my sewing case that held my favorite needles and threads as a bank vault holds gold. I put the loose pencils I'd left on my table into the case as well.

"What are you doing, Ginevra?" Anna asked, rising as well.

My hands did not stop their work. "I am doing what I must do. The only thing my heart and soul tells me to do.

With my bags packed, I shook the hand of each sister, who

seemed to have lost the capability to talk.

"I will always be so grateful for the opportunity you gave me."

Despite the squeaks and squawks they hurled at my back, begging me to turn back, I didn't.

I rode the ferry the whole way, the Providence to Newport ferry. The cold wind slapped me, but it did little to relieve me of the heat of my anger, the fire of my fear.

What would Osborn say? What would my father think? How could I carry on without showing my children the right way to live this life?

Why did they force me to choose between one dream and another? It was the question that branded me more than any other. Is it truly not within a person's grasp to have it all, all that one desires, all that one dreams of, all that one willingly works hard for?

The sea was calm yet dizziness tilted me, the questions whirled me home.

I followed my feet; they seemed to know better where I needed to be.

"*Cara figlia!*" my quiet father greeted me cheerfully. "So good you did yesterday. I watch-ed you. Did-a you see me?"

I shook my head. If I opened my mouth, if I spoke, it would be with tears. I'd be damned if I would trade one accent for that of a victim.

My silence, my rigid stance spoke for me. Papa took me by the hand and into the back room. For a time we sat in silence, the silence of waiting, watching, as we watched my father's young apprentices carve and mold the wood – a tiered top of a grand dining table, the almost sensual curve of a violin's scroll and pegbox – through the open arch of this small room.

He gave me what I needed, time.

After I had drunk enough of it, I told him, "I have left my place of work, Papa."

"The work you love?"

"*Sì.*"

He did not look at me but searched inside me still. "Tell."

I told him. He knew much of it... the march. He had been there, though I had not seen him. He knew as well my strong feelings of gaining suffrage. He had never said anything, one way or the other, on my stand on the subject. Of course, he had never said anything when he had learned the truth of the murder either. That time he had only held me longer than he ever had before or since. I do remember his shy grin when I told him I would be a part of those who worked for suffrage; pride and satisfaction had tickled it into place.

"They made you pick," Papa finally said after he had chewed upon my story. "You look into heart and found-a you answer. Brava, *figlia mia.*"

It took every ounce of strength left in me that day to keep my tears from making tracks down my face.

"What-a you do now?"

My shoulders rose and dropped. I shook my head as they did.

My papa looked at me, gaze like an arrow. "Perhaps you do as I do. Your own-a place. You the boss."

My eyes blinked, no fluttered. My papa gave me a thought – a lifeline – I had never considered.

One talented hand, gnarled from years of chiseling and carving, patted my knee.

"Think on it, Ginevra. Ask-a you mother."

My mother had been lost to us for nearly thirty years. We both spoke to her still.

I would ask her... I would think on it. I wondered if another dream had just been born.

Ginevra

March 1916

The space was small and without much life to it, but in my eyes, I could see how full it would be, how lovely it could be.

For now, the stench of dried ale rose up from the stained wooden floor and dirt and mold discolored the two side brick walls.

I had taken the lease on the building only three doors down on Broadway from my father's workshop mostly with my own money, and some from my husband. We had spent a merry night as he read a scolding note from his mother on the whole affair. As with Pearl and her gallery, it was my husband's name upon the lease, it was my husband's name that was attached to the business I would hopefully create; as an "invisible" person, I could not own my own business.

But hope alone did not make things happen.

"*Molto bene*," I applauded myself. "To work."

I picked up the bucket full of soapy water, picked up the harsh, steel-tipped brush, got down on my knees, and set to work.

I switched hands as each arm grew weary. I bunched my skirts beneath my aching knees. I heard not a sound, not even the church bells.

Until she came.

"Well, now that is a sight one should not see."

My back had been to the door; in my kneeling position, it meant that my backside – one jerking with each push of the brush – greeted her.

"Shouldn't you be at the gallery doing something useful, rather than pestering me?" I didn't turn, didn't stop scrubbing.

"Oh my dear, Ginny," Pearl twittered. Something was up; Pearl never twittered.

I sat back on my heels and turned around.

Pearl stood in the doorway. Just behind her, a flatbed carriage took up the whole of the street, its bed piled high with what only she knew, for it was covered with a heavy tarp. Standing next to it were the two maids who worked now and then at The Beeches.

"What are you about?" Now I pestered Pearl.

She laughed, which only made me want to pester her more.

"I am about you," she said simply and with a wave of her hand, the carriage driver threw back the tarp.

"*Dio mio*," I whispered. I rose to my feet. I groaned not a bit as my stiff body unfolded.

There were vases of many sizes, of many colors. There was artwork, some of Pearl's I recognized, some of beautiful women beautifully gowned, some in her new style; I thought it abrupt but liked it. There was a beautiful maroon and gold settee that would look stunning against the brick… once the brick was cleaned. So much of what she brought me came from The Beeches.

"Ladies," Pearl said a single word and the two maids walked in. One took the bucket by my feet, took the brush right out of my hand, while the other carried more buckets, more brushes, and rags in from the carriage.

Pearl came to me and took my arm in hers. "It will be mahvelous, dahling."

How I loved when Pearl mocked, when she pretended to be smug.

Her smile softened. She whispered to me, "We will be victorious… in all our battles. You'll see, Ginny."

155

I squeezed the arm wrapped around mine.

What would I have done without this woman and her daring spirit? Would I still be a servant or perhaps a menial manufacturing worker? Gratitude is not a word worthy of what I feel for her.

Pearl

April 1916

We hadn't seen Alva in Newport since before the march. When she popped in, like Jack out of his box, she took us all by surprise, she stunned us with what she had been doing. But when did Alva not stun and surprise?

"Here is a copy for every member of the PEA, dearies." Alva pointed to the stacks of slim books piled in the corner of the headquarters at 128 Bellevue. While most of the women in attendance, those holding positions of authority or action within our suffrage group, squinted to read the spines of those books, I studied Alva.

Though she wore her fur-trimmed jacket, she also wore jowls, a new accessory for her. At sixty-three she would still be considered attractive, but not even a Vanderbilt or a Belmont could stop the march of time. Did heroes grow old or do they just become more celebrated?

In my moments of musing, Ginevra had joined the rush and returned to her seat beside me, a book for each of us in her hands, including Mabel who once more sat with us, who once more wore the same dress as the last time we had seen her.

"If you have not read about this work," Alva lectured, never happier than in this role, "it is an operetta, a suffrage operetta that I wrote, with the help of Elsa Maxwell."

I flipped open the gold and black cover to the inside title page. Alva spoke the truth, in her manner. Her name was listed – and listed first – as one of the authors of the work, as was Elsa Maxwell. But Elsa was also listed as the author of the music and lyrics. The story – the concept – I had no doubt came from the complex and concentrated mind of Alva Vanderbilt Belmont while Elsa had given it life.

"In New York, we performed this operetta but once," Alva continued, "and in doing so, we raised nearly 8,000 dollars for the cause."

That brought our noses out of the books.

Alva slapped one down on the table before her.

"I think we can do better, right here in Newport."

That brought out fish-mouths and outraged gasps.

"Oh please, dearies." Alva would have none of it. "After all we've done, you will now cower?"

"I won't." I meant to whisper these words to Ginevra; I said them loud enough for the whole room to hear.

Along with her cackle, I found myself at the end of Alva's pointed finger. "I knew I could count on you, Pearl, you would never back down from any challenge, would you now?"

She and I became stone, staring statues alone in the full room. She looked deep inside me. I wondered what she saw, what she knew to be the truth. Yes, surprise was one of Alva's most potent weapons. It would not surprise me at all if she knew that I, and not Ginevra, had killed Herbert Butterworth.

Did she extort me with that stare? I couldn't take the chance.

"Of course, Alva," I said with an ease I acted, my first performance. "You can count me in."

"You are in, dearie, you can bet you are." Every word she spoke relieved a layer of my dubiety and replaced it with certainty. Somehow I would find out when and how *she* came to be certain.

I did not include nor speak for Ginevra; not only had I learned from the last time I had volunteered both of us without consulting her, I knew that such public speaking and performing did not suit my dearest friend. Her talents lay elsewhere.

"Will you help with the costumes?" I leaned toward her, hiding my lips and my words behind the opened book. "It could do much to bring customers to your business."

Ginevra did not look up from her perusal of the book, though I knew she did not read it. "Sometimes, Pearl, you simply do not play fair."

I bucked my shoulder against hers and saw her small, half-smile, as I straightened up.

"This is all rather outrageous," Mabel hissed, outraged but not brave enough to have Alva hear of it. "I do not mind marching but-but acting, on a stage… scandalous. My husband's family would be appalled."

I patted her hand. "You need do only what you feel comfortable doing," I assured her. "Only what your family would approve of." I thought our very struggle here was to give us the right to do just the opposite, to do that which we knew was right in the face of any and all opposition. Clearly Mabel – and one or two other women at the meeting that afternoon who also harrumphed at the suggestion – was not made of such "deviant" substance as I.

"Oh, that I will," Mabel huffed, closing the book with a snap, crossing her arms like a shield upon her chest. "That I am."

"Humph," I heard from my other side, finding Ginevra studying our friend through the lens of disapproval.

"I have always wanted to act," this from Sarah Eddy, on the other side of Ginevra, her tow blonde head leaned forward to whisper to us all. "But my family would never have forgiven me."

"And now," Mabel snapped the question, "will they not still find such behavior unforgivable?"

"Perhaps," Sarah said with a waggle of nearly invisible brows on her pale skin, "but it is for a cause – our cause. And I am a grown woman. They will simply have to."

"Humph," Mabel grunted as I winked at Sarah.

"I leave you to study the work at your leisure," Alva declared. She should just have said be quiet now and let me talk, which is what she meant. "Let me tell you the gist of the tale."

Like obedient students, we closed our books and gave her our full attention.

"We join Mr. and Mrs. John Pepper from Oshkosh out West," Alva began and we tittered appropriately. "They are about to hold a gala, one to welcome home their eight daughters from finishing school abroad. During their time away, each daughter had mastered a necessary skill, not only to get them married off…" Someone in the room coughed. It might have been a clumsily concealed comment on what Alva had done to Consuelo to marry her off to an abusive duke or it might just have been my imagination. "They had become a classical dancer, a ballroom dancer, a singer, a poet, a comedienne, and a tragic actress. Another is a whiz at sports, running, swimming, even golf." Alva walked back and forth before us, ticking the daughters' names and talents off on her fingers. She stopped when she had ticked seven fingers. She stopped. "And what becomes of the eighth, of Melinda herself..?" She held us enthralled. She swam in our suspension. "She became a suffragette!"

Ginevra and I joined in the applause.

"I hate to admit it," I whispered to her, "but I'm intrigued."

"I am impressed," Ginevra said with that honesty of hers that rankled me at times. "Alva has more talents than even she imagines she does." But then she brings me back to love with her humor. "But truthfully, it is quite an accomplishment to write a book."

"Bah," I grunted. "Anyone can write a book, or so I've been told."

"There are the gossips of the town, the reverend, the physician…

you know, the typical players in any small typical town," Alva continued as the applause faded away. "But Melinda has not served her talents – the play does not end – until she has converted everyone into suffragists and suffragettes."

More applause and more laughter followed, all deserving if I were to be truthful.

"I believe I am going to enjoy this," I told Ginevra and I meant it.

"Do you have time for it? I'm sure Alva will cast you in a main role."

"Do I have time? You know I have nothing but time."

Too much time. Since the march, patronage at the gallery was lower than when we first opened it and though the event had given my mind pictures I could have painted for years, I knew no one who would have bought them. While Ginevra struggled to find customers for her fashion house, one open for only a month, I struggled to find purpose. No artist existed, of any type, did they not want their art contributing to the world and the world of culture. My world was untethered in so many ways then; Alva's operetta could be just what I needed to feel alive again.

Our lives came second to that of Melinda and her sisters. Alva had set the date of the performance for the end of June when the richest of the rich would be in their summer cottages. That meant we had only two months to learn our dialogue, the songs, the dancing, build sets, and craft the costumes.

Ginevra's prediction had come true – Alva did cast me as Melinda. I think Ginevra had a much easier time of it than I did. She was no fool, my Ginny; she had agreed to create the costumes only if the cast went to her shop and not she to the theatre.

The day I went to Costa Couture, a name her husband loved as much as the rest of us did, though perhaps not nearly as much as Felice, I could barely get in the door. I stood at it and watched her, so vibrantly alive I wished for a dress made of her colors. Women and men took up all the space, standing on the raised platform before a three-beveled mirror, lounging on the settee and chairs as they waited their turn and thumbing through Ginevra's design book as they did.

"Oh, I must have this one," I heard a fashionable young woman say, the one that would play the dancing sister.

Ginevra's head tilted her way as she snuck the woman a glance out of the side of her gaze. She would remember the woman's face and she would make her that dress.

My friend must have caught sight of me as well, for she raised her shoulders and her brows and offered me a wide smile full of tucking pins.

I laughed, waved, and mouthed, "later," to her, before leaving her to her paying customers, rather pleased with myself, and went back to rehearsal, ever mindful of the days hurtling us to performance night.

Somehow we had done it; somehow I found myself backstage in the dusty, old theatre that had originally been built as the Zion Episcopal Church in 1834, becoming St. Joseph's Catholic Church in 1885, and now serving as the Layfette Theater, a theater offering live performances of all types.

I would not go on until halfway into the show, which only seemed to make my stage fright worse. I knew there were Vanderbilts and Belmonts, Astors and Havemeyers in the audience as well as my family and dearest friends. I paced, I murmured my lines silently to myself, and I sang my songs in my head.

"Do you hear that?" Somehow she found me. From the shadows, Ginevra demanded I withdraw from my head and listen. I heard laughter and applause and yes, even cheers. "They will be all warmed up for you and you will give them the best of it."

I took her hand and held it until my cue came. I hesitated. She pushed. I was out on stage. I became Melinda Pepper, a young woman daring to buck the social constraints of her age. It didn't take much acting on my part.

I walked on to the stage and into the role. With my hand, I raised a suffrage flag and, as I marched off the stage, down one aisle and back up, the other "people" in the audience came to march behind me, actors who symbolized laborers, factory girls, sales ladies, and even the poor. They followed me on stage as I concluded the song, "I Am Melinda."

"Good heavens," one of the actresses on stage portraying a town gossip gasped, "I actually believe the creature's a suffragette!"

To the rousing laughter, I lost myself to the play and my part in it.

Until the heckling began.

I did not hear it at first – I was far too wrapped up in my role.

I noticed strange movements by my fellow performers... heads snapping toward the door in the distance, some flubbed lines, and some even left the stage before it was their time to do so.

As I sang one of my songs, one that brought me to the very front of the stage, it was hard not to notice – even with the glare of lights in my eyes – so many heads turned away from the stage rather than towards it.

"You spit on your true purpose as given by God!"

Was it irony or planning that such words came on my refrain of, *"Girls, girls, put away your curls... we're done with teas and balls!"*

I kept singing though perhaps I shouldn't have.

"You will destroy the sanctity of family!"

"Men have ruled us women East and West, from the caveman in his lair, to

163

the flyer in the air, to keep us women down they thought best."

Though I was not meant to, I left the stage even as I continued to sing. I acted as if it was part of the act... that I was meant to sing directly to people in the audience as if to recruit them to my cause.

I wanted the glare of the light out of eyes. I wanted to see who dared to act so beastly, to hurl rocks of words.

"But turned now is the tide, and we cannot be denied, we are coming in our millions to enhance..."

"Sappho! Leave us alone!"

Sappho? I nearly laughed aloud; if they only knew how much I enjoyed the pleasures of the flesh with my husband. And what business was it of theirs where I found my pleasure?

I could see them now and they could see me – they clogged the doors. No one could have left did they wanted to. They wore sashes as did those for suffrage, like the one I wore now as I sang, but theirs read, "My husband votes for me," or my father, or my brother. I kept walking toward them.

"Pearl!"

The sharp call of my name did not stop me.

"For they need us great and small, and we'll gladly give our all, to show what we can do if we've the chance!"

As if hitting my mark, I ended my last note as I took my last step to stand before them.

"You," I drew the word out as I eyed the ones I could see. Lips snarled back, eyes narrowed, so full of hate. The dogs were upon us. "You, none of you, bought a ticket to this show."

"We don't need a ticket. We come doing God's work." The blonde, dainty woman growled like the sailors who come to port for some fun.

"Indeed?" I asked. "Your God teaches you to act like animals?"

"He teaches us to do anything to spread His word."

I heard the murmurs in the audience grow louder… squeaks of fear, squawks of anger.

"Anything?"

A tall woman stepped forward, nudging two of her companions aside to get to me.

"Yes, anything."

She shoved. My head flopped forward, snapped back.

I fell backward against the last row of seats.

Someone in them pushed me forward, back toward her. Their force put more force behind my cocked right arm and the fist at the end of it.

The last thing I remembered was the pain exploding on my knuckles as they collided with her face, as the large woman barely flinched from my strike, falling on me, tearing at my sash, my hair, while I swung now two balled fists at her head.

"Hah!" I barked a laugh as I entered the jail's visitor room and saw who awaited me there. "They sent you, did they?"

"Oh no." Ginevra did her very best not to laugh with me, but she failed miserably. "I volunteered. It seemed only right. You know, because—"

"Because you wanted to relish the reversal of our roles? To see me sitting in the hoosegow?" I sat at the table between us, pulling the rough, no doubt flea-infested blanket closer around my shoulders and the tattered clothing still upon me.

Like a flash, our laughter faded as the memories flooded. All those months she sat in prison for a crime I had committed, I had visited her as often as I could. With memories, it was a truth, the darker they were, the more powerful they were and the longer they stayed, no matter how unwelcome they were.

"Are you well, Pearl? Have they treated you well?"

I nodded even as I lay gentle fingers on my throbbing cheekbone. "They gave me some ice." I tried to smile; I failed. It hurt.

"Perhaps it might be best if you don't look in a mirror for a while," Ginevra looked at me with such pity, I didn't even ask – didn't want to know – what remnants of last night's tussle I wore. I dropped my head in the cradle of a cupped palm... I, Pearl Worthington Wright, had been in an actual tussle. Not only in it, but in the center of it. My mother vomited in her grave.

"You might think about some cosmetics, perhaps, like those—"

The door behind me opened abruptly and with it, Ginevra's eyes rose and she gaped.

I turned and smiled.

"Officer O'Leary," I greeted the large man, understanding my friend's look, "we meet again."

The policeman tipped his hat to me. "Dat we do, ma'am. Though oi'm not as 'appy ter clap yer as oi ought ter be."

"Nor I," I assured him. I introduced the policeman to my friend, explaining how we knew each other. Ginevra relaxed stiff muscles back into the care of her chair with a sigh.

"Yer re free ter go, missus," Colm O'Leary said after a nod to her.

"Did you bail me out?" I asked Ginevra.

"No, I didn't—"

"Why ever—"

"Peter is coming with the money, but I don't think he's arrived yet." Ginevra finally finished a sentence in our contracted conversation.

"Well, then how..." I turned to my new friend, Office O'Leary. "Did you?"

"On a policeman's salary?" His bushy red brows slanted askew on his forehead.

I felt my chagrin warm my bruised face. O'Leary must have enjoyed it for he laughed as he told me the truth of things. "We are lettin' yer go. De mayor wants as wee attenshun broot ter dis tin' as possable."

"He's letting everyone go, sir?" Ginevra asked a good question.

"He is. But wan at a time. Oi wus able ter convince de captain ter let yer go 'ome first." Officer O'Leary stood taller, if that was even possible, though he narrowed his eyes at me. "An' that's wha you'll go, roi, straight 'ome?"

I stood, rose on tiptoes, and kissed his cheek, turning the Irishman's skin a brighter red than his hair.

"I promise." I crossed my heart.

He led me out of the room and to the free part of the jail where Ginevra waited for me. We thanked him again, both of us, and profusely, and walked out into the sunshine.

With her arm about mine, Ginevra walked me home.

"You will tell me what that policeman said, yes? I don't know how you understand a word with that accent of his."

I could only have laughed harder if it didn't hurt my face quite so much.

Pearl

October 1916

Both wars of the age were heating up, as hot as the Indian summer that kept our windows wide open, that kept us drenched in the sweat of all kinds.

More suffragettes than ever marched, picketed, and were arrested, and yet once more, the amendment's failure was predicted in the upcoming vote.

On the first of the month, Germany had launched major counterattacks on British soldiers in Polygon Wood, West Flanders, and Belgium. Since July, the Allies had been fighting the German Empire for control of the Belgian city of Ypres in West Flanders, with no end in sight.

The weight of it all sucked creativity from my soul as surely as the tide sucks the waves out to sea twice a day. I had heard of this, the depletion of the soul as the murderer of creativity. Art is born in the soul; if the soul is depleted, what has art to feed upon?

I sat in the backroom of our empty gallery. There were no customers to greet, to talk to of art, to sell any piece to. My suffrage activities, my arrest, I knew were, in part, to blame, though Peter would never agree.

The canvas before me mocked me with its blankness, denounced me as a fraud with no true talent.

Not even my husband was there at the gallery. I had no idea where he was. I knew only that he was not with me. He had been spending less and less time at work. If he were another man, I would have worried there was another woman. But his never quenchable desire for me and his impeccable honor allayed such qualms. No, I did not fear any philandering on Peter's part. I feared something much worse.

I had fallen into a dark abyss. Even if I tried looking up, I could see no light.

"Pearl!"

I had never heard my husband yell my name so, speak so with a tone that would bring fear into any that heard it, that could stop a thief in mid-snatch.

"I'm here," I yelled back. I ran.

We collided in the middle of the hidden corridor behind one gallery wall.

I found a man I barely knew. Peter's soft curls were a nest for rats; his disheveled clothes bore sweat stains. The beauty of his face had been ravaged as if by fire or disease.

"What is it? What has happened? Are you all right?"

I didn't know what I needed to know, so I asked every question that burst in my mind as my eyes scoured him for any sign of injury.

"There is..." he panted. He flopped his hands upon my shoulders and allowed me to give him what support I could.

"What? What?"

"There is a German U-boat... here in Newport... at the Naval Station!"

I stepped back as if I could run from his words.

"Are we under attack?"

169

His head shook; sweat drops flew through the air.

"They are…" Peter's frightened tone became a snarl full of hate. "We escorted them into port… they are socializing with the American officers."

My life had been a series of the ridiculous, but surely I had not heard him correctly, surely this was far too absurd to be true, even in the context of my life, a life littered with the strange and absurd.

As we closed and locked the gallery, as we trotted to our home, Peter tried to explain that which defied logical explanation.

"I don't know how or, more importantly, why," Peter began. The fingers of the hand that gripped my arm dug into my flesh as he hurried me along. I had no idea why we rushed. "But while I was at the base, they—"

"Why in heavens were you at the base?" I knew – I thought I knew. I denied my knowledge.

"They, the Germans, were being escorted into port by one of our submarines. I ran to watch like everyone else. I could not believe my eyes, Pearl, it was like something out of one of my nightmares."

He hadn't answered my question. I don't think he heard me or could hear me. I let him talk.

Peter's blue eyes filled with the red of fire.

"Then…" He shook his head, he chuckled – actually chuckled – but with no mirth. "Then the damned captain, Kapitanleutnant Hans Rose to be precise, actually rowed ashore and called upon the officers of the base. I had just been speaking with the base commander, with Admiral Knight…"

Oh, you will tell me the why of that! I refuse to remain in the dark.

"We were standing together as the man came ashore. The German spoke to the Admiral in English, very good English, right there on American soil. I tell you, Pearl, I didn't know if I had died and gone to hell. I stepped back, but not too far. I heard every word that passed between them."

We had arrived home. Thankfully, Mary was still at the park with Sarah.

I dropped like a stone into the first chair I saw, the one in the foyer by the small console table. Peter paced the short length of the hall as he babbled on.

"We, the United States, we are still neutral in this war, if you can believe it. The Admiral has little choice but to be cordial, cautiously cordial. And he was that. I give him credit, for that at the least.

"He, Rose, claimed his ship required a short repair, or so he said when the Admiral asked him why Rose had come so close to our shore. I don't think the Admiral believes him. I don't. But we're still neutral, what can the Admiral do? He asked the German how long the repair would take and then granted him that time, no more than a few hours, to stay in port. They have to be gone by six o'clock."

I looked around the corner and into the sitting room. The finely scrolled grandfather clock Felice had made us for a wedding present told me it was but ten minutes until three. They would be here – the most aggressive of combatants the world was coming to know – would be in our city for another three hours. I bent my dizzied head down between my knees.

"Rose heartedly agreed to it. And then... and then..."

Peter began to remove his tie, then his jacket.

"What the hell are you doing?" I had never cursed at my husband before. I had never cursed in his presence, ever.

"I am changing my clothes," Peter blathered as he continued to undress, right there in the hall. "You must change. We are joining them... aboard the German boat."

My husband had gone mad. It was the only explanation. Oh, how I wished it was the only explanation. I didn't move, couldn't.

"Rose invited the Admiral and a few of the other officers and their wives, to tour the ship. For some hellish reason, the Admiral agreed. I couldn't take it, Pearl, I couldn't stand any more of it. I started away, I was almost at the gate out when I was stopped by a private who informed me that the Admiral wanted me – us – to join them, the party going aboard."

"What the hell for?"

For the first time since he came to me at the gallery, Peter stopped moving, stopped talking. Agitation of every sort fled. He wrapped himself in a thick suit of armor, one I had never seen him wear.

He stopped right in front of me where I hadn't moved from my chair. He bent down so that his eyes were on the same level as mine.

"My Pearl, I cannot tell you." He kissed me. "Not yet."

I was no fool. I will grant that for all the wealth I had been brought up with, lived with, it was a very small world that I had lived in. Even my college experience was highly structured, disciplined, and hemmed in by a long list of rules.

But there had been books, lots and lots of books. And in books, the world is limitless.

In times of war, if someone cannot tell you what they are about, they are about the business of war, in some form or another.

The tips of my fingers began to tingle. I had to put my head back down between my knees.

"You don't have time for that, Pearl. You don't have time to be anything but that strong, resilient woman I know you are, that I have seen you are."

Gently this time, he took me by the arm, helped me upstairs where I changed into my most authoritarian-looking, most serious-looking suit, bearing the label *Costa Couture*.

"Pearl, I need you to really be Pearl," Peter whispered in my ear as we approached the dock that would bring us to the ramp to board the unsubmerged boat. The knot in my stomach tightened when I heard the music the German crew played on a Victrola, as they waved to the crowd, one growing larger and larger by the minute, gawking at the foreign sailors from the shore as if they were at a zoo caught up short by the sight of an unknown creature.

My patience with my husband thinned, by the fear of the truth of him I had been guessing at for some time, by the nonsensical words he tossed at me. I sneered at him.

"I am going to have your head examined as soon as this is over," I snapped. "Whatever are you asking of me?"

"When I first saw you, first met you, I thought I had never seen anyone so alive. Everyone else in that pub that night disappeared." Peter smiled as he spoke such words to me. My anger only grew as he touched my heart so, when he once more whispered, "I need you to make me disappear."

I tried to swallow but couldn't, nor talk. I could barely breathe. I knew exactly what he meant. I hated it, but I would do it.

"Ah, zis must be one of ze vonderful beauties of Newport I haffe read so much about," Kapitanleutnant Hans Rose said as he took my hand, bowing over it, a feather brush of his lips upon the glove that covered it.

"Oh, you flatter me so, Captain," I flirted. In another life at another ime, I might have actually flirted with him.

He looked to be about my age, perhaps a bit younger, tall, with lovely cheekbones and full lips between a dashing mustache and an intricately shaped goatee. His eyes were the color of the ocean he sailed upon.

But his hand on mine made me long to jump in the sea to wash any remnant of him off me. Nausea I had known when carrying Mary reintroduced itself to me. I swallowed it down as best I could.

"I am so interested to see your ship, Captain. I have a new interest in ships these last couple of years." If he had known why, he would have known.

"It vill be mien pleasure, Madame."

Captain Rose and I led the small band of chosen ones on the tour. As he droned on about the size of the ship and how it was powered, as he pointed out crew quarters and officers' cabins, I slipped my gaze toward both my husband and the Admiral whenever the Captain would not see. They looked at more than what Captain Rose showed, they listened much more diligently than I.

"I saw some very large guns on deck, Captain." Oh, how men loved to talk about the size of their "guns." "Are they the only weapons you carry?"

"Nein." He couldn't stop himself, narcissists rarely can. "Zere are torpedoes as vell."

"Torpedoes?" I put a gloved hand over the circle my lips formed. "Are there many of them? Are we in danger of blowing up?"

I staggered a bit, threw my hand upon my heart; it was the perfect performance of a coquette, all those who had always annoyed me so.

The Captain threw back his head and laughed. I longed to kick him between the legs.

"Now, now, Madame. Such questions vill make me zink you are ein spy," he laughed again.

I fake-laughed with him. "Oh, I am no spy, I assure you. I am a painter," my voice changed in an instant, it became the one I used when tussling with the antis, "and a suffragette."

"Pearl."

The hiss came from just behind me. I didn't turn.

"Ah ja, I haffe read about suffragettes. Our women work for the vote as vell, though I believe zey are closer to success than American women."

And with that smug comment, this American had joined the war against the Germans.

"Perhaps you should read about what the German women are doing, Pearl. Perhaps you might gain some insight." Peter jumped into the conversation before I could jump off this ship, this farcical ride he had forced me to take, bringing the Captain to the bottom of the sea with me.

"Perhaps I should do a great many things, dear husband," I said to Peter as I showed him my teeth.

There was a deadlock between our gaze. Before I could do something stupid, something to put my husband and me in jeopardy, an American private stumbled quickly through the tight environment of the ship toward us.

"As requested, Captain."

There was something in the young man's failure to look the German captain in the eye that told him of his displeasure at a task just completed, though I didn't understand why giving the foreign captain a copy of the *New York Times* disturbed him so.

Captain Rose, who had informed me his name was pronounced Roos-uh, quickly folded the paper and tucked it under his arm.

His ill-disguised flirting became hurried; he hurried us through the remainder of the tour of his ship.

In less than an hour aboard, he escorted us off. Within less than a half-hour, close to half-past-five in the evening, the boat pulled away from our shore.

"Thank the good Lord," I sighed as Peter and I waved them merrily on their way. I was all too glad to see the back of that ship.

"Indeed," Peter agreed. He was Peter again, my Peter, though there was a look upon him as if I painted his portrait with two very different colors – one of exhausted relief and one of possibilities – a look I had never seen upon his lovely face before, one he turned directly to me. "You did very well, my Pearl, under very difficult circumstances. Thank you so very much." He kissed my cheek.

I wanted him to talk as much and as fast as he had before. I wanted – needed – to ask him so many questions. But I knew now was not the time.

"And you, my love? How did you do?" I leaned into him, his arm wrapping about my waist. I looked up to him with all my questions, all my needs, shining from my eyes.

"Well enough," he said. "Well enough."

He took me home and made me forget, if only for a few hours, everything that had happened that day, all that had been seen that day and all that it meant.

The next day every newspaper told us about the six ships the U-53 and Captain Rose had sunk off the Massachusetts coast, how they sank south of the Nantucket Lightship, which placed them clearly outside American territorial limits. The six ships belonged to the British, the French, and the Dutch. It was if he knew where the ships would be and how best to sink them.

In war, as in life, there are rarely coincidences.

In the days that followed, Peter spent less and less time with me at the gallery.

Ginevra

January 1917

"I believe we should, once more, mirror the form of protest that our leaders are currently conducting in Washington right here in Rhode Island, directly in front of the State House."

Pearl stood at the podium more and more often of late as Alva stood at it less and less.

Something was happening with my dearest friend, something I understood, and something that I didn't. The something that I didn't, scared me. It had been five years since she lost her family and it had been five years since we had joined the suffrage movement. Pearl's involvement had grown more frequent as did her anger; she seemed forever ill at ease. I would follow her, as I always had, as I always would, but I found now I did so to keep an eye on her.

"We will work in concert with our sisters in the Rhode Island Equal Suffrage Association. As they are based in Providence, it will be much easier for them to get to the capitol building," Pearl passed out copies of the *New York Times* as she told us of the next protest for the Political Equality Association of Newport. "What a shame it is that the Capitol no longer resides here in Newport as it once did. That would have made things much easier."

I knew she kept talking but I heard little of it. I could barely take my eyes – my mind – off the words and pictures in front of me.

The newspaper called them the Silent Sentinels because this protest, unlike all others that had come before it, they conducted in absolute silence. In thick heavy coats with their sashes over them, before the tall, iron picket gate of the White House, these women simply stood in silence and let their banners and signs speak for them.

Mr. President How Long Must Women Wait for Liberty?

Mr. President What Will You do for Woman Suffrage?

"They have been there since the tenth of this month, put in place by Alice Paul after her disastrous meeting with the President. We are but two days away from the end of the month. It is time we joined this stage of the fight." Pearl slammed her copy of the newspaper down on the podium before her; more than a few women jumped as paper slammed upon wood.

I did not jump, I did not stop reading. I had come to the part of the article that related what President Wilson had said to Alice Paul when she asked for his support of suffrage. Though he favored it, he did little to promote it, influence the movement desperately needed. While the President had given them little hope for his backing, he had given them a call to arms, though I doubt if he knew it at the time.

"Ladies," the paper recounted he had called to them just as they were leaving the Oval Office, "concert public opinion on behalf of woman suffrage."

Though English was not my native tongue, I knew it well enough to assume the women's interpretation of "concert public opinion" was that we needed ever more women on our side. We needed to increase our power while limiting that of the antis. Yet our two groups, both made up mostly of women, seemed to be growing at an even pace.

"Will Alva be joining us?" I heard a voice from behind me call out, though whose I couldn't tell for sure, perhaps that Minnie something, for it was that sort of girlish snob voice of hers. Whoever it was, she asked a good question.

"She will not," Pearl said, not nearly as righteous as just moments before. "I wrote to her of it and, while she is fully in favor of it, her age and the cold prohibit her from taking part."

If in my mind, Alva was the Alva from my difficult adolescence, I would have sneered at her response, one that sounded merely like an excuse. But these past five years working by her side had allowed me to see her aging and it was not an attractive journey she now made – there are few of us for whom it was.

"But she has sent us two thousand dollars for us to make more signs and banners and sashes."

Pearl held up the check, swiftly and smartly turning the negative into a positive. I had a front-row seat to Pearl's transformation from painter to politician. I was unsure if I would give it a good review or not.

"She seems so angry," Mabel whispered from beside me. She always seemed to sit with us and none of the other women.

"Hmm." I wondered the same but something kept me from sharing my concern.

"I don't see why Pearl would be so angry," Mabel said like a whiny child.

"I—," I had no chance to respond.

"And most importantly, we must keep our plans and those of our Providence sisters a secret until our first day of protest, two weeks from today." Darkness stained Pearl's creamy skin even as her voice rose in a rousing rallying cry. "I know we will get much coverage from the newspapers, we will have our women in charge of such things make sure we do, but the worst thing that can happen is for the antis to learn of it too soon."

In that, I couldn't agree with Pearl more. Not one of us wished for a repeat of the disaster that happened on the night of the play.

Both Pearl and I had now spent time in prison; neither one of us ever wanted to return.

"Two weeks, ladies." Pearl walked from the podium, through our ranks, to the back corner of the room. "We have two weeks to enlist as many women as possible, assuring them they will be used on a rotating basis. And we have two weeks to make new signs and banners."

For the first time since the meeting started, one of Pearl's genuine smiles lit up her face.

"This is the one I have chosen and written for myself."

With flair, the Pearl of her debutante days returned, and she spun the sign around.

The room exploded with applause and laughter. It was the perfect sign to hold up in front of the State House and its golden ornamentation upon the very top of its dome.

When will the Independent Man become the Independent Woman?

"How can you, Ginny? How can you even think of it?"

Osborn and I had been married for nearly fifteen years; it seemed he was gaining some of my fiery Italian temperament. I had never seen him so agitated, so bursting with it, as I did that night when I told him of our plans.

"I do no understand, *caro*," I responded truthfully. "I have been involved in this for over five years now, why are you suddenly—"

"Because now women are being arrested!" Osborn slammed his large hand upon the table between us. I looked to the ceiling as if I could see through the wood and the beams and know whether he had woken the children or not. At thirteen, Felix rarely fell asleep as early as he used to, he rarely did not understand adult talk as he used to, either.

Osborn understood my upward glance. Removing glasses he had recently started to wear – their dark rims made his eyes look even bluer, I thought – my husband ran clawed fingers through his straight blond hair, hair just starting to include small plumes of bright white strands.

"What if it had been you? If you had been put back in jail when Pearl had?"

His tall body curved round as his elbows landed on his knees; his head shook back and forth and back again, the pendulum of a clock, one ticking down his patience.

When he looked at me, when he lifted his face, I wished he hadn't. Blood shot its way through the whites of his eyes, fear splotched his skin from hairline to neck. His fear jolted me as surely as if it were an arrow shot directly into my heart.

"I dream of it, you know? Visions of hell's making. It breaks me, Ginny, it breaks me."

I went to him, knelt by him. My face had grown so wet. I do not know when.

"But I survived, *mi amore*. Pearl saved me."

Without taking his head from the ragged basket of shaking hands, his eyes of blue and red veins – of purple almost; the color of his rage, passion, turmoil – found mine.

"You mean *you* saved *her*?"

I forgot how to breathe, or if I did I would have shattered with each inhalation.

He knows. He's always known.

"I do no—"

"Don't, Ginny." I hated the bitter smile forming on his lips. "Do not even try. *We've* always known.

My knees failed me. I fell back upon my feet, a stone tumbling down a bottomless well.

Until he lifted me, till his arms turned to flesh again and wrapped themselves around me.

"We saved each other," I whispered into his neck, my head

collapsing on his wide, firm shoulder.

"I know," came his only reply.

"Damnation! I cannot believe they are here!" Pearl swore as she did more and more lately. Across from our picket line on Smith Street, the wide lane that ran in front of the State House in Providence, a long row of antis were already in place. They held signs, as we did, but unlike ours, they rallied against the vote, *The Women Who Love the Home do Not Want the Vote*, read one such sign. Apparently, they were incapable of loving more than one thing at a time.

"They began showing up just minutes after we did," one Mrs. Agnes M. Jenks, the current president of the Rhode Island Equal Suffrage Association, informed us. Though she lived in Massachusetts, she bore the rough and tumble look of one born in the woods of her home state of New Hampshire.

"Has your organization kept it a secret, as we did?" Pearl demanded.

Agnes merely glowered at her

"I believe that means yes," I whispered in Pearl's ear, doing my best to rein in my friend's obvious frustration.

"I believe," Agnes interjected, "that there is an infiltrator among us. Either in your organization or mine."

Pearl's head bobbed up and down, though her eyes shone with fiery denial. "Then we must suss out who she—"

"Or he..." Now both Pearl and Agnes glowered at me.

"Who *she* is," Pearl finished, eyes racking the line of women on the suffrage side as if she searched for a criminal in a police lineup.

The names of one or two women jumped into my head, but I would not accuse with no more than my gut feelings. I had been at the opposite end of those, I would not subject someone else to them.

"Well," Agnes said as she turned, "I hope they are made of as stern stuff as we. This looks to be a long road ahead."

With mutual agreement, Pearl and I fell into the silence of the Sentinels. If only the antis stuck to the same form of protest.

We both felt the need to do it, to pay this call, to check on the woman who had led us down this glorious, hazardous road, to check on her health. And if such were fine, to ask for her involvement once more.

Pearl had sent her card ahead, by the hand of Hazel, and though we had not heard from Alva, we made for Marble House just the same. Surely, Alva wouldn't turn us away.

The door was opened not by Alva's butler, but by a woman, one with a stern, serious bearing.

"May I help you?" she asked, not welcoming but not unfriendly.

"Why, um, yes." Pearl recovered faster than I. "I am Pearl Worthington Wright and this is Ginevra Costa Taylor. We are... friends of Alva's. I sent my card yesterday to let her know we would be calling on her today."

"I know nothing about that," the woman replied but opened the door to us. "She is having lemonade in the Teahouse. Perhaps she is awaiting your arrival."

The woman led us silently through the large foyer, up each small flight of stairs of the many levels of the opening vestibule, through the main floor hallway, and out to the terrace.

"I don't believe we are acquainted, Miss..?"

"Field," she said, her manner so removed she could have been speaking of someone else. "Miss Sara Bard Field."

"Oh!" I chirped like an adolescent schoolgirl; my feelings belonged to the sound. "We have not met, but I am an admirer of your work. I find your articles in the *Woman's Journal* to be among the best.

And your slogan, "No Vote, No Babies," well, that was…was simply genius."

"You're that Miss Field?" It was Pearl's turn to chirp. She held out her hand to the woman. Miss Field looked at it for a moment before accepting it. "It is indeed a pleasure to make your acquaintance. I take it you're a guest…"

The woman snorted and my unblinking eyes darted a sidelong glance at her.

She did not look like one of Alva's typical guests. Her plain dress of blouse buttoned high and long skirt matched her plain, almost hard face, a face exposed by the drawn-back curtain of dense, dark hair, parted in the middle and brought to the sides of her head with little fanfare. It was the style of the day, though she wore it as if it belonged to a previous decade.

"Are you here on suffrage business?" Pearl tried a different tack to engage the woman.

"I am assisting Mrs. B in the writing of her memoir," Miss Field stated.

We walked slowly across the long expanse of grass from terrace to teahouse, a meandering course that suited me. I would never take this view for granted, the one from the western cliffs of the small island and across the ocean. I would never take any of the magnificent views this small piece of land gave as a gift from Mother Earth.

"That must be an interesting undertaking," I suggested, hoping to draw something out of this subdued woman. From her many articles, no one could doubt Miss Fields's intellect or her dedication to the suffrage cause.

"Interesting… hmm… that is one word for it." Miss Field was as outspoken in person as she was on paper. She stopped suddenly; we almost tripped to stop with her. She looked at us for the first time.

"I haven't seen you among Mrs. B's typical set."

I couldn't tell if that was a statement or a question yet I felt as I had when the police questioned me in those long-ago days.

Pearl snickered. "I grew up in that set, it is true. But when I left, without my mother's support or permission, to attend college, I lost my membership."

Pearl surprised even me with her contracted confessional.

The inquisitive woman's head tilted to the side. Her gaze never left Pearl's face.

That targeted gaze fell on me.

"And you?"

"I-a—"

"Ginevra immigrated to this country as a child. She was once my lady's maid until she, too, walked away from that life and into college. She is one of the country's most up-and-coming fashion designers." Pearl took a step closer to the sternly posed women. "But, most of all, she is my dearest friend, my sister in all but blood."

It was almost a dare. To be Italian in those days was almost as bad as being a colored person; we were despised for nothing more than our darker coloring and our place of birth. We were looked down upon, thought to be dirty and diseased, prejudiced against in so many ways. Pearl made sure this woman did not even attempt to treat me in such a way. I dropped my chin so neither of them could see my grin, one of both pride and amusement.

"Well," Miss Field huffed, "I'll be damned. Call me Sara."

"Thank you, Sara," I finally found my tongue. I would eventually learn the rest of this woman's connection to Alva; her very demeanor made it clear it was not a simple thing. "Are you not inspired by your work with Alva?"

Sara's folded arms dropped to her side; she turned a face of impassive features to the sea.

"My real work has yet to begin. At this point, I am taking notes while Mrs. B talks. And talks."

"Yes, she is quite good at it, isn't she?" Pearl laughed.

"That she is." She had us walking again, but even slower than before; she would make the trek to the Teahouse last as long as could make it. "She is also hard, flinty, and brutal to her inferiors, which is how she sees me merely because she pays me."

"Do not take it personally," I tried to assure her. "There are very few people who Alva does not deem as inferior."

"Nor is it entirely her fault," Pearl came to Alva's defense. "It was how she was raised, what she was raised to be. Some people find it harder to shake off the shackles of their childhood than others."

"So I have learned. The woman is sharp and calculating despite her years. And she has done much good for the suffrage cause," Sara admitted.

"It must be especially difficult for you," Pearl seemed to be musing aloud, "with your socialist beliefs."

Sara looked for signs of insult on Pearl's face but found none.

"It is difficult to witness so few possessing so much," Sara admitted. "Mrs. B even seems to acquire people. If she deems one worthy, she takes possession of them. I came here with the expectation of being a co-author of work of literature and find myself on one hand being forced to act as her personal secretary while on the other being trotted out to social events as her most polished pet."

"Well," it was Pearl's turn to look pensively out to sea, "I will tell you that I know almost as much about Alva as Alva herself. Her daughter was one of my dearest childhood friends, a friend I still call my own." It was Pearl's turn to stop us. "I ask this of you, do not let your disapproval of the socialite overshadow your respect for the suffragette. In my eyes, in many, Alva has done her penance and resurrected herself. She has a right to glorification for that alone as well as her dedication to the cause."

Once more, the questioning look in Sara's eyes scurried over Pearl's face.

"You make a fine point. As a journalist, it is as I ought to approach it." Sara, having seen sense and logic in Pearl's words, started walking again. "Might I call upon you, Pearl, should I need to get another's thoughts on certain particulars of Mrs. B's life?"

"I am at your service," Pearl replied graciously. "And feel free to call upon us should you merely need to get away from the hoi-polloi. We shall take you to the White Horse Tavern where you can meet the real people of Newport."

At last, we learned that this serious woman could, in fact, smile. "I'd like that very much. Thank you."

"Pearl! Ginevra! My dahlings!" Alva called out to us from her chaise within the shade of her red-and-black-lacquer teahouse. "I completely forgot you were coming to call today."

We might have believed her did we not find her in her frothiest day gown, hair primped and pinned to perfection, and with the perfect number of cut crystal glasses that sat upon the table beside the pitcher of fruit-filled lemonade.

Pearl and I each kissed a cheek and took a seat, one on each side, as the chairs' arrangement demanded.

"I see you have met my Sara?"

From over the rim of my glass, I shot a sympathetic glance at the talented writer. She told us true, Alva had "collected" her.

"We have," I replied, "and we're honored to have made her acquaintance. Her work is to be greatly admired."

"Of course. I would have no one but the best to help me tell my story." Alva was an expert at making another's expertise somehow seem her own. "Do you think it too distasteful of me... writing a memoir?"

And suddenly the Alva she had become, the one who had seen real life amid the trauma of infidelity, divorce, and widowhood, returned, her wall of pretense crumbling in the company of those she could trust.

Pearl reached out and patted her hand. "If yours was a life far less ordinary than it has been, perhaps. But you have earned the right to it. In my eyes, at least."

Alva gave Pearl her gratitude in a quivering smile. As sweet as it was, it caused me concern; such an overt sign of emotion was further proof of time marching faster for our Alva.

"What you have done, the work and devotion to the cause, is worthy of note," I added. "And it is the reason for our visit."

"It is." Pearl suddenly seemed to remember the why of it as well. "We have been sentinels at the State House for a few months now, Alva. I fear our message is not being taken seriously… without you by our side."

"Stuff and nonsense." Alva wiggled her round buttocks higher upon her chaise. "I have seen the pictures, read the accounts. You are all doing quite well without me."

"But I'm sure we—"

"My health won't allow it, I'm afraid." Alva did not even give Pearl even the chance to plead our case. She stopped it with a truth little others knew. "It started, oh, last year or so, I believe. My breath thins with the least little exertion. Some doctors say it is my heart, others my lungs. The one thing they can all agree on is I must slow down."

We did not question it as truth; we did not have to. The slump of her shoulders, the smile that had become a frown, all spoke to her disappointment the years brought upon her. Alva Erskine Smith Vanderbilt Belmont had never lived "slowly". Now she was forced to learn how and how to accept it. An acceptance we all must make at some point if we are blessed enough to live long enough.

Pearl and I shared a glance; we would let the subject drop. We respected this woman – though our younger selves never would have believed it – far too much to make her speak of her failing health more.

"How are Consuelo and her boys?" Pearl asked wisely, for there is little else that could happily distract a woman's mind than to speak of grandchildren.

We talked then, not as suffragettes or socialites or servants, we spoke as mothers. Even Sara could join that conversation. We talked until we saw Alva begin to tire.

"I fear we must get back to our children." I rose, with Pearl quick to follow. "Thank you, dear Alva, for everything," I told her but it was not the conversation or the lemonade I spoke of and she knew it.

"We will always be grateful to you," Pearl said, once more kissing a wrinkled cheek.

"I did it for you," Alva shocked us. "Not you, in particular, but for all the women who would come after me. So many women who had started this fight, who have fought this fight, have passed on. But when we do, we can but hope that our actions will make the lives of the women to come next a bit better. It is the best purpose my life has known."

I leaned down to kiss her goodbye. "Put that in your book, Alva. It deserves to be said."

She thanked me with a nod and turned to Sara with another, a motion for the woman to walk us to the door. We were but a few steps away when she called our names, turned us back to her.

"And while I might never have imagined it, I could not have chosen two better women than you to carry on for me. There are none better." And with that, she waved goodbye.

The three of us walked back across the lawn, silence came with us for a bit, till Sara broke it.

"She is a different woman when she is with you. I had not seen this woman yet. You have allowed me to see her differently," she confessed.

"People are like that. If you think the worst of them, the worst you will get," Pearl said, as she could have said of so many women of her childhood.

"And if you think the best of them, they will give it to you," I assured her.

"Then I will say good day to you, ladies, but not goodbye." Sara brought us to the door. "And the next time we meet, you will see the best of me."

We did not doubt it.

Pearl

April 1917

Warmer air started to find us at last. The days of standing silently before the State House became slightly more bearable, though it took all the resolve I had to suffer the antis' verbal slings without vocal retaliation. Ginevra brought me through each day that was our turn to stand in the line. She could silence me with a look, keep me from stomping across the street with a single hand upon my arm.

I fell on to my favorite settee the moment I returned home. It took me a few minutes to realize my home – though I knew both Peter and Mary were here – was as silent as our protest.

"I'm home," I called out, hoping to bring them out, hoping to hear them. I heard not a sound.

I stood again, though my swollen feet hated me for it, and looked up from the bottom of the stairs.

"Peter? Mary? Are you here?" I knew they were and yet I asked.

Sounds did come then, murmurs, a closing door, and soft footfalls till I glimpsed my husband at the top of the stairs.

"Tere you are. I thought perhaps—"

Something on his dashing face, ever more dashing as the years passed, silenced me.

"Peter? What is it? Is Mary all right?" I started to rush up the stairs but a hand gesture and his descent kept me at the bottom.

"Mary is just fine, my Pearl." He gathered me in his arms as he reached the floor I stood shakily upon. He bent his knees slightly, straightening as he held me still; my feet came off the floor and I released myself into his keeping. It was a distinct embrace of my tall husband that both soothed and aroused. Marriage did many things to people, good and bad. A long and good marriage allowed us to hear our spouses without them saying a word. I did not want to hear this silence of my husband's.

"Tell me, Peter," I demanded even as he still cradled me. "Tell me now."

He said not a word but lowered my feet back to earth and led me back into the sitting room, back on to the settee. He poured us both a glass of amber liquid from the cut crystal decanters on the sideboard table. I put the glass he handed me down without taking a sip.

Peter threw the entire contents of his glass down his throat before sitting beside me.

"I'm quite surprised you did not hear of it on the train or even on the ferry."

"Because I slept through most of the journey!" I snapped at him. He delayed and I would have none of it and he knew it.

I could not tell what was to come as he turned to me, as he, at last, looked me in the eye.

"President Wilson has signed a declaration of war." He said the words simply as if they were simple.

"The President…" I couldn't hear my own words over the painful hum that suddenly screeched in my ears.

Peter took my hand. "America has joined the war."

We sat there for a time, how long I hadn't a clue. I digested his words and all their implications; he gave me the time and silence to do so.

I picked up the forgotten glass and threw the contents down my throat as he had done.

"What does it mean?" I croaked through the sting of the whiskey on my throat.

"It means the United States—"

I almost threw the glass still in my hand at his head.

"What does it mean... *for us?*"

He needed time now. It was almost as if I could see the lawyer wheels in his head turning – the one who would choose his words carefully. I would see through them.

"It could mean conscription will begin again."

"Hah!" It was nasty of me, but I laughed. "You are too old and are married with a child. They will not conscript you."

"They won't have to, my Pearl."

Realization struck as did lightning scorch the earth.

"Don't call me that!" I did throw the glass then. I stood up and threw it against the stone of the fireplace. The shattering echoed through our very lives. "Do not call me that while you try to tell me you are going off to war. Don't you dare!"

I fell into the arms that were somehow already there to catch me.

For the sake of Mary, we both acted at dinner that night, behaving as if nothing were changing, pretending as if her father weren't knowingly intending to put his life in mortal danger. She knew, of course, that he was going. He had been telling her when I arrived home. But at twelve years old, and so very much my daughter, she didn't accept or enjoy our performance. She left the table without having barely eaten a bite, went to her room, and closed the door.

We followed shortly after. It was as if we all suffered the exhaustion the coming days would force upon us. Though my body begged me to, I could not sleep. I lay wide awake in the crook of my husband's arm.

"How long do we have?" I asked without the need for further explanation.

"We have the rest of our lives, my Pearl, the rest of our very long lives."

"How... long... Peter?" I demanded.

He gave up his claptrap, though I knew he meant well by it.

"Two months." I heard him say over the thumping of my heart in my ears.

Two months. In the fourteen years of our marriage, we hadn't been apart for more than two days. In two months, he would be on the other side of the world.

Anger had kept them at bay, now it failed me and the tears fell freely down my face, dripping off my chin, and on to his chest.

Somehow the words in my mind were able to slip through my tight throat.

"You are all I have, Peter. You are all I have left."

My husband dared to smile in the face of my torment, smile and shake his head back and forth upon the pillow.

"You have Mary. And you have Ginevra."

I sat up sharply, pushing against him. My arms flew up in the air. I didn't bother or care to dry my face. "One is a child and the other a friend."

Peter sat up beside me; for the first time that day I saw splinters in his composure, but they were made of anger, and at me.

"First..." he pointed a finger at me, "Mary is *your* child, your flesh and blood, our flesh and blood. And secondly, friends do not do what Ginevra did for you. They do not sit in jail for months for a crime their 'friend' committed."

My rage evaporated into a sweat that drenched me. I jumped up from the bed.

"She would do the same for me, as I would have done for you, both you and Osborn too."

He blathered but I could not hear his words over those screaming in my head.

He knows. He knows the truth.

I paced the circle of the rug in jerks and fits, stops and starts. My tongue became a dry sponge crammed down my throat.

Peter came to me, cupping my face in the warm basket of his hands.

"And I would have taken that shot as well. What you did was right and just, my Pearl."

Before I could fall, I caught myself on him.

"If that is not family," his gently moving lips feathered against my ear, "I do not know what is."

I hated how much I loved him in his uniform. Damn such men that wore their death shroud so well.

The awful greenish-brown of it seared my eyes in the bright June sun. He would not tell me what type of uniform it was; though similar to those worn by the hundreds of other men milling about the water's edge of the base saying goodbye to their families as Peter did, there were enough small differences that told me what he could not say.

His hat was not entirely cloth and brimless like that most of the men wore. His was a proper cap with a visor that hung rakishly over his eyes. His jacket was tailored and belted and his pants were wider at the top than the others, though they all wore boots up to their knees.

"You must be sweltering in that clothing in this heat what I am going to do without you?"

He laughed as he took off his hat and captured it between arm and body, his hazel eyes appeared as containers for every color from blue to grey to amber. My oval face felt like a child's as he cupped it in the hands of a man, a chalice of warmth and love.

"You can do this, my Pearl." His gaze bore through me,

demanding my soul to listen.

My gaze held nothing but confusion and fear. My darling – the only man I ever completely loved – was leaving for war, most certainly to kill, quite possibly to be killed. What was I to do that could compare to that? That which I must endure shrank beside it.

"I have never known anyone – not man nor woman – as strong as you."

His beauty swam before me, a Seurat painting in motion.

"You will care for our Mary and our gallery. You will paint the greatest of masterpieces. And you will fight on." Strong hands moved to my shoulders, fingers dug into my arms, he almost shook me. "Fight on for your rights, my Pearl, promise me."

I fell against his chest.

"I will."

And then he was gone.

Ginevra

June 1917

The sameness of the days dragged us all into a wakeful sleeping walking, a stroll to a destination unknown as we held our breaths.

Pearl and I and the other PEA women continued to take our turns as Silent Sentinels at the State House, continued to suffer the insults of the women on the other side of the lane. In contrast to what our men overseas suffered, it was less than the sting of a bee.

On days when we weren't at our posts, I sat in my fashion house, my empty fashion house, and sketched designs I might well never make, for I had no customers to make them for, save for a handful of the socialites who continued to come to me through the summer. Now they too had gone. If not for my husband's help and that of my father, and my dwindling savings from earnings while at Tirocchi's, I might have questioned if I could last through the war. All would depend on how long it lasted, but war can never be calculated in days.

Life itself changed little, save for all the men who came through Newport, through the training school and the base. Thousands and thousands of them. The single women of Newport must have thought Christmas had come to stay.

We were encouraged to cut back on certain foods so that the rations could go to feed our soldiers.

Food Will Win the War!

A man called Herbert Hoover, put in charge of the country's food administration by President Wilson, had the posters plastered everywhere. They encouraged us to cut back on meat, wheat, and sugar.

"What else is there?" Hazel lamented whenever we shopped together.

Living in a state with so many farms, we had vegetables aplenty and we both learned to make filling stews from them. Knowing Pearl's husband might not get a good meal made it easy to give up one for myself.

So I sat and I sketched. I took the changes in fashion – the higher hemlines, the disappearance of the high-button boot, the new type of coat some were calling a trench – and I took them further... three hems, each one higher than the one beneath it. To the pump, as the new shoe was being called, I gave a curved heel or a perfectly placed bow. And that coat. I adored it. But not as a coat. I used the almost military form of styling... the buttons and the belt and the epaulets on the shoulders and turned them into dresses and suits.

I made one for Pearl and one for myself as well. We loved them so much we had to make sure we didn't wear them at the same time. We were bored but we were bored and fashionable.

And I read. I read and read everything I could get my hands on... newspapers for the latest on the war, and every suffrage publication available, however many they were. We could not let the war overshadow or stall our battle.

The *Women's Column* was a weekly journal that came out of Boston and published by Alice Stone Blackwell – one of the formidable and fiery suffragette leaders. I found the articles included in it not only informative but entertaining. The front page of this week's edition had its smattering of typical headlines... *A Victory for Women*, about a fundraising event to give women money to attend medical school at Johns Hopkins University, *Lessons from New York*, describing the latest strategies being used by the headquarters of the national organization.

I set aside my sketching, made myself some coffee, which I now drank with no sugar, and picked up the *Women's Column*, intrigued by a different sort of headline… *A Wise Girl*. I sat down to read.

"You see how it is, my dear," he said, taking her soft hand, which had never done very hard work, and patting it reassuringly: "I'm poor – only a thousand a year, dear – and we shall have a struggle to get along at first—"

"I don't mind that in the least," she interrupted, stoutly, rubbing her cheek softly against his hand.

What *is* this? Its tone seemed very odd in this publication. But I read on.

"And," he pursued, having graciously allowed her interruption, "we shall have to come down to strict economy. But if you can only manage as my mother does, we shall put through nicely."

"And how does your mother manage, dear?" she asked, smiling – but very happily – at the notion of the mother-in-law cropping out already.

"I don't know," replied the lover, radiantly; "but she always manages to have everything neat and cheerful, and something delicious to eat; and she does it all herself, you know! So that we always get along beautifully, and make both ends meet, and father and I still have plenty of spending money. You see, when a woman is always hiring her laundry work done, and her gowns and bonnets made, and her scrubbing and stove-blacking done, and all that sort of thing – why, it just walks into a man's income, and takes his breath away."

I was starting to get an inkling of where this was going and admired the way the author was getting there.

The young woman looked for a moment as if her breath was also inclined for a vacation; but she wisely concealed her dismay, and, being one of the stout-hearted of the earth, she determined to learn a few things of John's mother, and so went to her for a long visit the next day. Upon the termination of this visit, one fine morning John received, to his blank amazement, a little package containing his engagement ring, accompanied by the following letter:

"I have learned how your mother 'manages,' and I am going to explain it to

you, since you have confessed you didn't know. I find that she is a wife, a mother, a housekeeper, a business manager, a hired girl, a laundress, a seamstress, a mender and patcher, a dairy maid, a cook, a nurse, a kitchen gardener, and a general slave for a family of five. She works from five in the morning until ten at night; and I almost wept when I kissed her hand, it was so hard and wrinkled, and corded, and unkissed. When I saw her polishing the stoves, carrying big buckets of water and great armfuls of wood, often splitting the latter, I asked her why John didn't do such things for her. "John!" she repeated, "John!"—and she sat down with a perfectly dazed look, as if I had asked why the angels didn't come down and scrub for her. "Why—John"—she said, in a trembling, bewildered way—"he works in the office from nine until four o'clock, you know, and when he comes home he is very tired, or else—or else—he goes downtown."

Now, I have become strongly imbued with the conviction that I do not care to be so good a 'manager' as your mother. If the wife must do all sorts of drudgery, so must the husband; if she must cook, he must carry the wood; if she must scrub, he must carry the water; if she must make butter, he must also milk the cows. You have allowed your mother to do everything, and all that you have to say of her is that she is an 'excellent manager.' I do not care for such a reputation, unless my husband earned the name also; and judging from your lack of consideration for your mother, I am quite sure that you are not the man I thought you were, or one whom I should care to marry. 'As the son is, the husband is,' is a safe and happy rule to follow."

So the letter closed, and John pondered…and he is pondering yet.

"Marvelous," I laughed out loud as the witty parable ended. I laughed so hard I nearly spilled my coffee. "What in—"

I jumped to my feet. I did spill my coffee then, all over the floor, my skirt. I rushed out the door of my shop without a jacket, without a thought, and stomped to the Brick Market as if I were a soldier in the war, the news journal still in my hand, bunched tight and crinkled.

It was well there were no customers inside, for when I threw the door open so hard, the knob of it hit the wall of the corridor. She was there, just her, in the main room, hanging a painting.

"Are you out of your God-a damn mind-a?" I screeched, yes, screeched at her.

"And a good day to you, Ginny," Pearl said with a smile.

I gnashed my teeth. I thrust the crumpled paper out as I took stomp after stomp closer to her. "Explain this," I demanded, oh yes I did. The name at the end of the article that had amused me so – the author of it – was one Pearl Worthington Wright.

With the raised brows of one vaguely interested, Pearl glanced at the journal in my hand, then just as casually at me.

"Well you see, Ginny, I thought approaching the topic from the backward perspective would be a more powerful—"

The paper crackled, as did my anger—that which she poked with her sarcasm – as I shook it before her face. "Stop your nonsense. You know right-a well what I mean. What are you doing publishing under your real name?"

"Why should I not?" Pearl's fists, balls of bone and flesh, found her hips.

"Why... why..?" Why did she goad me? "Hmm, let me think. Because our activities have already changed our lives in damaging ways, let me count them... I lost my job because of our march and you customers." I swept the empty gallery with my hand. "Our houses were vandalized. You were put in prison because you got into fisticuffs – fisticuffs! – at the play. We are insulted every day we stand silently in that protest line. Do you want more such challenges? Is that why you wrote this? Is that why you used-a you own—"

Bending at the waist, Pearl thrust her chin at me. "I *want* the amendment passed so that we might get the justice we deserve, so that all of this..." She flicked the paper still in my hand with one of hers, "...is no longer necessary. I want to find something in this world beautiful enough for my brush. And I *want* – I need – my husband to come home!"

We stood, toe to toe, snarl to snarl, just as two quarreling sisters would.

Pearl and I rarely argued. When we did, we rarely argued for long.

The need she spoke of, kicked against, the desperation I saw in her moist eyes, in the grey strands that threaded her hair that had not been there just months before, in the trembling of her bottom lip, slain me, almost unfairly.

I dropped the paper and gathered her quick and hard in my arms. I let her have the cry she so obviously needed.

"I'm sorry, Pearly," I sighed in her ear. "I mean only to think of your protection, to keep you safe."

I felt her head nod against mine, heard her sobs fade to sniffles and hiccups.

She pulled a few inches away, yet stayed within the circle of our embrace.

"Did you like it?"

I laughed through her tears.

"I loved it!"

Pearl

I painted him. Over and over again I would set myself before canvas and easel, a solitary sailboat floating on the sparkling ocean off in the distance in my mind, or the two lines of women in protest, those of us for, those of them against. And yet when I did dip the brush in paint, when the brush found the canvas, it was always him that emerged. I painted Peter not as I had last seen him, in that wretched uniform, but in all the other and magical ways I had looked upon him, as a groom waiting for me at the end of the long aisle, as a lover hovering just above me, and as a joyful boy when he beheld our daughter for the first time.

Painting him became an obsession, one of sweet pain – and unprofitability, as I could not put a single one up for sale. I knew I had to do something else, set my whirling thoughts upon something different.

That's when I began to write. I was no Alva Vanderbilt Belmont, but I thought I could craft words well enough to overcome my lower status, my lack of influence when looked at in contrast.

When my first little "story" had been published in the Last Laughs portion of the *Women's Journal*, I found an acerbic outlet for my dedication to the cause and frustration at the slow progress we made.

I knew Ginevra read the journal cover to cover; it surprised me it had taken her so long to discover what I was up to. As she lashed me with her fear, my lash was of frustrated fear. Once plied, both were dropped. She would continue to fear for me and I would continue to write… and to paint him.

"He looks very young, Mother," my darling Mary's voice skidded my brush upon the canvas. She had entered the gallery, made her way to my studio, while I painted on obliviously in the nowhere in which I seemed to exist.

With a smile, I beckoned her to me. Now almost thirteen years old and I could see the beautiful woman in the adorable girl who stood beside me. "He was young, then. We were at a dance held at Brown University while we were both still in school." I did not bother to tell her it was the moment I fell in love with him. I did not need to; she had eyes and my brush was nothing if not a confessional.

With the same sort of sigh, we stared at the most important man in our lives.

"What brings you here, merry Mary?" I asked her, pulling us both back to the present as much as we would try to avoid it. "Should you not be at home studying?"

Sarah was still with us, though Mary was of such an age that she did not require constant looking after. Sarah came to us every day though I could rarely afford to pay her. I had access to "Peter's" funds – those he had inherited upon my family's passing – but I was stingy with them as were so many in times of war. Who knew how long this conflict would last? I kept us fed and clothed, I kept the gallery from closing, and I still clung to ownership of The Beeches, the last the largest drain, but I still could not let it go. I couldn't have sold it then even if I wanted to; it "belonged" to Peter, and only Peter could sell it.

The smile Mary had greeted me and the image of her father with, trickled down to a grimace. She held a rolled newspaper out to me. "I thought you should… I knew you'd want to see this."

SUFFRAGE PICKETS ARRESTED AT THE WHITE HOUSE

The headline burnt itself across the front page of *The New York*

Times. With Mary still by my side, if forgotten, I read as fast as I could.

"Obstructing sidewalk traffic?" I yelled as if the author of the article could hear me, as if the police who had made the arrest could. "This is not to be borne!"

"It is just an excuse, isn't it, Mother?"

I looked at the daughter I suddenly remembered.

"They just wanted to get them off the street and didn't have any other good reason to do it." My daughter stared at me. "Is that right?"

I stared back at her, my merry Mary, my daughter who strode ever faster toward womanhood, my daughter the suffragette.

"That is right, Mary, and it is very wrong."

Pearl

November 1917

Every day from that one onward, we would dine with Ginevra and her family, at their house or ours. Every day we read of the terrifying journey these women endured.

"They try to justify their actions by denouncing those of the women as inappropriate in a time of war." Osborn, ever on our side, found much to fuel his anger with the obvious obfuscation coming from the President and the police in the country's capital city. Osborn feared the loss of his best friend almost as keenly as I feared the loss of my husband. To use our soldiers – our soldier – as a legitimization stung like a hangnail, an ever-constant annoyance.

"I don't understand why they are keeping these women so long, Father." Felix, at fourteen, had inherited his parents' leanings towards equitable justice. "They had made arrests before but let them go the next day. Why hold these women so long?"

"The Kaiser sign," Ginevra answered her son. The rest of us agreed.

It was an erudite comparison made on a protestor's sign, one too apt, too true. The sign that broke the President's patience compared the president to the German emperor, intending to point out Wilson's hypocrisy – he supported the cause of freedom for the German people but not for the freedom of the women of his own country.

Though artfully clever, it pushed passersby to their edge of patience.

"But it was the women who were attacked." At eleven, even Angelina understood unethical treatment.

For three days the women had been attacked by a mob grown angry, but only suffragettes felt the cold steel of policemen's handcuffs, only they had been sentenced to sixty days in the Occoquan Workhouse. Alice Paul had not been on the line at the time. As soon as she stepped upon it in October, they arrested her as well. Now, in all, thirty-three women were still imprisoned in one of the country's most barbaric prisons, sharing cells with those infected with syphilis and fed food spiced with worms.

"Workhouse, my a—"

"Osborn!"

"Sorry, my dear."

And so it went night after night, as more and more information came out of that prison disguised as a workhouse, as the women within went on a hunger strike, until that night.

Ginevra's family had come to our home armed with enough copies of the newspaper for all – the children, Sarah and Hazel as well. No one cooked food that would go uneaten.

Together we read of the night, a night some were calling the Night of Terror.

There was no logic to what we read, the words forming incomprehensible images. There was no order in which we read aloud, only that which our outrage demanded.

Alice Paul was taken from her bed, carried to another room, and forced into a chair, bound with sheets and sat upon bodily by a fat murderess, whose duty it was to keep her still. The prison doctor, assisted by two women attendants, placed a rubber tube up her nostrils and pumped liquid food through it in the stomach.

Angelina gasped like a baby bird fallen from the nest too soon.

"Should we stop?" I softly asked Ginevra; she just shook her head, read another passage.

Guards burst into a holding area and drag, carry, push, and beat women back into their cells. Lucy Burns was handcuffed to the cell bars all night with arms far above her head.

Dorothy Day was slammed down on the arm of an iron bench, twice.

Dora Lewis lost consciousness after her head was smashed into an iron bed.

Of a sudden Felix stood so fast, his chair flew out from under him as words hurtled from him.

"This is… this is inhumane, cruel. These men are…" I thought he would curse; he would be right if he did, "…dirty, bloody animals." He did curse, an English word he had learned from Peter.

He gave it to us then, every girl and woman in the world; he gave us a gift of a lifetime.

"Mama, Aunt Pearl…" his mother's big eyes in his stricken face took in the others, gliding slowly over Mary, staying on me and his mother.

"You have shown me all a person, any person, can do, is able to do." He stood tall over his mother where she sat in the conflict of raising a good man, of him being one with strong legs that could take him far from her. "The women in my life have, always will have, my deepest respect."

She said nothing, couldn't I'm sure. Lifting a hand now larger than her own, Ginevra kissed the back of it, held it to her cheek.

As I watched, I thought I saw Ginevra's mother, her grandmother, doing the same, in the watery gaze in which I looked upon them.

Osborn freed himself from the immobility his son's outburst had lain upon him, walked to him; he, at least, stood taller than his son. He did not throw the boy in shadow but in a silhouette that almost fit.

Without needless words, the father shook the son's hand.

I leaned closer to Ginevra beside me on the settee. I wiped a tear that sparkled upon her cheek.

"What we do, we do for them all."

She gave me her half-smile… and her hand.

Hazel, a newspaper close to her nose, read more, *Alice Cosu suffered a heart attack; received no medical attention.*

"Enough!" Osborn shouted. I had never heard him shout before. Our emotions rode a merry-go-round in those days. "Enough," he cried again, as he stomped about the room, snatching the paper from each of our hands.

"But—" Ginevra tried.

"No, dearest. It is enough," Osborn said a tad more calmly, though we could all see his chest rising and falling rapidly. "We have read enough. These women… these poor women…" his gaze fluttered over all the women in the room, especially his wife and daughter.

Did he picture us undergoing such violent, vicious treatment? Did he picture the women he loved most being tortured? Would not any decent man who read of these atrocities?

"They have endured enough." With that he stomped out of the room, leaving the rest of us silent in wonder. In seconds, he returned, thrusting blank writing paper and ink powder-filled fountain pens into hands from which he had pulled the newspapers.

"Write." It was an order and nothing less. "Write to Senator Lippit and Senator Gerry. Write to Congressman Colt. Write to the damned President."

Ginevra did not even part her lips to protest his language.

"But what should we write, Father?" Angelina asked, looking at her father for the first time with fear.

He saw it too, he must have. Osborn knelt by his daughter, the youngest of us, and took her into a gentle hug, whispering to her softly, "Tell them what upsets you most, sweet pea. Tell them why you think what they are doing is wrong."

Angelina smiled, that smile like the grandmother she had never met whose name she bore, the smile that suited her name. Osborn let her go with a tweak of her nose and the young girl set immediately to the task, as did we all.

Ours were not the only voices raised in furious protest. Voices that grew louder and louder as more atrocities were perpetrated on these women, as the papers reported it all. In less than two weeks from that night of terror, all the women had been pardoned and released. But the damage had been done.

Some of the women never recovered good health after what they had endured. Some never returned to the suffrage cause.

President Wilson and those who ran the federal government suffered great harm to their reputations.

On the day we read of the women's pending release, Mary and I walked to the beach. It was one of those golden fall days where a heavy coat kept the wind, turning ever colder with each passing day, from our bodies but not the warmth still in the sun from our faces.

We stood at the water's edge, as we often did, staring out to sea as if we could see Peter on the other side. But that day we looked at something different.

We watched as the tide began to turn.

Ginevra

January 1918

We lived on the headlines those days, those on our war, those on the war.

SUFFRAGE VICTORY IN THE HOUSE
PLEASES ALL BUT ANTIS

"They only want re-election," Pearl mumbled as we rumbled upon the train taking us to the State House and the silent picket line. Despite the brutality that had happened, we still stood, all in a row, silent as pickets in a fence, just as they still did in Washington. It became more challenging and the temperatures became more brutally cold. We tried to get others who would stand so we should all stand less often, expose ourselves to the climate fewer times. There were times – such as days like these – when my thoughts were very uncharitable to those who refused to stand on the line, women like Mabel and Minnie.

I could not argue with Pearl's accusation, both because I agreed and because she had taught me the inner workings of the American government system... what should *be* the workings and what *were* the workings.

The year 1918 was an election year, a "mid-term" election year; a concept I still struggled with. But I understood what needed to be most understood... our government officials cared as much for their re-election as for making and enforcing laws that would improve the lives

211

of those they represented. After the horror of the Night of Terror, after the criticism brought upon those in office for it, many people who had straddled the for-or-against-suffrage fence had fallen on the side of for.

"Does the why of it matter?" I asked though I think Pearl had spoken to herself. "Does it matter as long as the law is passed?"

Pearl looked out the window of the train, where the snow-covered landscape was a blur of white. The dingy gray sky did little to make it as bright as it could be.

"No. No, it doesn't matter." Her cloak of hopelessness muffled her voice. "It would simply have been wonderful did they do it for honorable reasons, because it is the right and ethical thing to do."

I nodded with a tinge of self-pride even though my religion considered it a sin. I was pleased my thoughts on the issue were correct.

"This time, Pearl, this time it will pass the... the..."

"Senate."

"*Sì*, the Senate."

I had hoped our conversation, this news, would relieve Pearl of her wearying worry. She stared out the window as the world hurried by, but she looked farther, looked to wherever Peter might be. She had not had a letter in too many months

HUNS STARVE AND RIDICULE U.S. CAPTIVES

That headline was the only one she truly cared about and she didn't need to tell me so. We all felt it, we all wondered... had Peter been captured? Was that the reason for his lack of letters home?

Like a child, I turned my mind's eye from the thought as if not seeing it made it invisible. I turned all my focus to suffrage's long battle. Pearl could not.

While it was written that President Wilson had urged members of the House to pass the amendment, he had also produced an elaborate plan for peace. Whether either would be adopted or not we would have to wait and see.

Such was our life in those days; we existed in the purgatory of waiting.

Pearl

I couldn't seem to get warm. I sat on the floor in front of the fire in my too-empty bedroom. It had been such a cold day on the line. It felt as if the bitter temperature had wormed its way into my bones. As kindling fed a fire, his silence fed the cold within me.

Mary slept peacefully in her room. Perhaps I could make money as an actress for she seemed to believe the hopeful persona I played whenever we were together. Or perhaps she was the consummate actress.

Only when she was asleep did I indulge. I did not want her to see me doing so.

From the pocket of the thick dressing gown I wore over my flannel nightgown, I pulled the letter, the last letter I had received from him four months ago. His letters had never arrived more than a month apart. But that was before. The lack of more made this one more dear. I kept it on me no matter what I wore, no matter where I went. The creases were getting thinner with so many folds and unfolds.

Shall I spare you, my Pearl, or will your eye, the one that looks within, see the truth of my words, no matter which I use?

I tell you the worst my body has suffered resides in my feet and my gut. I can never seem to keep my feet dry, none of us can. I consider myself lucky that my feet have turned red while the feet of some of my comrades have turned blue. Besides your love, please send me more socks.

They tell me I do not have influenza or malaria, but I cannot seem to keep food in my belly. It often finds its way out of me through two methods. You will find me but a rail upon my return, which I pray is soon.

My mind suffers with yours and our Mary's. I know I need not describe, I know you suffer as I do, the pain of longing. But, as your letters tell me, we battle on.

We are not meant to leave this world worse than we came to it, my Pearl. No, we are blessed and cursed with a compulsion to leave it far better. To use the power of our times as the tools of change. I saw it in you the first time my eyes laid on you... a fire that could warm or blaze. It drew me to you. Well, that and your bountiful br—

A knock that did not wait for my answer opened the door. Hazel's head popped around it.

"I'm for my bed, missus." She had started to sleep in our home now and again, not long after Peter left, insisting Mary and I should not be alone. I think her aloneness in a time of war brought her here. Whatever the reason, I was glad for her company. "Is there anything I can do for you before I turn in?"

"No, thank you. You get to bed."

I had tucked the letter under me as fast as possible at her interruption. But not fast enough. She eyed me with pity tinted rebuke.

"Get some sleep, missus. You don't want dark circles around your eyes when your man comes home."

I gave her what little of a smile I could muster.

Hazel clucked her tongue and left me to my letter.

Your determination in the face of so much acrimony has only made me stronger, braver. I am the luckiest man on Earth to have found a woman such as you. A fighter like you. Yes, we must fight on. If not we two, then who? For our Mary and those who come after, we must fight on.

I soldier on, my Pearl, with you ever in my heart and mind.

I rubbed a finger over the letters his hand had formed. Once more, I folded it up. Cradling it against my chest, I lay down on the floor where I sat and hoped for a dreamless sleep.

Ginevra

July 1918

"Ginevra!"

Osborn's voice crashed against the brick walls as loudly as the door slammed shut behind him. It was the middle of the day, yet he came to my place of work when he should have been at his. He screamed my name in a voice I had never heard, a voice that belonged to a man chased by some horrid monster.

"Here, Osborn. I'm here." I ran out of the back room where I sketched to find him standing in the door, sweat dripping down his forehead into his eyes. "What is wrong? Are you all right? What has happened?" My voice became a screech; what I saw on his face scared me all the more. Tears. In eyes blazing with pain, on a face twisted and gruesome, glistened tears. He told me all with one word.

"Peter."

Someone kicked me, kicked hard and fast, right in my stomach. My stomach tried to hurl my small lunch back up. I suddenly wore a drenching coat of sweat.

"No, no." I shook my head again and again. I stepped backward as if I could step back in time. "No, do not say it. Please, *Dio mio*, it cannot be true."

Osborn reached me in a few steps, grabbed me, and pulled me against him. He sobbed upon my shoulder.

Still, I shook my head. My mind shut like the windows in winter, shut, shuttered, and nailed tight. Osborn opened them with one other word.

Pulling back, his pained face now so close to mine.

"Pearl."

Did he slap me? It felt so. It was meant to.

I ran.

I ran and ran. I fell. The cobbles ripped the skin from my palms. Still, I ran.

I ran through the fence gate. I heard the sobbing through the open windows. Mary's sobbing. Hazel's sobbing.

I ran into the house.

They were there together. Hazel holding Mary. Mary holding Hazel.

My head twisted in more ways than it was meant to.

Hazel pointed a single finger upward.

I ran up the stairs.

I rushed through the closed door.

She lay on the floor. She lay so still, a fist the size of a boulder latched on to my heart, squeezed. It felt about to burst.

I ran to her. I rolled her over. Eyes so swollen, they were lumps upon the beauty of her face, opened to me.

"Thank you, dear God. Thank you." I gathered Pearl into my arms. Held her against my chest though her limp form fought me. I rocked her. "I thought you were dead, too."

Pearl moved. She moved her head, turned her ravaged face up to me.

"I am."

Pearl

Red. Red and wet. Red liquid covered everything.

Hats, like camping dishes upside down, flew here and there, everywhere.

Smoke breathed fire. The sky above a swirling vortex of hell.

Spiked and barbed trees with no leaves stabbed the sky.

The screams. Dear God, the screams, a torrent of torturous pain.

Running and running. Can't breathe. Can't find any air.

Fear craved vomiting.

Shooting and shooting. Shooting anything, anyone.

Silence. Explosion deafened.

Sloness.

Buckling. Knees buckling. Falling. Reaching. Evaporating.

Gone.

"Peter!" I screamed and screamed. "Peter! Peter!"

My scream became the portal from the dreaming world to wakefulness. Still, I screamed.

She bolted up from where she slept in a chair by my bed, where she had been for over a month.

Ginevra wiped the sweat from me, cooed at me. Pulling back the thin linen, she climbed into bed with me, propping my quivering body in the crook of her arm and shoulder.

I leaned into it, sank into it. Still, she cooed.

Her cooing grew softer. Sleep flirted with us both.

"Go back home to your family, Ginny," I mumbled but did not lift myself from her. "Go home."

Ginevra didn't open her eyes.

"I am home."

I woke to find her no longer in my bed. I woke to the rumble of voices in the room below me. I found some strength, barely enough to throw the twisted linens off me, to tiptoe to the door and crack it open. I listened. Some words climbed the stairs better than others.

Marne. Ludendorff. Second offensive. Lasted three days. One more day, that's all he needed.

I denied those words. Threw them back down the stairs.

More than 12,000.

Just Americans.

Over 100,000 allies in all.

I staggered back to bed. My husband had not died alone. He had died with so many others. Did that help? I couldn't decide. I crawled back under the linens.

It took longer for the armed services to return my husband's body to me than it had to scrape my family off the ocean's floor. At least they returned him to me already in a coffin. I was thankful Osborn had stopped me when I tried to prop it open, to see Peter, to hold him once more.

"It is not the man you married," he had whispered to me. "It is only the vessel that held him. He is still here." He'd placed a hand upon my heaving chest and led me away. It was only much later that I learned the Peter they returned to me was a Peter in pieces, shattered by tank fire, by an explosion.

"I am so sorry for your loss, my darling," a woman that looked so familiar to me said, leaning down to where I sat to kiss my cheek.

"Thank you," I mumbled. "They were... I mean..."

Who was I burying? It had been more than six years, yet I was confusing my husband's funeral with that of my family. I heard the cry of a seagull out the window. I was in Newport. I buried my husband.

"She will know you were here, Consuelo," Ginevra stepped out from behind me, consoling the crying woman.

It was Consuelo, I hadn't known her.

"Dearest Pearl, I am so sorry." This woman I knew, her straw-like reddish-blonde hair gave her away. I thought she looked like a mop. My thoughts wandered strangely. Mabel sobbed, almost as deeply as I had and did again and again. "No matter... I mean... it doesn't matter what—"

"Come, Mabel." Ginevra took the woman's arm. "Let me get you something to drink. Is your husband with you?"

"N-no. He... um…. he had…"

Mabel's words trailed away as I lost interest, as Ginevra led her away. I seemed to have lost the ability to focus on any one thing for long.

Long. The line of them was so long.

Did the line of sympathizers end? That didn't seem right. I could see them lined up at the door; at the door, out the door, and around the corner.

Osborn sat down in the chair beside me, picking up one of my limp hands from my lap.

"Let us have a bit of a breather, shall we, Pearl?" He asked as if he too suffered; he did. He'd lost what was to him my Ginevra.

"Look how my Felix dotes on her."

His words led me to a corner of the large room at The Beeches, the only place I owned large enough for all the people they told me would come.

Looking so grown up and a bit dapper in his suit and bow tie, Osborn's son brought a drink to my daughter, stood over her until she had drunk enough to satisfy him.

"He's going to be such a good man," I sighed, wondering if I would ever smile again, laugh again. "As good as his father."

Osborn shook his head. "No, a better one."

He surprised me; he didn't do that often. "You are a good man."

"I could have been better. I could have gone... I should have gone... with Peter."

My other hand lifted to cup his in both of mine. I shook my head. "Then you'd both be dead."

Osborn shrugged his shoulders without a word.

"Besides," I continued. Our gazes stayed on our children and our thoughts on the same burden. "I think it's my fault he's dead."

"Pearl!" Osborn exclaimed even as he whispered. "How can you even—?"

"Because of what I did, because I killed Herbert."

I knew he knew. I think he was surprised to learn I did.

"I... uh..." Osborn forced his voice to drop back down; he had almost yelled at me. "Do not—"

"I am being punished for what I did." I denied him his argument.

For a moment he said nothing, did nothing. Then he leaned closer to me, whispered softer, "Do you see that man over there?"

With a jut of his chin, Osborn led my gaze to a bulbous man whose red-veined nose was almost as round and large as his gut, one threatening to pop the buttons of his three-piece suit. The high, stiff collar of his shirt dug into a fleshy neck, a large fabric hand choking him.

"He came to me at the bank, getting a loan for a real estate venture. A loan that was ultimately approved against my recommendation to those above me. He has been evicting women and children, some who, like you, have lost their husbands to this war and some that are still hoping for theirs to return." A sneer bit his sweet

221

face… an Osborn I barely knew. "Yes, he threw them out of their homes without so much as a by-your-leave so that he could tear them down and build a hotel."

For a while, we both stared at the man, one I had known since my childhood.

"If there is punishment in this life, if there is hell for the living, it belongs to men like that. Not to a woman who saved her dearest friend."

I sighed again, though this one sounded just a bit different.

"There you are." The gruff voice pulled both my friend and me from our wonderings. I looked up into the hard face of my father-in-law.

Osborn had been wrong after all. Hell had just found me.

He leaned down as the others had, he kissed my cheek just like them, but Erasmus Wright whispered no words of comfort to me.

"You have taken him from me, twice now," He put his yellowing teeth on view, pulling his lips back in a parody of a smile. "You insisted on living here in Newport instead of in Albany with us. You—"

"I did not. No." My head shook with my voice. "No. He wanted—"

"Stop your prattle. I know he did not." He took my hand in his – a grotesquely twisted branch – pretending to shake it. I could feel bone pressing against bone in the crush of his hand. "And now you keep him here, in the ground here instead of where he belongs beside his mother."

"See here, sir." Osborn stood, a knight rushing to a crying damsel's distress. "This is neither the place nor time for—"

"If I wanted your opinion, I would have requested it." Erasmus did not even look at Osborn as he dismissed him.

"In my boy's passing, I will exact my revenge upon you." The man, so like my husband though age-hardened and hate-darkened, straightened. His piercing gaze, dry and tearless and pinched with acrimony, took in the large and opulent sitting room. "I think I shall enjoy summering here... once this belongs to me."

I bolted out of my chair. If I had the strength, if I had the reach, I think I would have wrapped my hands around his throat.

"You will never—"

Spinning and spinning... his face, all the faces, the paintings, the tapestries. Wobbling, legs of rubber. Osborn's arms around me.

"You will take yourself from here this minute," I heard Osborn demand.

"That you will, sir."

I knew that voice, had heard it since my childhood. Mr. Birch.

"Hah!" He laughed. Erasmus Wright actually laughed, at his own son's funeral. "I will leave. But you will see me again, and soon."

"I know Peter had a will, I signed it as a witness myself." Osborn sat across from me at the dining table that was just the right size in my real home on Farewell Street.

"I remember," I agreed. It seemed there *was* a panacea for grief – survival. "He had it done while we were in New York that last time, when we buried my family. I remember he apologized for not having done it sooner, when Mary was born."

Like us all when we are young, we never believe the wraith of death will come to call upon us. Trauma often serves to remind us that there is no certainty, at any age. The loss of my entire family, the reversion of all my family's wealth to my husband and not to me had prompted him to do it then, and quickly.

"Then where is it?" Ginevra whined, pacing about the table I sat with Osborn.

"When Henry Wilson died, four years ago now, I believe, they turned over all our legalities to another attorney. But they failed, the firm, without Wilson at its head. A year or so ago. I have sent letters to the names of the other lawyers who are still practicing. Hopefully, one of them knows something. Hopefully one of them will get back to me soon."

I had written those letters that very morning when I received the one from my father-in-law's attorney, the letter Ginevra and Osborn passed back and forth between them like the last drops of water to be found in a dessert. Its masthead of Burdick and Burdick was intimidating in and of itself. The senior Burdick, a man named Clark, was now serving in government while his son, also named Clark, practiced law, ran the firm his father had established. They both wore their power loudly in this city.

"You may not have that much time, I fear." Osborn studied the letter as if he were to take an exam upon its contents. Strands of his straight hair stuck out will-nilly on a head too busy at thought. "They have requested expedition, citing your father-in-law's ill-health."

"The only thing ill about that man is his temper," Ginevra spat. "But, dearest, explain this Dower law to me."

Osborn's shoulder rose to his ears, brought back down by his suspenders and ignorance. "I am a banker, not an attorney. But I had always thought it a law meant to protect a widow, not the other way around. It looks here as if—"

A knock upon my front door interrupted him.

"Ah." Osborn rose to answer it. "Here is the man who can truly answer our questions."

William Harvey, a fellow student of both Peter and Osborn's during their undergraduate years at Brown, was a short yet comely man. Dark hair and dark keen eyes shone out of pale yet creamy skin. He moved quickly through the door and into the room on muscular legs that matched the rest of him.

"Mrs. Wright, a pleasure, if under these trying circumstances," he said as he shook my hand. "I will do everything in my power and the law's to help you."

I appreciated that he did not simper sympathies as everyone did when they saw me in those days. He was a man who got down to business.

"Thank you, Mr. Harvey."

"Bill, please, madam. May I see the letter?" He asked of us all; the mess of papers strewn across the table made it indistinguishable. Ginevra handed it to him. It seemed we all had forgotten how to breathe in the short time it took him to read it.

"Humph," he grunted as he finished reading it, keeping it in his hands, but sat back in his chair.

"I was just trying to explain this Dower law, Bill, but I'm woefully ignorant of its full implications and how it is being used *against* Pearl." The pleading need to help me in Osborn's voice put one small sutra in a piece of my shattered heart.

"It is being used against her in a despicable contortion of its intent." Mr. Harvey's denunciation began his explanation.

The Dower law was indeed meant to protect the widow should her husband die intestate – without a will. To give a widow at least a third of her husband's property lest his family takes it all.

"What the law also states is that the other portion belongs to surviving descendants or, if there are no descendants or descendants of the age of maturity, then the surviving parent gets the rest." Bill leaned toward us, elbows on the table, hands splayed there too. "As I understand it, the majority of that 'property,' something of a fortune, if I read the papers correctly, in truth belongs to you, Mrs. Wright."

"Please call me Pearl," I asked of him as I nodded. "Yes, the majority of it came to us… to Peter… when I lost…"

Bill's hand shot out across the table to take mine. I noticed the fine hairs on the bottom parts of his fingers. "You have had more than your fair share of it, haven't you, Pearl."

I could only nod, grateful I did not have to speak the words.

"The mansion, what was left of her father's business, the proceeds from the sale of their Fifth Avenue house," Ginevra spoke for me, righteously so. "It all went to Peter as Pearl was a married woman and so no a person at all."

I could see how angry the creep of her accent made her as Ginevra closed her mouth, pinched her lips tightly together.

Bill's penetrating gaze smiled at her. "It is an outdated law. Just one of the many you women are fighting against, and rightly so."

"You support suffrage?" Ginevra's brows rose like an impatient crooked sun, crinkling her forehead.

"Indeed I do. I have three sisters and two daughters. But even did I not, I am a believer in justice."

I wished I could have kissed Osborn's cheek, right then and there. Bringing this man – this sort of man – to my assistance was a great gift he gave me.

"My daughter is thirteen years old. Is that not considered above the age of maturity, in legal terms?" I entreated. "She is old enough to marry legally if I were insane enough to allow it, which I assure you I am not. Does that not define what is and what is not the age of maturity?"

"It does," Bill nodded. "But I fear it is once more a question of gender. They are claiming your father-in-law's right to his share on two counts, that there is no will and that the surviving descendent is a female and therefore is not a citizen in the eyes of the law, not one old enough is their claim."

"But Peter did make a will," Ginevra blurted.

"And exactly what does he think his 'share' constitutes?" I asked. If I could buy the man off, I would. I needed to rid myself of Erasmus, of all the traumas of my life and somehow get on with living.

For the first time since his arrival, Bill Harvey avoided everyone's eyes.

"As the law dictates," he replied, for the first time sounding subdued, "he would be entitled to 50 percent after the first 50,000. As an example, if Peter's estate is worth 200,000, his father, if this case is awarded in his favor, would receive 75,000 dollars."

"*Bafangu chooch!*" Ginevra flung her hands in the air, jumped back up, and walked away from the table. I thought it a good thing none of us understood Italian.

"The estate is worth far more than 200,000," I stated flatly.

"I assumed," replied Bill.

"But most of it is not liquid."

Bill's gaze returned to me. "Understood."

We three fell into silence. Ginevra returned to us, though her walk about the house did not wipe anger's redness from her face.

"Then there is but one thing to do," Bill told us all, "we must find Peter's will."

From the instant Bill Harvey left the house, we began. Ginevra and Osborn opened every drawer, tipping them upside down. The papers that fell out of them, if there were any, were put in a pile on the table before me. I went through them with painstaking methodology, reading every word, the useless, the interesting, the lovely, and heartbreaking. By the time Hazel brought Mary back from some shopping and some playing in the park, the house looked like an old glove turned inside out, its seams and tatters naked to the eye.

"What in the name of—"

"Nothing to worry about, Hazel. Just a little organizing." That's what I said. What I told her with my eyes was something far different. "Why don't you and Mary start cooking, if you wouldn't mind. I think we've all worked up quite the appetite."

We searched the entire time they prepared a meal for us, even as our bellies rumbled in response to the enticing aromas. We searched in vain. We all ate little of the lovely meal.

Osborn sat to my right, Bill Harvey to my left. Across the table from me, still dressed in smug pomposity, were my father-in-law and two other men, introduced to me as Clark Burdick and that man's assistant, Benjamin something; I didn't care a whit what his name was.

When I introduced Osborn, calling him my banker rather than merely my friend, it still elicited a flurry of objections from the other side of the table, noted and dismissed. There was little they could do about it at this particular table.

That Erasmus had agreed to mediation surprised me; it was a new form of legal jurisprudence developed during all the labor disputes with the newly unionized workers that had arisen in the last decade. That he insisted upon it so quickly did not. I had no doubt he would disagree with everything and anything we proposed but he would be able to tell the judge he had tried when he took me to court. People do many things for the sake of pretense.

"I am here for two very legitimate reasons," Osborn raised his voice above the disparaging din. "Not only can I give evidence to state of the Wright family's finances but I can state emphatically that Peter did draw a will and that document returned Mrs. Worthington's fortune to her upon his passing, returned it to where it rightly belongs."

Clark Burdick raised his brows – his ridiculous brows that looked more like caterpillars stuck to his forehead. "I endeavored to contact Mr. Peter Wright's last attorney of record and found he had passed away and that his firm has been dissolved."

"That is true." My attorney took up the wrangling. "But, as Mr. Taylor has stated, a will does exist. We merely need time to uncover a copy of it."

"Nothing exists if it cannot be read by a judge, not in a court of law."

"Which is why, if you force us to, we will be petitioning the court to grant us more time to find it based on Mr. Taylor's assurance that it exists."

The wrangling became a shouting match. Grief still held me apart, alone in roomfuls of people. I stared out the window of the Colony House, across from the Brick Market.

As if a god had sent a vision to lift my spirits, life me further out of the muck and mire oozing around me, I spied Ginevra walking in circles on the lawn of the Great Common between the two buildings.

Ginevra

I walked round and round in circles. She would only let Osborn accompany her and Bill Harvey to the meeting with that wretched man who had somehow helped bring the lovely Peter into this world. I did not doubt she was afraid of more off-color Italian words from me. The older I grew, the easier those words came to me though I had only heard them spoke when my elders thought I did not listen; it was such words children seemed to hear the loudest. I wore my armor as Pearl's protector a bit too well. I knew the truth of it… that the meeting was only for those with a legal basis to be there. If love and devotion were not the highest law of the land, then justice was indeed blind.

"Peter made a will, that we know," I spoke aloud as I walked those circles in the Great Common. People stared at me as if I were not in possession of a sound mind. The truth was the exact opposite. I had a sharp mind, my mother had always told me so. All that I had achieved, how far I had come in this country that was not the land of my birth, had proved her to be correct. I merely had a different way of thinking hard than others did. But think hard I did.

"A copy would have been kept at the lawyer's office, the one who drew it up. But that office no longer exists and none of his fellow workers knows what became of it."

I was smart enough not to say the Italian word for what I thought of those people out loud.

"Still, Peter would have been given a copy of his own will. Osborn and I have copies of ours. But what is a will? A will is a document where we tell the world who we want our precious things to go to when we die." Around and around, my walk, my thoughts; they traveled in the same circle. "Precious things, precious things…" There was something in those words that tickled the edges of my mind like a not-so-obvious clue in one of those Sherlock Holmes stories that Osborn loved and read to me.

"What are some precious things? Yes, yes, our children," I argued with myself as if I were two people. "Things, not people. Jewels… yes, that's what I mean, that's the sort of precious things one would put in a will. Where are jewels kept when they are not being worn?"

The only woman I knew who had had a great many jewels was Pearl's mother. They were still at The Beeches, still in the…

"Safe!" I screamed the word, a victory cry of a soldier who had beaten all to the top of the highest hill.

I ran.

Pearl and Peter did not have a safe in their own home. Pearl had mentioned that she kept her mother's jewels, kept them for Mary as Pearl only wore a few now and again, in the safe at The Beeches. If Pearl used the safe at The Beeches, did it not follow that Peter might have as well?

I ran faster.

"Will I always be running for you, Pearl Worthington Wright?"

Perhaps I deserved the looks I received as I yelled and ran were warranted.

Dodging putt-putting automobiles, carriages, horses, and the steaming piles those animals left behind, I ran. I ran like the forty-year-old woman that I was, that Pearl and I had turned into in July, momentous birthdays celebrated quietly. Peter's absence made anything else seem distasteful. Now our birth month would always be thought of as the month of his death.

By the time I reached The Beeches, putrid greenish sweat stains spotted my summer yellow walking suit. I must have looked like a bowl of rotting fruit. My chest heaved with each breath; the hill up to Bellevue had taken all my wind.

As I rounded to the north side of the mansion and the servants' entrance, I massaged the stitch in my side. The front doors would be locked with no one in residence but the staff door would always be open, at least until the night fell.

I flung open the door, flung myself through it, and flung myself into the arms of Mrs. Briggs, the bent and bellicose Mrs. Briggs.

"Whateva ah you doing, girl?"

Forty years old and she still called me girl. She knew my name; I'd bet she'd never forget it.

"I'm so sorry, Mrs. Briggs." And I was, very sorry I had encountered her at all. She was the last person I'd wish to run into on my urgent quest. A quest it was, for I did not know if my hunch would bring success. But the flip-flopping in my stomach hinted at its reliability.

"I must get to Mr. Worthington's library." I started for the stairs that would take me to the first floor. Till she yanked me back. Till she plopped herself between me and the stairs.

"Now what business could you possibly have there?"

Some people just ooze with hate, as if it came out of the very pores of their skin. They craved it as some do love. Mrs. Briggs was such a person and I her favorite target. But I was no longer that frightened fifteen-year-old girl who had come to this house with but a few words of English upon my tongue, wearing fear as loudly as my poverty and my tattered clothes.

She hated me for my ethnicity, the things Pearl and I had done, but most of all she hated me for all I had achieved. Envy is always the portal to hate, especially for those who hate themselves. If she had wanted more from this life, she should have fought for it, as I had. No one just hands you a life of "more."

"I am here on an errand for Pearl, Mrs. Briggs. One that—"

"Nonsense," she spat from lips circled by a web of deep wrinkles. "The missus would have told me you were—"

"Mrs. Briggs, I do not have time for your twaddle," I chastised her, oh yes I did. Enough was enough. Her face nearly exploded, mouth agape, eye slits were slits no more. "What I am doing, I do to save Pearl, to save her from financial ruin." I mimicked the housekeeper's pinched face and demeaning stare. "And what I do will save you your home, the place in which you simply live and get paid for it. Now get out of my way or I will get you out of my way."

Like a dog in the road with a carriage barreling toward it, she scurried aside. Once more I ran, up the stairs and down the long marble hallway.

I stood in the doorway of Mr. Worthington's library. The smell of him… of pipe tobacco, leather, and despair hit me like waves during a storm. I had to close away my sadness, my missing him.

My eyes scuttled about, over the fine leather furniture covered in pristine white sheets, there the desk, there the two chairs and the table between that always held his decanter of whiskey. It was too dark with the closed curtains to see much else.

I rushed into the room, throwing open the heavy damask draperies, till sunlight shone through all three, then whirled to face the room once more.

His desk. On the wall behind his desk hung the last family portrait the Worthingtons had taken together, the one from Clarence's wedding. There had always been a family portrait there.

"There had always been a family portrait there, always," I said the words aloud as I walked toward it. I pulled on one side, then the other. It didn't budge.

I dropped my elbows on the fireplace mantel just below the

portrait, dropped my head into my hands, defeat made it heavy.

"Where the hell else could it be?" I muttered.

"On the bottom."

I jolted. I whirled.

Mrs. Briggs stood in the doorway. I had no idea how long she'd been standing there. I knew only that she came to help. She shocked me in more ways than one.

"There's a latch on the bottom of the frame."

My hand flicked out, my fingers scurried and searched. A click, a pull, and there it was.

"Well, go on." Mrs. Briggs stood beside me now, urging me on with typical impatience.

"It's... I need..." I stared at the safe and its dial of numbers.

"1890." The deep, warbling voice of Mr. Birch made us both jump. We must have stared at him as one would a great work of art or a train wreck. "The year this cottage was built. 1, 8, 9, 0," he repeated with almost condescending slowness. "Left to one, right to... oh, just move out of the way."

Mrs. Briggs and I did just that, jumping out of the way as the large, though elderly, man barged into the room.

He spun the dial, we heard the click, the safe popped open.

"What are you trying to find?" he asked without turning around.

"A will, Peter's will."

That brought both pairs of eyes to me, eyes suddenly full of understanding.

Mr. Birch pulled out all the stacks of paper and the thick brown folders tied shut with strings to match.

Mrs. Briggs and I yanked the sheet off the glorious old desk, one with all of Mr. Worthington's things still upon it, fountain pen and inkpot, blotting-pad and datebook, and his pipe sitting with tobacco still in it in a cut-crystal ash urn as if he had just taken a puff.

We three had never been part of the same team, though we had all been servants, no matter our ranks within that ranking. As if we had planned it, Mr. Birch handed stacks to Mrs. Briggs, who laid them on the table while I sorted them. That day we worked as a team.

Osborn and Pearl will think me mad when I tell them of this.

I almost giggled. Instead, I set to my work.

Paper edges sliced my fingers. A headache formed between my eyes as they strained to read all the documents. I did not stop for a moment – a single moment can change a life.

"Budget, Inventory," I muttered aloud as I read each paper's headings, "Schedule, Last Will and...*alla buon'ora!*" The last I yelped out. I had found it, I had finally found it.

"Is that it?" Mrs. Briggs pressed close to me.

"Is it Master Peter's?" Mr. Birch loomed over our shoulders.

We all read... the Last Will and Testament of Peter Erasmus Wright. *To my wife...* my eyes scurried faster.

"*Grazie, Dio cara, grazie mille.*" I'd found it, and it was indeed the weapon to slay the dragon.

I dumped some other papers out of one of those brown folders and put the will inside. Before I rushed from the room, I kissed them both, a kiss for each cheek. Mrs. Briggs paled and wobbled. Mr. Birch's tired face took on a rosy red glow.

I ran for the door, stopped, rushed back in, and grabbed Mr. Worthington's pipe.

"For my Papa," I cried over my shoulder as I rushed once more for the door.

The last thing I saw, the last thing they both did, was to gift me with a smile, the first I'd ever received from either of them.

***

"You can't go in there," the clerk sitting in the lone chair outside the room held up a hand at me like a policeman directing a crowd. I could have been a beggar off the street, such was the look he gave me. I didn't give a thought to my appearance; I was afraid to.

"I will and you will have to pick me up and carry me from this building if you mean to stop me."

In the time it took for his chin to drop toward the floor, I slipped past him and threw the door open.

"I have it! I have it!"

"Ginevra?"

My husband and my dearest friend yelped my name as if they didn't know me, know the me I was at that moment.

"It's… right… here," I panted, breath thin for all my running, for the excitement that made my heart feel it would burst in my chest. "Peter's will."

"What?"

"You found it?"

"Give that to us, if you please?"

This last came from the man sitting beside Erasmus Wright.

With an Alva Vanderbilt Belmont smile purposefully upon my lips, I opened the folder, took the thick document out, and handed it to Bill Harvey. My smile widened as Erasmus scowled; he'd tasted something bitter and its name was defeat.

Time stood still as each person at the table took their turn reading the document. Bill pointed things out to Pearl and Osborn but I could not listen, I could not take in those words. Once more I walked circles, this time in the corner of the room. This time I prayed.

"Do not think for a moment that this is the end of it," Erasmus growled, pulling me out of my pilgrimage. "You will pay, one way or another, for what you did to my son."

"Get out!" Pearl slammed her hands upon the table so hard it silenced everyone in the room. "You have no right to be here, you have nothing to stake your evil on."

Osborn and Bill stepped back, gave her the moment she deserved. Never had a woman been so glorious in her righteousness.

"I did not insist we live in Newport. Your son wanted it as much as I. And do you know why?" She leaned over the table. Were she a snake, a long, split tongue would have snapped out to strike the man upon whom she plied her venomous outrage. "You. He wanted to stay away from you. Your nastiness, your constant criticism—"

"I do not—" Erasmus yelled as he paled, as he became shorter with rounded shoulders. He tried... a futile attempt.

"I am speaking," Pearl demanded his attention. "This is what he wanted." One hand slammed upon the table again. "Newport is what he wanted." The other hand slammed. "And I am what he wanted.

"Now go. Leave us be. But as you do so, know that you have not only lost this fight, you have lost the only connection to your son that remains... your granddaughter, for I will never allow you to see her again. You did not care that she would be a casualty in your war against me. She will know of it and it will be your end."

The dragon curled with defeat, the fatal blow plied. Pearl had slain him with the weapon I gave her, with the truth of what happens to those who set out to hurt.

We watched in silence as Erasmus Wright and his attorneys left the room, pretending possession of pride.

The door closed behind them. Pearl fell into her chair. Bill and Osborn shook hands.

"I ask one thing of you, Pearl," Bill Harvey said to Pearl as he took her hand. "When you get the vote, and I have no doubt you will, you must help us rid our country of these harmful laws."

"I gladly make that promise. Or perhaps it will be my daughter that will see it to fruition," Pearl replied. "Thank you, Bill."

With a head tip to us all, the lawyer left us.

I still stood in my corner... till she reached out to me.

I ran to her, for her, yet again. I took her hand and knelt by her side.

Without a word, she laid her head upon my shoulder. I would always accept its weight, whenever there was a need.

"We must get the vote, Ginny," she said without lifting it. "We cannot let this sort of thing continue."

"No, we cannot," I agreed. "We must not."

Pearl

The lilting notes from the piano woke me. Her sweet voice as it sang along brought me to her.

So, send me away with a smile little girl
Brush the tears from eyes of brown
It's all for the best
And I'm off with the rest
With the boys from my hometown.
It may be forever we part little girl
But it may be for only a while.
But if fight here we must
Then in God is our trust.
So, send me away with a smile.

Mary sat at the piano, morning's low, golden sunlight casting a halo about her as she sang. She didn't hear me as I came down the stairs, as I walked to her. Only when I sat beside her upon the piano bench did she see me; only when I saw her face did I see she sang through her tears.

Of course, she would play that song, *Daddy Mine*. What I didn't know was if I should stop her. Oh, how I worried she would be lost forever in the death of her father, a tender and affectionate father who meant so much to her.

But then I remembered, though I don't remember at which funeral it was said to me or by whom. I knew only that it had made sense to me… *the only way to get past grief is to go through it.*

My Mary and I would go through it together, armed with precious memories, with love so great it would never – could never – be forgotten.

She knew I sat beside her, yet Mary kept playing, kept singing.

I turned the pages of the sheet music for her.

Pearl

November 11, 1918

We heard the shouting first. Hazel came running from the kitchen into the sitting room where Mary and I sat on the floor and played with her dolls. Her Aunt Ginevra had made them new clothes; the lack of customers in these years of war gave her the time.

Winter had not quite come to Newport, though fall began to bow to it. Despite the chill, we opened the windows to try to hear better. We couldn't. Just voices, a jumble of loud voices.

"Do you think we are under attack?" Hazel twisted and squeezed the cleaning cloth in her hands. "Is it the Germans again? Are they attacking us?"

My daughter's eyes beseeched me more with the woman's every word.

"Now Hazel." I couldn't completely chide her. We had all been on worried guard after the German U-boat left us as friends only to sink ships off neighboring shores. "You know the fire brigade would be knocking on our door should such a thing be happening."

I didn't lie; it was the notification method decided upon by the city officials. I always wondered, however, were we truly under attack, how they would get to us all. That thought I didn't share.

"It sounds like cheering," Mary said, her head still hanging out the open window, her long, curly hair twirling down like a lovely vine. "I think I hear—"

"The war is over! The war is over!"

Those words brought all our heads out the window. A boy, no

older than Mary, ran up and down the streets, arms whirling like a many-colored pin-wheel, adolescent voice cracking and squeaking as he jumped and skipped his way down the street, as he cried words that brought us all to relieved tears.

"The war is over," I repeated, I whispered, slipping back inside, sliding down on to the sofa. I did cry, and for so many reasons. Relief of such magnitude gave blood to the heart, breath to constricted lungs. It drove away fear, fear of my child's life, fear of deprivation – drove it away as surely as the sun did the moon.

But my eyes spilled bitter tears as well.

Four months. If he had just survived for four more months…

It would be a thought that would forever haunt my mind.

"Celebration at the Common." The young crier continued to spread his cheerful news.

"Can we go, Mother?" Mary asked, too young to realize how close we came to having Peter back, to recognize the irony within this moment.

"Why not?" I said, as merrily as I could muster.

We wrapped ourselves in coats and hats, even Hazel, and made our way to the Common, following the band music that grew louder as we drew closer. It sounded as if every band in the city had come out to serenade us with songs of patriotism and victory.

What we saw when we turned the corner, when the Common came into view, brought out the laughter in us all.

Men, women, and children danced about as if they were drunk. I suspect many of them were, even the older children. They danced in groups, in couples, and even alone, just for the joy of it.

"There is Sarah, and for heaven's sake, she's dancing!" Hazel exclaimed as she pointed her finger.

"Do you see the Taylors?"

Hazel stood on tiptoes for a moment. "No, Missus. Only Sarah.

May I—"

"You don't need to ask, Hazel," I threw the arm that did not hold Mary around her shoulders. "Go. Have fun, have fun all night long, if you wish."

Hazel twittered as only elderly women seemed to do and took herself off to Sarah. Within minutes, we watched and laughed as the two of them danced a jig together.

And why should she not? Why shouldn't Mary and I? We deserved to – had we not sacrificed for the sake of this victory?

Yet I could not, as much as part of me longed to. I let Mary join a group of children of her age who did their unlearned form of joyful abandoned dancing not far from me where I sat on a patch of grass just outside the bustle of the celebration.

"She is going to be such a beauty, Peter, as beautiful as she is smart," I spoke to my husband. It was not the first time; it would not be the last.

I saw other women, women like me. Our heads wore two faces, those of joy that the war was over, those that grieved for our men that never made it home.

"Pearl?"

I turned to the soft feminine voice. I knew the face of the tall, thin woman with the most glorious blonde hair I'd ever seen. I could not remember her name.

"It's Minnie, Minnie Johnson," said she. One or both of my faces must have shown my confusion.

"Of course, Minnie. I… I…" I had seen her at a suffrage meeting or two; she was hard to miss, though I couldn't recall if she marched or picketed with us. I remembered questioning her commitment to the cause.

"Don't worry yourself, Pearl," Minnie said graciously, pulling me into her arms. "I lost my Arthur as well."

I could have kicked myself for my unkind thoughts. "I'm sorry, Minnie." I pulled out of her embrace. I saw then she wore two faces as well. "I'm sorry for us all."

Minnie turned her moist green gaze to the revelry bursting all around us.

"At least it was not for naught. At least we lost them for a good cause."

I squeezed her hand. It would not be the first or last time I was to hear such a sentiment. It would not be the last time I questioned it.

"Yes. At least there is a victory."

"Take good care of yourself, Pearl." Minnie kissed my cheek and walked away.

I could only raise my hand in parting as she walked from me.

"Pearl?" A male voice came from somewhere. "Is that you, Pearl?"

I turned and saw them. I nearly cried.

I jumped up and ran to them. I hugged them both and both at the same time.

"You're here. You're here and you're alive."

Consuelo's brothers, childhood friends so dear to me, I held in my quivering arms. Survival of loved ones could almost overcome the loss of others. Almost.

They laughed as I stepped back, but not too far. I didn't want to let them go; I held each of their hands.

"How dashing you both look in your uniforms!" In truth, I appraised their bodies for injury, thanking the Lord when I saw none.

"Well, I do," Willie, the older of the two, joked. Harry, younger by eight years, gave his brother a playful punch on the arm.

"How long have you been home? Surely, the government is not so efficient as to have you returned on the day of Armistice?"

"We were discharged four months ago, actually," Harry informed me. "Though we had been hearing all the talk of a peace treaty in the trenches, we didn't believe it until they started sending regiments home."

"Pearl, I..." Willie started and stopped. Conflicting emotions turned the corners of his lips downward; he twisted his cap in his hands.

"What is it, Willie? You can tell me anything, you know that." If my mother had had her way, Willie would have been my husband. Alva would never let my mother have her way.

"I was in his r-regiment," he stammered. "In Peter's regiment."

How thankful I was my hands were still in theirs; they kept me from falling.

"It must have been good for you both, to have a familiar face to..." I faltered.

"Let's sit, shall we?" Harry led me back to my spot on the grass, to my view of my dancing daughter. The brothers sat, one on each side of me.

Willie began to talk, to tell me of what he and Peter lived through.

"What he did that day, Pearl," Willie shook himself. He had seen it but it seemed as if he still didn't believe it. "He heard the tanks coming before anyone else. He sent us all back. He took all our grenades and sent us back, while he... while he..." Tears flowed silently down his face. Many a soldier would cry after many a war. It was the longest-lasting effect of war.

I did not know they flowed upon my face as well until Harry handed me his handkerchief.

"He held them off, you see, Pearl," Harry picked up the story where Willie could not. "One man and armfuls of grenades saved over fifty lives, maybe more."

"It was the most courageous thing I have ever seen," Willie whispered, "that I shall ever see."

I took their words, I took the last moments of my husband's life, from them with both gratitude and heartbreak.

"Thank you," I could but say softly.

We sat there, the three of us, three childhood friends. We were all scarred and injured in ways that could not be seen. We watched the celebrations before us. We had all learned that no matter the outcome of a war, no matter the victory, it was a wicked and evil thing.

Pearl

January 1919

As in the wake of the War Between the States, prosperity came to us in the aftermath of what had come to be known as the Great War. When will men learn there is nothing great about war?

My renderings of my Peter as a soldier drew more and more people to the gallery and my work sold for more and faster than it ever had, though I would not put on display or sell those of him as the man I knew before he became a soldier, before he died as one.

I might be an artist but not a foolish one. I plied my brush as often and as quickly as I could, using the pictures from the newspapers as my guide, the ones of the soldiers in "glorious" battle, the ones of them marching home in victory. Brilliant colors and stark, hard strokes defined this phase of my work. Its grandeur, its homage to our victory, appealed to those whose pockets started to fill and those whose pockets had always been deep. I needed more time, more time off the gallery floor talking and selling the work to customers and more time creating it. The satisfaction I found was not only in my growing financial self-sufficiency but for the outlet of my frustrations and emotions, my need and my grief.

Ruth Chase had received her degree in art history from my alma mater the previous June. She was personable, knowledgeable, eager, and a suffragist. She was exactly what I needed and I thanked our time on the picket line for bringing her to me, for giving me the chance to hire her as my assistant at the gallery.

She would work the gallery floor while I worked the paint in the backroom, save for the days we spent on the line. We took turns when it was our turn. After what I had gone through, the nearly fatal blow of Erasmus Wright had stoked the flames of my suffrage fires. In the evenings at home with Mary, she did her homework while I wrote more articles.

"In some ways, I feel sorry for him," Ginevra said as she folded her newspaper, as we rumbled along on the train to Providence once more.

"Whatever for?" Her words brought me out of my half-dozing state, wrapped in my heaviest coat and a blanket to ward off January's cold.

"Well, he is trying to help."

"Help that has come a little too late, after he allowed so many to be harmed."

"Yes, but that speech, the one he made in September, it was quite moving."

I rolled my eyes, though I could recall the words of it, almost every one.

President Wilson had taken to the floor of the Senate on September 30 last year for the specific purpose of urging them to support the women's suffrage amendment that they would once more be voting on in October. It was a monumental occurrence; he became only the second president in history to speak before the Senate. A bold move, no doubt. Inspired by belief or guilt, I would forever ask that question.

*This war could not have been fought without the services of
our women. We have made partners of the women in this war...
Shall we admit them only to a partnership of suffering and*

sacrifice and toil and not to a partnership of privilege and right?

"Yes, it was quite stirring, but it didn't work. We are still fighting while the soldiers have stopped, are we not?"

Ginevra shrugged. She possessed the kindest heart I've ever known. Kindness can be a handicap when it renders one blind.

"You have to know, Pearly, you must know, I am more committed to this cause than ever. Let them drag me to prison, let them take all that I possess, as long as I have the love of my family. I will not rest until we cast our first ballot."

But then Ginevra was always full of surprises.

Ginevra

They came back and they came in droves. *Costa Couture's* doors opened and shut more and more often, inundated with clients, both new and old. At last, I could concentrate on my designs, proclaimed as "distinctive and innovative" by the local newspapers. Hems dropped again, but under my pencil, they curved around a woman's legs. Opulence returned with fur and jeweled beading, but I used them sparingly, making them the highlights of an outfit not the whole of it. It gave such fur and jewels the focus and attention they deserved. Fashion was how we expressed ourselves, not hid behind. It should always serve us; we should never serve fashion. Yes, I designed and designed, sketched and sketched, thanks to the end of the war and with the addition of a seamstress and a salesgirl.

In truth, I did not have the time for suffrage, for the protests and meetings and days on the picket line. But in my heart and soul, with my words and actions, I would sacrifice all my time to it.

When we made our way up the hill from the train station to the State House that day, we were greeted by a new sight, a new form of protest. The Watch Fires of Freedom had come to Providence.

They were first sparked by the national parties, first lit before the White House. That President Wilson's fine speech to the Senate had failed to get the amendment the number of votes needed had made his speech useless, made the words nothing but ink on paper. As the President toured Europe after the war, as he spoke of democracy and freedom, his every word mocked us, as if he'd turned a blind eye to our lack of democracy and freedom.

So the fires began. And a woman named Edith Ainge had started the first one, her words became those which were repeated as each suffrage group sparked their own flames.

> *We consign to flames the words of the President which have inspired women of other nations to strive for their freedom while their author refuses to do what lies in his power to do to liberate women of his own country. Meekly to submit to this dishonor would be treason to mankind. Mr. President, the paper currency of liberty which you hand to women is worthless fuel until it is backed by the gold of action.*

Rolled-up copies of the President's speech were set on fire and left to burn to ashes, in urns where we picketed, in front of as many public and government buildings as possible. Our banners would now proclaim the President as a hypocrite.

"You know this might well land us both in jail again," Pearl said to me as we stared into the first flames our hands had lit.

Well, at least we'll be in there together this time," I replied, delighting in her giggled response.

Pearl

June 1919

"Mother?"

I stirred. I heard my daughter's voice in my dreams.

"Mother, wake up."

I stirred more, my body rolling back and forth in my bed. But it wasn't a dream. It was my daughter.

I opened one eye, squinting at her in dawn's murky light. At fourteen, Mary had stepped over many a line that changed one from a girl to a woman, and yet she still rose early, as young children are wont to do, much too early for me. I might have missed the baby she once was but oh how delighted I was that she had become enough of an adult that I need not wake with her anymore. We were taking those first steps from mother and daughter to best friends, though one's child is always one's child, no matter their age, no matter the depth of the friendship.

"Are you all right, Mary? Are you hurt?"

"I'm fine, Mother, but—"

"But then I shall surely make you pay for waking me so early."

"Aunt Ginny is running up the street in her dressing gown, calling your name, and waving her arms in the air with something in her hands."

I bolted upright. I stared at my daughter, assuring myself she was fully awake and not babbling in some bizarre dream she might be having.

Her very smirk, one so very belonging to a fourteen-year-old, told me which was true.

I jumped out of bed, threw my wrap about me, and fled down the stairs, just as Ginevra began pounding on our front door.

"Pearl! Pearl! Let me in!"

"Are you mad?" I greeted her as I flung the door open and pulled her in before her lunatic cries woke the neighbors and set their tongues to waggling; we had always been a favored topic of wagging tongues.

"I am!" she cried. Grabbing my hand and Mary's too, she pulled us into the most bizarre ring-around-the-rosy I had ever experienced. "I am mad with joy! Mad with victory!"

Mary laughed her still merry laugh while I held my large, unbound breasts from bouncing too painfully.

"About what, you deranged woman?" If I could get her to talk, perhaps she would stop this circle of jumping and skipping.

She did stop. As if I had struck her with a log of wood, Ginevra stopped... stopped her jumping and her skipping and her raving cries.

With tears in her eyes, she held a crumpled newspaper out to me with both hands as if she gave me the keys to Heaven.

"It's happened, Pearl. It's passed."

My gaze could not move quickly enough between her glowing face and the blaring headline.

SENATE PASSES THE SUSAN B. ANTHONY AMENDMENT
56-25

I saw it, I read it with my own eyes.

I dropped to the floor, flattened the paper, and read it. I read it twice, once to myself, once aloud for Mary to hear every word.

My daughter joined me on the floor, as did Ginevra. Together we read it once more; together we shared tears of victory.

I don't know how long we sat there, how long we cried and

laughed, whooped and hollered, until the door opened. Until Hazel found us there.

"Have you all lost your minds?" she asked, looking as if she would back herself back out the door.

We three laughed through our tears. With a gentleness deserving of her age, I pulled Hazel down to the floor with us.

"As I live and breathe," she whispered. "I did not think I would live to see it. Oh, Pearl, Ginevra, all your hard work was not for naught. Bless you, bless you both." Her elderly hands quivered more than ever as she wiped her tears from her cheeks.

"Our fight is not over yet," I said with no diminished joy.

The perplexed glares from Mary and Hazel elicited a quick lesson in government, that in order for an amendment to become a true law of the land it had to first be passed by the House of Representatives – which it had in May – then by the Senate, and finally, it must be ratified – or approved – by at least thirty-six states.

"So you see, our fight has indeed not been for naught but it is not yet over."

"May I fight beside you, Mother?" Mary asked, gaze flashing to her Aunt Ginny, no doubt in hopes of support. She had no need of it.

I gathered her in my arms, rocking her as I did when she was but a babe though she no longer fit upon my lap.

"I can think of nothing that would bring me more joy."

Ginevra

I stood at the podium with her, a far more silent but no less determined leader of the Political Equality Association.

"As every suffrage organization in every state is doing, so shall we," Pearl's enthusiasm infected every one of the already enthused women, more than there had ever been, who heard her, who hung on her every word. Having her daughter in the gathering only added to her fervor.

"We must once more let our local government know that we demand – yes, demand – that they ratify the amendment. Once more we will take to the streets. We will march before the State House but we need no longer be silent. We will march before the homes of the governor and the mayors and the senators if we have to. But we *will* get Rhode Island to be among the first to ratify!"

Her rallying cry vibrated along the hallowed halls of the Colony House.

Women cheered. Some jumped from their chairs, their arms raised with fisted hands. The chanting began.

"Ratify! Ratify! Ratify!"

As Pearl took my hand in hers and raised them high, we chanted with them, our gaze rejoicing in the beauty and zeal in the women's faces.

Did I see a frown, a grimace, rather than a smile? No, it must have been my imagination.

"Ratify! Ratify!"

We joined our voices with those of our sisters.

Pearl

Time became marked not by the ticking of a clock, the turning of a calendar page, work, holidays, or even our children's lives, but by the states... the yeas and the nays.

In the short two-and-a-half weeks since the Senate had passed the amendment, nine states had ratified it, including our neighbors in Massachusetts.

"Come along, Mary," I cried up the stairs as I pulled on and buttoned my gloves, "I do not want to miss the early ferry. Aunt Ginny will be waiting and I want to get to the State House as early as possible."

The day had come. It would be our first day, armed with a passed amendment, to stand before the State House and demand the Rhode Island government to ratify it. I'd be damned if after all our work – all our sacrifices and those we'd imposed upon our families and our work – Rhode Island was not one of the thirty-six states that brought this amendment to law.

"Coming, Mother," came Mary's answering call, but I heard no footfalls coming toward me.

"You need not—"

The knock on our door prevented me from chastising my daughter further, who, I was sure, had decided to change her outfit once more. Her Aunt Ginny and that woman's world of fashion had made far too deep an impression on my budding woman of a daughter.

"What a surprise!" I cried with delight at the sight of the woman who stood on my stoop. "You've decided to join a demonstration at last. Well, you saved the best for—"

"I have not come to join you." Her voice crackled as if we spoke on the telephone and the connection was a poor one.

I looked at her, really looked, as I hadn't when I opened the door.

Her pink skin, dark and glum, held eyes narrowed to slits held in place by dark circles. She stood rigidly, shoulders squared, arms tight by her sides ending with fists. Once more, she wore the same dress we had always seen her in. Ginevra's eyes were forever keen, but what did it mean?

"Are you ill, dear?" I ushered her in. I felt as if I gripped a plank of wood as I led her by her arm.

"I have never before felt so well." She joked but with no true amusement in her voice.

I shut the door behind her and led her into the sitting room. I looked about for a fly that had possibly come through the door with her, so loud whizzed the buzz I thought I heard.

"Are you sure you don't wish to join us? We were just about to set off for the ferry or I'd offer you something. Would you like to sit?" She looked like she needed to. She looked as if did she not sit she would fall.

With her head shaking left and right, again and again, she refused my offer.

"I have not come to join you," her head kept shaking, her voice flat yet full of something I could not name. "I have come to stop you."

I stood there, just that and nothing more. I did not move or speak. I don't think or breathe.

What the devil did she say?

"I'm sorry. I'm not sure if I heard you correctly." I found my voice through the thick fog now surrounding me, filling the room.

"You heard me just fine."

Suddenly she no longer looked glum. Her fisted hands jumped to

257

her waist. Her neck thrust her forward.

"I will not let you cause any more damage. I will not let you lead any more women into depravity."

Such depravity belonged to her. I was as certain of it as I was my own name.

"Now, one moment, please. Let us talk reasonably." I spoke to her as one would a small pet one tried to coach into proper behavior. It was the wrong tack.

"Hah! There'll be no talking between us."

I squirmed and shivered at the sound of such laughter.

"You are the ringleader, the one they all follow," she moved a step closer to me. I kept my gaze on her face, her eyes. I had seen the face of madness before, on Herbert Butterworth as he tried to rape Ginevra. I stared at that face of such madness once more.

Where are you, Mary? Stay upstairs, please.

"Without you there, they will crumble and fall."

"No one is irreplaceable," I argued with truth. "There will be others there to lead this protest without me. Ginevra will—"

"Ginevra, that guinea, she is nothing without you."

I could have struck her – I should have. The heat of my blood pumped toward boiling. "I will not allow you to call her that. I will not allow you to speak such terrible language in my house."

"I tried to get her too, you know. But she made it to the ferry before I could catch her."

"I don't understand. Tell me why you are so upset, so angry with me." I stalled for time, for Hazel to come. But time could reveal Mary's presence in the house. I could not let that happen. The hateful madness had this woman firmly in its grasp. She had not given a thought to my almost-grown daughter.

"I have always been angry at you, as all antis who know of you are."

"An-antis?" Confusion reeled me. Understanding struck me, horrifying, heartbreaking understanding. I put a name and a face to the spy in our midst.

She laughed again. I longed to run from it as much as I did her.

I heard a creak upon the stairs. Mary? Did this woman in the throes of madness hear it too?

Stay there, Mary.

"Trusting, loving, Pearl," the woman taunted. "You hadn't a notion. Not once. You think yourself so high and mighty, the smartest one in our class."

"I-I knew you only as my friend, a friend of many years."

She spoke true, I had to admit it. All those meetings, all her work making the announcements and our signs. I had thought her devotion to be true. It all made sense now. Why she never joined us in public, marching or picketing. Why she could never be seen with us. For if she did, another anti, one who didn't know of her mission to thwart us – perhaps none of them did – might have given her away.

"I was your friend, until you became the Whore of Babylon, until you recruited all those other whores to—"

"How dare you?" I screamed back. My head thrummed with unrelenting drum beats; I saw little through blinding anger. "You wretched woman, I will—"

"You bring shame upon us all!" She accused me, her spittle stinging my face.

"Get out!" I bellowed. "Get out of my house this instant!" I knew my pointed finger shook on the end of my outstretched arm. I could not defeat it; I would not lower it. "Mab—"

It is the last thing I remember… that and the rise of her fist.

Donna Russo Morin

Ginevra

I boarded the ferry. What else could I do? I had no idea what might have delayed Pearl and Mary; I knew one of us had to be there early to act in the role of leader and organizer. Without one, those just joining us might question their involvement in the cause.

As the steamer pulled away from the dock, I stood at its stern, my gaze scouring the launch platform, praying for a glimpse of them.

Pearl

I woke up shivering. It felt like a fall day, not one in high summer.

I opened my eyes. A bad thing to do, for as I did, I opened myself to a swimming vision that churned my stomach and a thundering headache. My left eye did not seem able to open as wide as the right.

I tried to lift a hand to fell it but could not. My arms would not move. I looked up – up? – at them. They were shackled by rope wound round and round one of two marble columns, or at least one of the two I could see.

Marble. Expensive. Cottage?

Someone holds me prisoner. Who? Why? Where?

Stuttered thoughts roiling so hard to find answers.

I closed my eyes. Rested for a moment. Opened them again.

I could see enough to know I was not in my own home. I could see too much.

I sat on a dusty floor, one that looked hardly ever walked upon. There was half a room of furniture, of a sort: a chair by a table without its partnering chair, no lamp upon the table or anywhere, a circular rug with no cozy sofa upon it. A half of a room like a half of a life was a depressing sight to behold.

"She will be taught a lesson, oh yes she will."

The voice came from a different room, one not too far away.

I knew that voice; I'd heard it before. My wounded brain shuffled through memories – people and their voices – ever so slowly.

"They shall all learn. Damnable women who think they can take it all, have it all."

Anger, sharp and stabbing, bitter and dangerous.

Footsteps. Movement. Coming closer.

The silhouette appeared in the arched entryway. Long skirts. Piled hair. A woman.

"So." A grunt of a word. "You're awake."

She stepped closer. Long skirts kicking up dust. She walked on a cloud of it.

She stood before me. I looked up.

Mabel! Mabel… Mabel… I couldn't remember her last name, not the one of her birth or marriage.

"Mabel," I muttered, it was all I had.

"Look at you now, the beautiful Pearl Worthington Wright, the powerful suffragette." She squatted before me. "You look like a dog, a mutt, on a leash." Her lips a swerving gap in her face. A clown's mouth. A wicked clown's humor.

"Where?"

My eyes stayed open longer, wider. They saw nothing familiar.

"Why, you are at my house. The one you never deigned to call upon."

"Your house?" I heard her wrong. She was the wife of a rich man. The mother of many children. This was a place of aloneness and desolation. "Wh-where is your husband?"

We can never know how wrong our words can be until they're spoken.

"You took him!"

Her scream slammed like a hammer upon my skull.

"You." She pointed at me with a knife I did not know she had in her hand. "You took him and my children away. If you had come, if you had paid a call years ago, when we first saw each other again, he might not have left, he might have stayed."

Nonsense. She was speaking it. Or was I hearing it? It was

nonsense.

"I did no—"

Her fist came again. Struck me again. Blackness found me again.

Ginevra

The bell chimed. From the hill just to the west, the church spire rose up into the sky. The Baptist church had a steeple of five floors. Its bell rang and rang; it rang twelve times.

Midday. Midday and still without any sight of Pearl and Mary. Others from Newport had arrived on the later ferry. I asked every one of them but not a one had a word of her, of them, not a sight of them either.

I knew then that what I felt was true… something was wrong. Something had happened.

I put down my sign and walked off the line.

"Where are you going, Ginevra?" Sarah Eddy called out to me.

"I'm going to find Pearl," I said, not loud enough for any to hear. I just kept walking until I got to the ferry dock.

Pearl

I coughed and coughed; I choked. Drowning.

The frigid water thrown in my face dripped off my nose, my chin.

Awake again. Mabel stood right before me again.

"No more time for sleeping," the bucket clanged upon the hardwood floor as Mabel dropped it, "we need to get down to business."

"Wh-what business?"

Dear Lord, my head hurt so badly. With each throb came a wretched pounding in my ears. Each thought, each word, a struggle.

"The business of you getting me what I want."

She sat, actually sat, upon the floor in front of me. We were to negotiate? Did we sit across from each other at a desk?

"I w-will get you wh-whatever…" I had to say it. I didn't mean it.

"What I want is my husband back." Mabel leaned in close. The knife nestled in the cradle of her skirts. "He left me, you know. He took my children. He left me in this house all alone, with no money. My children. Oh, my babies."

She cried. Mabel sobbed and moaned and rocked herself back and forth. A disheveled, distraught child bemoaning the loss of her most cherished toys.

"S-so sorry. Wh-where?" I had to sound acquiescent, sound friendly.

"The where doesn't matter!" Pitiable Mabel snapped back to raging wretch. "It's who. The question is who took him."

I complied. "Who?"

"A suffragette, who else? Minnie Johnson!" Her face only inches from mine. My bruised skin stung by the heat of her fury. "One of your damnable suffragettes! You want this, you want that, you want the vote, you want other women's husbands… you want everything!"

Ginevra

The steamer did not move fast enough. If only it could have used the steam of my worry, it would have flown.

It gave me time though, time I needed to think, to plan.

As soon as the ferry docked in Newport, I rushed from it, ran home, seeing little save my children playing in the garden behind the house.

"Sara?" I yelled before the front door closed behind me.

"Ginevra?" My husband's voice answered me. He came rushing round from his study through the sitting room.

"What are you doing here? I thought you were at work?"

"What are you doing here? I thought you were at the State House?"

Our confusion layered upon each other's.

"I left some papers—"

"Pearl didn't show up."

"What?" Osborn balked, wide smile trembled, faded; sparkling eyes darkened, narrowed. I had his attention. My answer trumped his. "She didn't go to the State House? But it was your plan – her plan – the start of the new program."

"Exactly," I replied, rushing away from him. "Sara?" I called again. This time, short quick footsteps brought her down the stairs, brought her to me.

"Missus? What's wrong?"

I could only imagine what a wreck I looked, a wreck matching the thoughts whirling in my mind. I spared no time to explain.

"Have any messages come? Any messages from Pearl?"

Sara shook her head, her lengthening jowls wobbling. "No. Nothing."

I turned on my heels, heading out the door I had just entered.

"Where are you going?" Osborn called to me.

"To Pearl's."

"Wait for me."

My husband came fast on my heels, beside me as we hurried the two blocks to Pearl's house.

I knocked once, and again. Nothing.

Osborn reached out, gripping the handle, turning it. The door opened. I rushed in. I found a frightening stillness.

"Pearl? Pearl, are you here? Pearl, I—"

"Wait." Osborn held me. "Listen. What is that?"

Rustling and scraping. The sounds came from nearby. We inched further into the house.

Scratching and squeaking. The door to the cubby beneath the stairs cracked open. One dark eye peered out at us.

"Mary?" I cooed softly, moving slowly toward her. "It's—"

"Aunt Ginny!"

Mary launched herself into my arms. I caught her, held her tight.

"It's all right. It's all right now." I stroked her curly dark hair.

"No. No, it isn't." Mary pulled away from me. My breath caught at the sight of her. Pale as winter's snow, eyes swollen and red, puffiness distorting her sweet face.

Osborn hunched over, hands on his knees, gaze on a level with Mary's.

"What has happened, dear Mary? We are here to help."

Mary released her grip upon me, fell into Osborn's larger embrace. She quivered there. His eyes rose to mine. I looked into a mirror and saw my terror

"She-she took her. A w-women came. They argued. Then-then she hit Mother. Hit her, then took her."

Worry fed, cruelly satisfied.

"Who, Mary? What woman?" I joined their embrace, my hand stroked Mary's back. "Did you know her?"

Mary shook her head.

"Did you see her?" this from Osborn. "Did you get a look at her?"

Mary nodded.

"Tell us what she looked like."

"Sh-sh…" The child hiccupped sobs.

I took her hands, demanded her gaze with my own. "We must try to be calm. It's the only way we'll find her. And we will, Mary. We'll find your mama and bring her back to you."

Mary swallowed, taking deep breaths. I watched as the fearful child became a focused young woman.

"She was short, shorter than Mother." Mary closed her eyes, looked at what her mind and her memories showed her. "Short and rather plump. Blonde hair but not a nice blonde, not a glowing blonde."

Three women came quickly to mind. I needed a bit more.

"Tell us all you saw, all you heard."

She did, slowly, precisely. Mary's tale began in the middle of events. She had been upstairs, changing her clothes, nose in her wardrobe looking for just the right dress.

"She called Mother awful names and that made Mother very angry. She screamed back at the woman, demanded the woman leave our house. But then… then…"

Mary's eyes burst wide, two bright full moons.

"She, Mother, started to say her name, I think, just before the woman hit her." Mary dug her fingers into my arms as the sights and sounds haunted her. "The last thing my mother said was 'mab'."

"Mab?" Osborn blurted, face a cobweb of skeptical crinkles. "Um… could it have been 'maybe'?"

I shook my head before Mary said another word. I knew. "Mabel. Mabel Tucker Washburn. Remember," this I asked of my husband, "she was at college with us. You met her. She fits the description, though you wouldn't know her with how ploomp she become."

I stood, pulling on Osborn's arm to stand with me. I leaned close to him. "Take Mary home, to our house. Sara will care for her, as will our children. Then—"

"What are you going to do?" Alarm clang in my husband's voice; he knew me too well.

"Then-a go to police station," it was at the very end of the street we were on. "Ask for Officer… Officer…" my mind ached as I searched it for the name. Tall, red-haired, Irish acc—, "O'Leary, Officer O'Leary. Tell him it's Pearl. He knows her, us."

We all started for the door, Mary's hand firmly in Osborn's.

"What are you going to do, Ginevra?" This time he did not ask, he demanded.

I said nothing as I moved through the gate, heading left where they would head right. My head whipped back as Osborn grabbed me by the arm, his blue eyes grey and beseeching, eyes I longed to fall into, but couldn't.

"No, Ginevra. No." His head shook so fast his features blurred. "Oh no, you will not. You will wait for me, wait for the police."

I shook off his arm and ran for the trolley stop.

"I can no wait. It may already be too late!"

Pearl

"What do you expect me to do, Mabel?"

She had given me some water, held the glass while I drank though I implored her to let loose my hands. They tingled at the loss of blood flow, ached with the bite of the rope.

"You will come with me, of course," Mabel answered as if I were a daft child. "You talked her into this, into stealing another woman's husband, you will talk her out of it."

"I b-barely know the woman." It wasn't a lie. The water had washed away some of the fuzziness in my head. "Yes, she is a suffragette and part of the Political Equality Association. I've s-seen her at meetings, at events. But I've barely said a few words to her. I never persuaded or urged her to take your husband."

Minnie Johnson was that kind of woman; when you were raised as a socialite, when you watched our elders switch husbands and wives with each other like they switched hats five times a day, you grew to be either repulsed by such behavior or you embraced it. When you were a beautiful socialite, as Minnie had always been, it was almost expected. She had always seemed to be a bit on the make. I was not surprised to hear Minnie had embraced it, especially after losing her own husband in the war.

"Of course you did," Mabel rebuked me, waggling the tip of her knife before my face, barely an inch from my nose. "You preached and preached, wrote article after article, about the rights of women, that we should have the right to do whatever we want. But I know, I know the truth."

She sat on the floor before me, once more running her free hand through her already disheveled hair. It looked more like straw than ever, strands sticking out like the bristles of an old, overused broom.

"Suffrage is an insult to the family, it is the path to immorality. They told me so."

Through my swollen eyes, I saw her better than I ever had, seeing so much I should have seen before. The quirky, jerky movements of her hands, her eyes; these signs were there from the moment we were reunited. Her quietness of one moment forgotten by loud exuberance in the next.

Mabel had been what we called a "flighty" kind of girl while we were in college. Now, through eyes that pained and a mind strained, I saw the truth: she had always been unhinged. Hers was not a logical, reasonable mind… and it never had been. To argue with a lunatic was lunacy. I knew it with certainty.

What I didn't know, what I could not fathom, was what to say, what to do to appease her, to get away from her unharmed… to get away alive.

Ginevra

Must you stop at every stop?

Some trolleys did, others did not. I had gotten on the wrong one. A silly, stupid mistake that could hurt dearest Pearl. I couldn't know what Mabel wanted from Pearl, if my dearest friend was in true danger. I knew only that Mabel had struck Pearl once already. I knew that strange feeling I had had whenever in Mabel's company from the moment she rushed back into our lives.

Portsmouth was the town on the northernmost tip of Aquidneck Island, where the island comprised mostly of Newport ended in a curl of land around a large cove. It had been nothing but coal mines until a few years ago and Mabel's husband had owned one of those mines. That was how he had made his money, or so Mabel had told us.

I knew nothing about where on Portsmouth Mabel lived. We had never visited as we said we would. Was that enough to make her so very angry, to bring her to violence? No, I didn't think so and I didn't need to try to figure out where she lived.

I had seen the sign, seen the "Washburn" name on the gate as we approached the very first trolley stop once in Portsmouth. A portion of land stretched out beyond the gate as far as my eye could see, the land Mabel had told us her husband attempted to turn into a farm. Little of that mattered. What did was that it was at the beginning of Portsmouth, not around the whole cove at the tip.

"You're gonna get yourself killed!" The trolley conductor squawked at me as I jumped off before he brought it to a full stop. I didn't bother to acknowledge his warning. I stumbled away.

I ran for the gate. I could just see a few glimpses of the large ochre stone house at the end of a long drive. I saw no workers in the fields. I saw no children at play, though it was a beautiful day and Mabel had a great many children.

I ran for the house. I ran and, as I did, I realized I had no idea what I would do when I got there. Could my appearance push Mabel toward more violence? It was the last thing I wanted. Were they even here? Had Mabel brought Pearl here or somewhere else? The one thing I did know was that I had nowhere else to start.

The closer I got the more I saw truth unspoken by any words. Beautiful flowering bushes in front of the tall windows of the first floor sprouted overgrowth or haphazard withered sprigs, toys spattered with mud lay here and there on the ground, their pathetic appearance crying out for attention they hadn't had in many a day. And that land, all that land that was supposed to be a farm, lay fallow and ignored, pathetic with its growth burnt to waning yellow by the sun and untended by any hand.

"Something has happened to Mabel's family," I muttered to myself, panting, thinking, running. For a woman of delicate nerves – a woman like Mabel – it could be the trigger to send those nerves into frenzies.

"Get up, I said!"

The scream tore through the afternoon stillness like shears through thin linen. Mabel's scream.

The house stood only a few steps before me. I heard no answer from Pearl, all I heard was my footsteps on the gravel drive. I jumped off it on to the dirt. I heard my steps no longer.

"*Grazie, Dio,*" I whispered. Those overgrown bushes in front of the windows were worthy of my thanks to God. They were all open, beckoning any breeze the heat of the day may offer… they allowed me to hear that scream. They could give me a glimpse into the house –

into whatever may be happening in there – without being seen.

The bushes rustled, complaining as I disturbed them, but they did not complain too loudly. I threw my hat and its far-too-visible plume to the ground.

Through the first window, I saw only a large foyer with not a single piece of furniture, neither a coat rack nor console.

A large drawing room, walls dressed in beautiful maroon brocade, I viewed through the second window. I saw only a single chair, not a glimpse of Mabel or Pearl. But I did see dust, a waft of swirling dust. It meant one thing… movement.

I moved to the next window.

I clamped both hands on my mouth, a gag of my own making, one so horridly necessary.

I'd found them, found her.

Mabel stood over Pearl, a knife in her hands. Pearl struggled to stand, arms tied at the wrists with wounds of rope. And her face, *Dio mio,* her face. The deep red bruises, the swelling. I bit my hands – it was that or a scream.

"I-I'm trying," Pearl croaked. "I am… so weak."

She fell back down upon the floor. Mabel kicked her. Kicked her!

My shock and fear exploded into rage. I glanced over my shoulder, desperate for any sign of Osborn and Officer O'Leary. A wasted glance.

"You lie!" Mabel screamed. Birds fluttered from the treetops in fear.

"If I c-could just have a little more water," Pearl whimpered, "just a little more. It could help."

Yes, it could. It could give enough time for the men to arrive, it could give me enough time to find a way into the house without Mabel knowing it.

275

"What a Dumb Dora you are," Mabel jeered, stomping out of the room and out of my sight.

With barely a pause, with swollen eyes closed, Pearl set her teeth to the rope on her wrists, forehead wrinkling with effort and pain. She made little progress, stopped, and slumped. Mabel's footsteps grew louder again.

"Here. Drink it. And be quick about it."

Pearl drank, sloshing water on herself and the floor as the tied hands holding the glass shook.

A sigh. The close of her eyes. A moment's respite.

"Where-where are you... are we going?" she asked between sips.

"Why, to that Minnie's house, of course," Mabel quipped. "It's a mansion, or so I hear. Money always marries money. She got the house and the money. Plenty for my man and my children. That witch," Mabel cursed, cast one; she'd become a witch. "I said hurry up."

Pearl moaned. "I c-can't. My stomach."

Mabel dropped to her knees and grabbed the glass with one hand. With the other, she grabbed Pearl's mouth, wrenching it open, pouring the water down Pearl's throat.

Pearl coughed and spluttered... then heaved. The water and whatever she had eaten that day exploded from her mouth, all over her, all over Mabel, all over the floor.

"Stupid bitch!" Mabel exploded, jumping up and away from the still retching Pearl, her wretched dress covered in putrid chunks and liquid. "I have to clean up, clean you up now, before we can go." She stomped away again, still muttering to herself.

My poor Pearl, how badly I felt for her misery, how glad I was for it. It sent the witch off to fetch her broom.

With one last look down the long drive, yet another empty gaze, I made for the front door. The handle didn't budge. My fingernails bit into my palms as my frustration did my mind. There had to be a back door, but it looked as if Mabel had gone to the back of the house. I couldn't be sure of either. I went.

I spied a door, down at the furthest corner of the back of the large house, just before a trellis of the same height as the building it lay upon. The ground was nothing but dirt and weeds; my footsteps would not be heard.

I made for the door, ducking at each window I passed, peeping into them. I saw nothing in any of them. Wherever Mabel was, I could not see her through a single one of them.

I almost crowed, reaching the door undetected. But then I almost sobbed – the handle wouldn't turn. I lay my body against the building, head against the stone, shoulder poked by a trellis arm.

A trellis arm. I picked my head up, put my hand on the arm, and pulled down; it didn't move.

"*Sono pazzo.*" As I picked up my skirts, as I tied them as best I could around my hips, I knew I must be crazy even to be thinking of doing what I was about to do. There was nothing else *to* do.

I climbed up the first steps up the rungs of the trellis easily. I moved faster. A foolish move. The trellis swayed. Would it tip? I slowed down. It was so hard to go slow, so hard not to see Pearl – battered and bruised – vomiting all over herself, over and over in my mind.

I reached the second-floor window next to the trellis. It was closed. "Of course it is," I hissed to myself in frustration. I prayed my attempt to gain entry wouldn't end there. "Amen," I sighed. The window wasn't locked.

Shimmying closer to it, curling one of my arms around a rung of the trellis to secure myself as best I could, I used my other hand to raise the window slowly.

Pearl

"You are taking m-me to Minnie's?" I couldn't trust my mind any longer. Lack of food and water, the battering of my head, my thoughts whirled. "Is that what you said?"

"It is," Mabel deadpanned as she cleaned my vomit from my skirt, her own damp but clean.

"But-but whatever are you g-going to do when we get there?"

She laughed, a vile sound. I winced, at the pain it caused, at the insanity it promised.

"*I* am not going to do anything." Finished with her cleaning, Mabel stood and stepped back. With hands on hips, she gloated. "You are going to do it. You are going to take this gun—"

"Don't, please!" I screamed at the sight of the black, oily metal weapon she pulled from her skirt pocket.

Mabel kicked me again, just hard enough to get me to take my still tied hands away from my face. I had thrown them there as if they could stop a bullet from blowing a hole in my stomach, my heart.

"Shut up!" Mabel bellowed. "I'm not going to shoot you. You are going to shoot Minnie."

I might as well have taken that bullet to the heart.

Ginevra

Somehow I caught myself, somehow I kept my body from crashing on the floor after wriggling through the half-opened window. I couldn't get it any further open. I almost fell to the ground getting it even halfway open. A loud thump on the floor and anything I tried to do for Pearl would be quickly undone.

With my hands on the floor, my legs still half out the window, I crept slowly further through on my palms. When only my toes remained outside, I brought first one foot in and then the other, slowly placing them on the floor. For the shortest of moments, I stood in silent gratitude. Then I took a step.

The thud of my heel upon wood sounded like the clang of a fire carriage bell.

I stopped again. Didn't move again. Waiting, sure Mabel had heard it. Excruciating seconds ticked by. I heard no footfalls on the stairs. I heard no screeching voice coming for me.

Bending over, I untied my boots, put them in my hands to carry. I looked at them in my hands, studied them. I saw them as something else. They were no longer shoes, but a tool and a weapon.

I crept to the door, peeked my head out of it, and looked down the long corridor to the left. There it was, the top of the staircase, the beginning of the steps that would lead me down to them. My tiptoed movements began.

"I-I cannot." It was Pearl's voice I heard. "I cannot kill someone, Mabel. There must b-be another way."

I almost tumbled down the stairs I had just reached. *Kill someone?* Insanity's shroud had fallen on us again. Would it always?

"There is no other way," Mabel's voice resounded as a high, piercing screech. "Jackson will see how deranged you are, how you dragged me to Minnie's house."

Mabel's screeching never ceased. Good. I used it. Used the sheer volume of the sound to make my way down the stairs ever so slowly, still on tiptoes. A large, gothic-shaped window over the door let the sunlight in, let me see down the drive. I saw no help on its way.

Below the balustrade, the hall ran past and around to the back of the stairs and whatever it may lead to from there. At the bottom of the stairs lay my first goal – the foyer. Its emptiness opened to two archways, one off each side. But which did I need?

"You will tell Jackson just what a terrible thing she did to me, to our children."

Mabel's blaring bellows led me to them.

"You will tell him that he must come back to me or you will shoot Minnie, you will kill her for the sake of your dear college friend."

"But-but you can't make me," Pearl's every word bounded off a sob. "You won't be able to f-force me to, n-not in front of them."

I made it halfway down the stairs. I heard them better, almost certain they were in the room on the right. If I did not have my shoes in my hand, I would have smacked my head. Of course they were in the room on the right; it was through windows to the left of the door that I had seen them. The other must be a formal dining room. It was how such homes were set – I knew, right then I knew what I would do. I continued my slither down.

Mabel laughed, the sound of a braying broken beast.

"I really don't know why everyone thinks you're so smart, Pearl Worthington Wright," she bit down on the final "t". "I will still have this. Either you kill Minnie or I kill you."

The knife. She still has the knife.

Just a few more steps.

"I can't, I can't, I can't," Pearl groaned again and again. "My daughter, my Mary, you will make her an orphan."

"You don't care about your daughter. Suffs don't care about their children at all. Everyone knows it's true. We said it, we antis, motherhood must come first. If you had put motherhood first, you'd be with your daughter this very minute."

I made it. My stockinged feet stepped off the last step, on to the floor. Somehow I moved a ghost.

"I-I did it for her, and for the daughter she might have one day."

I dared a peek into the room just as Mabel's open palm collided with Pearl's face, as Pearl's lip split wide, as blood gushed from it.

I could wait no longer.

I took two steps back... and threw one of my boots into the opposite room.

"Shut up, shut up, shut up!" Mabel bellowed. "Did you hear that?"

Her footsteps came at me, faster and faster. I ran as fast as I could, ran around the stairs, ducking in the slanted cubby beneath them, head perched on the corner of the wall, one eye peering out.

Mabel – a frightening specter of her – rushed out the one room, making for the other.

In a crouch, on stockinged toes, I made for her.

Mabel stood in the archway of the dining room, back to the foyer, head twitching this way and that. "Who's there?"

I snuck up behind her, raised the one shoe still in my hand, the hard wooden, two-inch heel pointed down like a knife.

Anger and fear made my arm tremble.

I closed my eyes, grit my teeth, and plunged it downward.

Only the sound of her grunt, of her body slumping upon the floor, opened my eyes again.

Mabel lay motionless at my stockinged feet. Dead or alive, I didn't care a whit.

I ran in the opposite direction. I ran to Pearl.

"Ginevra?" She stared at me yet not at me, at the disbelief of me. "Are you—?"

"*Sì, sì.* I'm here, dearest." I couldn't look straight at her, couldn't bear the brutality that marred her face… that rendered her so weak. I set upon the ropes, a struggle but a short one.

"Come, Pearl. Come. We must get out of here."

I put her arms around my neck.

"Ready?" I did look at her then, looked into her swollen eyes. They looked but barely saw, so unfocused they wavered in their sockets. "You just hold as tight as you can to me, I do the rest. One, two…"

I used every bit of strength in my legs to lift us both. Pearl hung on though her head hung back loosely on her neck.

Turning my body within the circle of her arms, I brought the brunt of her weight upon my back and made for the door.

"Are you with me, Pearl? You have to stay awake. We must-a get out of here." I looked over my shoulder at her even as I dragged her through the room, even as I brought us to the—

"You'll not be going anywhere."

Death itself stood before us, between us and the door, and it wore Mabel's face. It had a gun in its hand, aimed straight for us.

"I should have known you'd come, wop," Mabel plied an insult, a stupid one, one that did not apply to me. I had papers – I was a citizen. "Two peas in a…"

Mabel wavered. Her lids dropped; her head waggled on her neck, a neck that had a trickle of blood running down it.

"You're no good to me now, either of you."

Mabel raised the gun.

"Stop!" I shouted. "You can't—"

A bang, a crash.

The door burst open, smacking Mabel's back.

Her body lurched forward, thrown by a giant hand. Her arms flayed.

The gun exploded, light and sound blasted.

I closed my eyes, dropped to the floor, Pearl with me.

"Do naht move an inch."

I knew that voice, that accent.

I opened my eyes.

Officer O'Leary stood above Mabel, stood on Mabel, one foot at least. His own gun trained on her back, right where her heart would be. Behind him, I saw my Osborn.

I did not try to get Pearl and me to our feet. I slumped fully on the floor. All the tears of all my fears flowed freely at last.

"*Grazie, Dio.* Thank you, God."

Pearl

I still cannot tell you why women do what they do to each other. In comparison to men, we love each other deeper… but we wound each other deeper still. But this I do know, if we do not stand together, we sure as hell will sit alone and wither for the rest of our lives.

Pearl

January 7, 1920

The cameras flashed, their pop, pop, pops almost drowning out the words of Governor Robert Livingston Beekman as he signed the ratification document. I wanted to hear everything he had to say. He had matched our courage with his, calling for a special legislative session of 1920 to start a day earlier than the official opening of the governing body, called it specifically for them to vote on ratification. That the governor was a Newporter, still dashing at fifty-four, was an added benefit for the four of us from the Political Equality Association who had been invited – who had been honored – to witness this moment.

In truth, I was proud of the entire legislative body of our state. The ratification had passed with an 89 to 3 vote in the House and a 39 to 1 vote in the Senate. Such overwhelming numbers told a story of their own, not only a story of how well we fought this fight but a story of all the men who supported us. Even those we had lost in the process.

On one side of me stood Sarah Eddy and Maud Howe Elliott. On the other stood Ginevra. How many times we would save each other, I could not know. I prayed for no more. I would not be here if it were not for her. I would not be here without her.

The tips of my fingers, the tips of my toes tingled, drowning out the itch of the wound upon my forehead that was now in its last stage of healing.

"I have never seen a more determined, a more cohesive campaign in all my years, ladies," Beekman gave us a broad smile full of bright, white teeth. "I may need to hire some of you for my next campaign."

He stopped… stopped smiling, stopped talking. He peered up at all of us.

"I want to tell you all, I hope you know, how well deserved this is, how every woman in our country will soon and should know true citizenship and active participation in *our* country, in *your* country."

True citizenship. Oh yes, we had earned that. And finally, though scarred, though tired, we were and from this moment on, to be true citizens of these United States.

His serious words spoken, the Governor bent his head and with his sparkling gold pen, signed the document of ratification of the 19th Amendment.

More than one woman cried though they tried to hide it. I squeezed Ginevra's hand. I knew what ran through her, a surge of an electric current, for it matched my own.

The Governor stood, seeing us out of the dark-paneled room. He shook the hand of every woman who filed past him, his clerk handing out gold pens that matched the one with which the Governor had signed the ratification. From the moment it came into my hand, I clutched it to my chest.

"You are well healed from your ordeal, Mrs. Wright?" The tall Beekman leaned down. His words were for me and me alone, though Ginevra did as she would, leaning in to hear.

"Not completely, sir," I answered honestly, "but this…" I lofted the pen, "this will do much to finish the job."

Beekman turned his pleased smile on Ginevra. "And you, Mrs. Taylor, you are the epitome of the American story, are you not?"

Ginevra tilted her head. "Your pardon?"

"Well, let's see," the Governor ticked his fingers off one by one. "An immigrant who became a servant who weathered cruelty of an unholy sort, a college graduate, a successful business owner, a suffragette, a loving wife and mother, and…" His smile reached his eyes, his gaze skipping to me then quickly back to her. "…And a savior of lives. You are a hero, in my eyes."

I thought she would not respond; I thought she could not. Once more, she proved me wrong.

"Grazie, Governatore."

How I loved that she spoke in her native tongue, how I admired her insightful intelligent perception.

"But is it not what a true citizen of these United States is supposed to be?"

Beekman threw back his hand, laughing with delight. "Indeed, it is."

We moved along, giving those women in the line behind us their turn with the Governor, though Beekman continued to chortle.

As we walked out onto the blazing white stone steps of the State House, we found a horde of more photographers, more newspaper writers.

"How do you feel, ladies?"

"Tell us what this means to you?"

"Do you believe the amendment will be federally ratified?"

They hurled their questions at us without a moment's pause, without a crack to allow an answer.

Mary B. Anthony, the lead representative of the Rhode Island Equal Suffrage Association, stepped forward, raised her hands, and kept them in the air until the questions ceased, until the quiet space for an answer became hers.

"It is with a feeling of profound satisfaction that I realize that Rhode Island has ratified. 'Little Rhody' is a fine State and here is the proof."

The women behind Mary cheered and applauded. The cameras before her flashed, pencils scribbled.

I thought she would say more but she did not. Oh, how I wish she had.

Instead, she stepped aside and turned to me.

"It's your turn, Pearl," she whispered.

My mouth filled with sand. I had planned nothing, expected to need nothing. To be there, to live that moment, was enough.

I gave her a barely perceptible shake of my head.

Mary gave me a mischievous, shy smile and a push.

I found myself front and center before the press, before the notebooks and flashing cameras.

I shoved them from my mind. I thought only of what I was feeling, the satisfaction, and the hope that grew like our beloved beech trees, reaching – striving – ever upward. I stepped up with my chin in the air.

"Rhode Island has opened wide her privileges to women. It remains now for the women to prove that they are ready to take up the responsibilities accorded to them and prepare themselves to work with their husbands, brothers, and sons to make the state, our state, one that shall be worthy of the long task and sacrifice of the many noble women who, through nearly a century, have fought for, have suffered for, the political freedom of womanhood."

The four of us were so quiet as we rode the train back to the ferry, especially strange for the talkative Sarah. The brilliance of this moment, in our lives and the life of our country, overwhelmed us all, shone brighter than any of our words could express. We closed our eyes and basked silently in the glow of it.

"I have an errand I'd like to see to when we return to the island," I mumbled to Ginevra in the seat beside me. I don't know if she opened her eyes for I didn't. "I was wondering if you'd come with me."

"Of course," came her soft reply. "Where are we off to?"

"Portsmouth," I said simply.

I did not need to open my eyes to know that hers were most definitely now open.

"This is a bit of insanity, no?" Ginevra asked as we made our way down the long gravel drive.

I didn't answer. I was too busy noticing all the changes.

Row upon row of crops, asleep in these winter months, striped land that once lay unsown and untended. The bushes had been trimmed, the toys picked up, and a beautiful evergreen wreath hung on the new front door, welcoming any who came before it. Few did.

"Perhaps," I mused. "But what we witnessed today, what we achieved this day, brought me many thoughts." I kicked the gravel at my feet, feeling it bite through the thin leather sole of my boot. "Yes, a great many thoughts, of justice served. I don't believe justice has been served here exactly as it ought."

Mabel Washburn, though arrested and charged with kidnapping and assault, would never see the inside of a court, nor that of a jail other than the small holding cell in the police station. I took the news first with a flinch followed by a shrug, for I knew the truth of her, and it agreed with the decision of the court. Any semblance of sanity that remained within Mabel had been stomped out, not only by Officer O'Leary's foot upon her back but mostly by the failure of her husband to bail her out of jail, his refusal to pay for any legal representation whatsoever. Not a single member of her family in Virginia came to her, to see to her. They, too, deserted her. And she had been destroyed by the condemnation of almost everyone who knew her or knew of her on the island.

While I could never, would never, forgive her for what she had done to me, the trauma she had perpetrated on my daughter, there was a small place in my mind that understood. I had been a first-hand witness to the damage that men and women can do to each other.

Our knock upon the door was answered by a jovial Minnie Johnson, soon to be Minnie Washburn. Her smile withered like the frosted crops in the field at the sight of us.

"Good afternoon, Minnie," I said brightly. "We thought we'd stop by and welcome you to our island."

"I... um..." Minnie's cupid bow of a mouth fluttered with little upon her tongue.

"Might Jackson be at home? I would wish just a quick word with him."

"Minnie mine?" A deep base voice echoed through the foyer now resplendent with rug, console, paintings, and tapestries. "Who's there?"

Half-pinned hair whirling, following the snap of her head, Minnie still seemed incapable of forming words. In answer to her soon-to-be husband, she simply stepped back, opening the door wider.

I smiled broadly as his gaze fell upon me, as his merriment vanished like the sun when a storm raged in.

"Good afternoon, Jackson," I called, stepping through the threshold without invitation. Ginevra followed but with only one step.

"L-ladies," Jackson Washburn had grown stouter since last I saw him; I was glad to see it. "How may we be of service?"

"Oh, it is we who have come to be of service to you," I chittered. "We have heard of your plans to marry, the two of you." How proud would my mother have been, not for what I did, but for the way I did it. "Of course, it will have to wait until your divorce from Mabel is finalized."

"Now see here," Jackson found some manhood. "She has been

judged unstable. I have every right to find some happiness in this life."

"*Stronzo,*" Ginevra hissed behind me. That one I knew and I knew too that Jackson greatly resembled that particular part of the human body.

"You do. Of course, you do. Both of you." I reached out and patted Minnie's hand. She pulled it back as if my touch scalded her. "You had no part in what happened to me, in what Mabel did. All *you* did was to cheat on her, take her children away, leaving her destitute, and abandoned the mother of your many children in the hour of her greatest need."

"You have no right—" Minnie found her tongue at last – too late.

"Hush," I snapped at her. "*You* took another man's husband, lay with him, I have no doubt."

Minnie sucked air, a hand fluttered to her chest.

"I told the police and the judge, I told them all." I turned to Ginevra. "Well, I had to, didn't I?"

She played along; she had figured out my justice. She raised both hands in the air, palms up. "You had no choice."

"See?" I turned back to the dazed couple. "I only came here today to tell you what my wedding present will be, though I'm sure you won't be inviting me to the event."

"You're damned—"

"I will give you what you gave Mabel." I would not be stopped now; I would not pause. The raging fire within me demanded me not too. "I will tell the whole of society for, as Pearl Worthington Wright, I still have a place in it. I will tell them everything I told the authorities." I stepped closer to them. I wanted to see their eyes. "You will receive what you gave Mabel... ostracism, desertion, perhaps even destitution."

"If God is good," Ginevra contributed.

Jackson and Minnie reeled. Her hand on his arm did little good as he was as unsteady as she.

"I do wish you both a very happy marriage." With that, I turned, wound my arm about Ginevra's, and made for the door.

We were at the bottom of the four front steps when our goodbye came.

"Go!" Jackson yowled, an injured animal. "Go chase yourself! Never darken my door again!"

"Hah!" I turned. "Why in the world would I ever step another foot in a house of such ill repute?"

Ginevra and I continued our stroll down the drive, a barrage of colorful epithets bouncing off our backs, falling to the ground without hitting their mark.

Ginevra

August 18, 1920

There was only one place to go, only one place we should go to mark the moment.

With our children, children on the cusp of adulthood, we walked to The Beeches. Vibrancy and new life buzzed in the hot summer air, as if it crackled with the news, with the wind of change that blew through the nation as the breeze did the tops of our trees.

Only Pearl and I climbed the waiting limb, now both of us of forty-two years, we climbed lower and lower. Felix, Angelina, and Mary sat in one of the teahouses, pretending a high tea, acting older while giggling younger.

Pearl unfurled the many times rolled and unrolled paper. Together we stared at the picture splashed across the front of it. A man – one named Lansing, the Secretary of State of the entire country – sat before a wide desk signing a piece of paper with a semicircle of smiling women standing behind him. But it wasn't just a piece of paper, nor would it ever be.

"Read it to me again," I begged Pearl. I closed my eyes as she did.

"*The right of citizens of the United States to vote shall not be denied or abridged by the United States or by any State on account of sex. Congress shall have power to enforce this article by appropriate legislation.*" Her voice grew stronger, louder, with each word.

"Thirty-nine," I said.

"Pardon?"

I opened my eyes to her confusion. "It is only thirty-nine words

293

and yet it will change the lives of every woman in the land."

Pearl chortled in her throat, leaning back to rest against the trunk of our tree. We watched as Felix picked a few of the array of flowers that grew in the edged garden between the two teahouses. We watched as he made a fanfare of presenting them to Mary, play-acting the role of suitor come to call. We watched his face, Mary's face.

"I don't think he only acts," I said, with an equal measure of surprise and wonder.

Pearl laughed outright. "Nor do I."

We knew so many forms of hope that day.

"Susan B. Anthony, Elizabeth Cady Stanton, Lucretia Mott."

Pearl puzzled me with the names, but only at first. Then I joined her in her prayers.

"Lucy Stone, Paulina Wright Davis, Amelia Bloomer."

We spoke of and to only those who had passed on, who had fought the same fight as we had but who had not survived to see this day of triumph.

"Sojourner Truth, Harriet Tubman, Julia Ward Howe."

"Frederick Douglass." I would not leave out the men, those who had believed in the cause from the first for, if we did, we became like the men who didn't. "Henry Brown Blackwell, Thomas M'Clintock."

We called out to all those we could remember. We prayed to those we couldn't.

"Did you think...?"

I shook my head. "Honestly? No."

Pearl laughed. "How terrible it must be to admit you were wrong."

I swatted her arm. Together we laughed, together our minds traveled back and forward.

"It is an end to an extraordinary fight," Pearl sighed, face aglow in the bright magenta of the lowering sun.

I answered with what I thought to be the truth.

"It is only the beginning."

Maria

1964

"What did you say it is called again?" Grandmother Pearl asked me, for the third time. I couldn't lose my patience with those rosy cheeks of hers beaming at me.

"The Equal Rights Amendment, Grandmother," I said, putting my gaze back upon the pages before me, pages and pages covered in ink, words upon words upon words, still not enough of them to capture the fullness of these women's lives, the boldness of them as they stood against every wind that would dare buffet them. They stood against blast after blast of it. They raised their hands, unafraid, and met each one with equal force. It was their story... and mine. "Your amendment brought women the vote, but we are still not paid the same, treated the same in the workplace or college. But this is an amendment for equal rights for all, women and men. For true equality."

"Equality," Nonni Ginevra sighed the word. "You fight for it, *sì?*"

"I do, Nonni... we do." I smiled and patted her hand, turning quickly back to the pages in front of me. "Tell me about that first time." I needed to bring these elderly though still sharp minds back into focus. "Tell me about the first time you cast a vote."

Nonni laughed. "Your grandmother here sobbed liked a baby."

"I did not!" Grandmother protested, then lowered her head as those cheeks grew rosier. "Perhaps a tear or two."

"Ah, *sì*, I told you," Nonni jeered with a loving wink, bright eyes as sharp as I ever remembered them being.

Together they told me... told me of the long lines, the insults hurled at them as they stood in them, of putting pen to paper, and yes, of crying tears of joy.

My vision blurred with a few of my own, but I was so damned proud of them, so proud of what they did, so proud to be their granddaughter.

"Did you celebrate afterward?" I asked, looking at each in turn.

"We did," Grandmother replied.

"Where did you go? What did you do?" I waited to put my pen back upon the page, but then I looked up, then I saw their amused if barbed stares on me. I answered my own question. "To the trees. You went to the trees."

Nonni patted my hand as if I was four years old rather than twenty-four.

"Are they still there?" she asked. "Are our trees still standing?"

"Yes, Nonni, they're still there."

"Are the children playing in them?" Grandmother pestered me.

"Yes, Grandmother. All your grandchildren and great-grandchildren play beneath the beeches."

It took all I had not to laugh or perhaps cry. They've been asking me that since we began this project together four years ago. I hated to think of the day when I wouldn't hear one of them, or either of them, ask it.

I made a few more scribbles in what was my tenth, thick notebook.

"Is that it, Grandmother? Nonni?"

"Indeed."

"*Sì, e finito.*"

I stood and helped each one to do the same. Each at the age of eighty-six, they had learned to accept such help graciously.

Nonni Ginevra reached out and took Grandmother Pearl's hand

with the ease of having done so for a lifetime.

"As Alva Vanderbilt Belmont would have said," Grandmother Pearl's age-warbled voice held a chuckle, "let them think of us what they will."

The End

"For too long, women were formally excluded from full participation in our society and our democracy. Because of the courage of so many bold women who dared transcend preconceived expectations and prove they were capable of doing all that a man could do and more,
advances were made,
discoveries were revealed,
barriers were broken,
and progress triumphed."

President Barack Obama proclaiming
Women's History Month in 2016

Author's Note

I never intended to write a sequel to GILDED SUMMERS, but the often-expressed desire for it from my readers made me consider it. In order for me to write any book, I must have a historical event that I am passionate about to wrap the story around. In the case of this book, it had to be an event that was a logical extension of the lives of Pearl and Ginevra. The 100th Anniversary of the passage of the 19th Amendment cried out to me for its historical significance. This book, at its core, is a celebration of that anniversary; it is a call for every woman to don the colors of gold, white, and purple on August 18, 2020, and celebrate the achievement made on that day one hundred years ago.

It also carries great personal significance. I grew up in the 1960s when the fight for rights – civil rights, racial rights, women's rights – was at the forefront of the news. I soaked it in like a sponge. Some might call me a radical feminist but it would not be the truth. I am a radical equalitist. It is my deepest belief that no human should ever be judged by their gender, the color of their skin, the amount of money in their bank account, or any other criteria except that of their behavior, their kindness and generosity to others, and their achievements alone. If I were a politician (heaven help me from that), I would demand that every application, whether it be for college entrance or any professional position or job, be completely devoid of such markers, that neither gender nor race could be identified, that only the applicant's grades and previous experience be the criteria upon which their application is reviewed. It is a dream, my dream, and one I shall probably not live to see. But when I leave this mortal plane,

I will do so knowing I did my best, what I could, to move humanity to such a just and equitable place.

I owe many thanks to Miika Hannila and every member of the Next Chapter Publishing team for supporting me and encouraging me to write this sequel, to help me get it written and published in the shortest amount of time I have ever done any of my books.

I can never thank Phillip Senecal, Linda Nott, Laura Murphy, Cynthia O'Malley, and everyone at the Preservation Society of Newport County for their unwavering support and the amazing number of opportunities they gave me to reach the thousands and thousands of visitors to Newport—from both America and many other nations—to put GILDED SUMMERS in so many readers' hands, the very readers who kept asking for this sequel.

To the Historical Fiction Authors crew… you are the best! And though we don't sit at desks side by side, though we don't stand around the "water cooler" together, you are always by my side and your support and friendship is something I will always treasure.

To my local friends – the gang of wonderful ladies I'm blessed to call friend – thank you for checking on me when I don't leave the house for days at a time; thank you for forcing me to get out of the house now and again.

To my readers… I think of you with every word I write and I thank you for giving me the platform to write them.

To my family, thank you for putting up with the craziness, the uncertainty, of living with a "creative". And most especially to my extraordinary sons. Devon and Dylan, you have become the sort of men I had always dreamed, always hoped you would be… intelligent, accomplished, loving, kind, and, most of all, believers in equal justice for all. You are true gentlemen in every sense of the word and you make me proud each and every day.

And lastly but foremost, I thank the women who fought this fight, the fight for suffrage and those whom I watched (and still watch) fight for equal pay for equal work, for "our seat at the table". We stand on your shoulders.

To the women and men who read this, do not let their fight be in vain. Make yourselves and your actions worthy for those who come after us to stand upon our shoulders and reach ever higher.

WHAT IS FACT AND WHAT IS FICTION
GILDED DREAMS

The people named as victims of the sinking of the Titanic, the Newporters, are historically correct. There were, in truth, more of them that appears in this book. Many are buried in Newport's historic cemeteries.

Everything about the Titanic body recovery and identification process is true as depicted, including the incident with the undertaker, Frank Newell. While the story and the horrors of the actual event are well known, little is ever spoken about, no movies extoll, the domino of horror that came after, that would haunt thousands of family members who had to find a way past the truth of the ravaging, unnecessary deaths of their loved ones. Please see the bibliography to delve deeper into this information.

Pearl's legal status (or lack thereof), as she was informed by her family lawyer, was indeed the law of the day. The laws of the day in terms of women's rights, or again the lack thereof, should be a matter of study for all so that we may see how far women's rights have progressed... and how far they haven't. Please see the bibliography for further reading.

Much of the dialogue attributed to Alva Vanderbilt Belmont, such as her comments to Pearl at the funeral and her speeches at suffrage meetings, came out of words she herself had written, either in her memoirs, letters, or newspaper articles.

Half-sisters Anna and Laura Tirocchi were indeed Italian immigrants who owned and operated a fashion house in Providence, Rhode Island from 1911 to 1947. A & L Tirocchi Gowns, also known as *Di Renaissance,* specialized in custom-designed, sumptuous gowns for the city's elite women. The sisters consistently hired Italian immigrants or daughters of them as seamstresses, or "girls" as the custom of the age referred to them. Their shop closed upon Anna's death in 1947 and in 1989, Laura's son donated the contents of their house – including some completed, opulent gowns – to the Rhode Island School of Design and the University of Rhode Island.

The particular US Open that Pearl and Ginevra's husbands traveled to watch did take place. Francis Ouimet, a native of Massachusetts and a golfer of amateur status, is a factual historical person. His remarkable story was beautifully depicted in the movie, *The Greatest Game Ever Played* (Walt Disney Pictures, 2005).

The Great Friends Meeting House – as it is known today – is a meeting house of the Religious Society of Friends (Quakers) built in 1699 in Newport, Rhode Island. The meeting house, which is part of the Newport Historic District, is currently open as a museum owned by the Newport Historical Society. It is the oldest surviving house of worship in Rhode Island.

There were anti-suffrage groups – women who strenuously opposed women gaining the vote – in at least five major countries. In the United States, they began to form as early as the 1870s. In addition to many state-formed organizations, the National Association Opposed to Woman Suffrage, the main party of opposition, had local chapters in even more states. The "antis" numbered in the tens of thousands.

The Political Equality Association, PEA, was established by Alva Vanderbilt Belmont. Its headquarters did reside at 128 Bellevue Avenue. The building no longer stands as it did then.

The conference depicted at Marble House is actually a merging of the two events Alva hosted there; the one in 1914 as well as the one in 1909. I have chosen to depict them as merged to show the lengths

AVB went to in her personal fight for suffrage and to give the reader a more entertaining picture of this affair. She did charge for admission and she did charge a higher price for those who wished to tour Marble House, an act looked upon as scandalous by many in the "set". The china used has continued to be reproduced and is available at any of the Newport mansion gifts shops or online.

Julia Ward Howe had died two years before the second conference, passing away in 1910 at the age of 91 at her home in Portsmouth, Rhode Island. Ms. Howe had been present at the first conference in 1909 and my esteem for her demanded that I include her "presence" at the conference depicted. Her daughter, Maud Howe Elliot, stood for her mother at the 1914 conference.

Mrs. Margaret Brown, the most famous of the Titanic survivors was an attendee at the Marble House conference. From 1913 to 1920, Mrs. Brown rented Mon Etui – small and more resembling of a true cottage – at 44 Bellevue Avenue owned by the Muenchinger-King Hotel. According to the *Newport Herald*, Margaret Brown was welcomed and revered by Newport society.

The Una, originally published in Providence, Rhode Island, was the first newspaper wholly owned and operated by women in the United States.

Melinda and Her Sisters is an actual suffrage operetta – or what we would call a short suffrage musical – written by Alva Vanderbilt Belmont and Elsa Maxwell. Alva also produced the single performance at the Waldorf Astoria on the night of February 18, 1916, singlehandedly. It was never performed in Newport until the Preservation Society of Newport County re-enacted it in August of 2010 in their celebration of the 90th anniversary of the 19th Amendment.

The entire German U-boat incident is completely factual, save for

Pearl's presence upon it, including that Americans gave the captain copies of the newspapers, that newspapers of a neutral country were, in those days, naïve enough to give detailed facts of on the types and locations of American ships, as well as those of other countries within American waters. Captain Rose, his ship and crew, did perpetrate the loss and causalities the very next day as cited in this book. It ought to be borne in mind that there was virtually no press censorship at the time because the United States was still a neutral nation. It was also common practice to print shipping news, the times of the comings and goings of cargo vessels – a nice piece of intelligence for a commerce raider on the prowl.

Sara Bard Field did work with Alva Vanderbilt Belmont to produce a memoir. It was one of three that Alva would produce with the help of other writers during her lifetime.

The Women's Column was a factual suffragette journal out of Boston. Alice Stone Blackwell was its editor. And the *Wise Girl* story did appear on its front page, in 1890. It was written by Ella Higginson. Many copies of the Women's Column are available online and at many of Boston's large libraries. They are worthy of our study and our praise.

The Night of Terror is a factual event and far worse than I have depicted it. I strongly encourage everyone – woman or man – to look up the detailed information on one of the darkest moments in our country's history. Read about it, discuss it, and perhaps someone may find a justifiable reason as to why this is not in the curriculum of every high school history class in the country.

The Dower law was a law that did exactly as it is explained within the context of this story. It was the law in almost every state and territory of the United States... until 1990. Read that again... 1990.

The Watch Fires of Liberty began burning in Washington, D. C. in January of 1919 and spread throughout the nation until June of that same year.

After failing five times to be passed in the Senate, over the course of so many years, the 19th Amendment did pass and by the vote stated in June of 1919.

The presence of suffragettes as Governor Robert Livingston Beekman ratified the amendment is at it happened. It was an honor repeated throughout each state as they ratified it. Mary B Anthony's statement to the press is historically accurate as depicted.

The words that Pearl speaks to the press in front of the State House of Rhode Island on January 7, 1920, the day the ratified amendment was signed by the governor, were taken from a letter sent from the vice-chairman of the Rhode Island Woman Suffrage Association, Annie H. Barus.

The 19th Amendment to the Constitution to the United States, once known as the Susan B. Anthony Amendment, is indeed only thirty-nine words long, the exact thirty-nine words that are quoted in this book. It was passed on August 18, 1920.

GILDED DREAMS
READING GROUP QUESTION GUIDES

Why was the mention of Pearl's mother the "mark" that broke Pearl's stony shock? Would this be considered a typical response to grief? If so, why? Or if not, why not?

While informative and engaging, what is the purpose of Pearl's loss of her entire family in the sinking of the Titanic? Is it merely a historically monumental event to mark the time setting of the story and to engage the reader quickly to the tale or does it have a deeper intention within the context of the story?

For readers both female and male, were you aware that one hundred years ago, married women had no entity in the eyes of law? If not, do you believe it is a part of women's history that should be taught in schools? Why or why not?

Pearl tells us that... *It was all right there, on every canvas I had covered with my paints… the question of who I am, what I am.* Why did she question her identity? Which two worlds did she live in? And why did this cause an internal struggle for her?

As Pearl and Ginevra are reading more about women's legal rights, or the lack thereof, it was stated of Ginevra that: "As an immigrant, her position was even more precarious than mine. We had learned that, were her husband to die, the government would send her back to Italy, a home she hadn't been to in almost twenty years, and without her children." Discuss the similarity to the laws of the land (at the time of this book's release). Does it represent a forward or backward movement in the handling of immigrants to the United States?

When the women attend their first suffrage meeting, Ginevra learns about the "antis", the women who opposed women getting the vote. Is it common knowledge that such organizations existed? Is it taught in schools? If not, why not?

Daniel Webster, a man devoted to the United States, who served it for much of his adult life, did say, *"It is by the promulgation of sound morals in the community, and more especially by the training and instruction of the young that woman performs her part toward the preservation of a free government."* Does this make him a man against women... a chauvinist or a misogynist? Why or why not? Discuss whether the use of such words was fair in the fight against suffrage.

Pearl asked Peter: "The real question, the only question, is this... does the artist create only that which would please others, make them money? Or is an artist's true calling to create what our soul tells us we must?" Discuss what is considered the right answer and/or what the correct answer is. Discuss agreements or disagreements

Pearl answers Ginevra's question about Pearl's mother. Discuss Pearl's answer: "I think there comes a time when we become old enough to see that our parents are not some sort of gods, that they are human with human faults and frailties." Is this true of all people? Why or why not? What are the effects of either event?

Discuss the implications and power of Dr. Anna Howard Shaw's famous quote, spoken at the Marble House conference: "A gentleman opposed to our enfranchisement once said to me, women have never produced anything of any value to the world. I told him the chief product of the women had been the men, and left it to him to decide whether the product was of any value." What is its most powerful message? If desired, return to her full speech.

Before their march in Newport, Ginevra tells us: "If one is lucky, there are moments in life that you know, not when looking back but when looking from within them, that what you do is a great thing, a powerful thing." Discuss what she meant by these words, their full implications. Discuss any first-hand experiences of the same sort as what she felt at that moment.

During the march, one of the women's hems catches fire. Who is it implied started the fire and how? As it is based on a factual occurrence during such a march, discuss the implications of it.

Do you agree or disagree with Ginevra's statement: "Is it truly not within a person's grasp to have it all, all that one desires, all that one dreams of, all that one willingly works hard for?" Discuss whether this is a quandary modern women must face as well or not.

From what can be gleaned of Alva Vanderbilt Belmont at this time in her life, discuss whether – if she did indeed know the truth of who murdered Herbert Butterworth in *Gilded Summers* – she would disapprove or not. Why or why not?

By the time America enters World War I, it has been made clear that both husbands knew the truth about the murder of Herbert Butterworth. Discuss the possible reasons why they never revealed their knowledge sooner. Is their acceptance of the truth surprising? Why or why not?

Discuss the events of the Night of Terror. Did you have any previous knowledge of this horrific moment in America's history? If so, from where did this knowledge come? If not, discuss the reasons for its lack.

In Peter's letter to Pearl, he wrote: *"We are not meant to leave this world worse than we came to it, my Pearl. No, we are blessed and cursed with a compulsion to leave it far better. To use the power of our times as the tools of change."* Discuss the validity of his statement: Are there people who are born with this "compulsion"? Why or why not? Who, in the modern-day, might be said to be such a person?

Did Mrs. Briggs's behavior, when she helped Ginevra find Peter's will, come as a surprise? Discuss the possible motives for such behavior and which is the most likely.

When Mabel is revealed as an anti and as the spy within the ranks of the suffragettes, did it come as a surprise? Discuss the validity of her actions.

Perhaps the most important discussion of all is the nature and status of women in America. Discuss how far that status has evolved since the passage of the 19th Amendment in 1920 and how far we still have to go in the year of this publication, 2020 and beyond.

GILDED DREAMS BIBLIOGRAPHY

BOOKS

Belmont, Alva, and Elsa Maxwell. *Melinda and Her Sisters*. Miami, FL: HardPress Publishing, Reprint 2012.

Conkling, Winifred. *VOTES FOR WOMEN!: American Suffragists and the Battle for the Ballot*. S.l.: Algonquin Books of Chapel Hill, 2020.

Hoffert, Sylvia D. *Alva Vanderbilt Belmont: Unlikely Champion of Women's Rights*. Bloomington: Indiana University Press, 2012.

Stanton, Elizabeth Cady, Susan B. Anthony, Matilda Joslyn Gage, and Ida Husted Harper. *History of Woman Suffrage*. Salem, NH: Ayer Co., 1985.

Weiss, Elaine F. *The Woman's Hour: The Great Fight to Win the Vote*. New York: Penguin Books, an imprint of Penguin Random House LLC, 2019.

ARTICLES: NEWSPAPERS/MAGAZINES/JOURNALS/WEBSITES

"A Woman of Genius." The Project Gutenberg eBook of A Woman Of Genius, by Mary Austin. Accessed February 6, 2020. http://www.gutenberg.org/files/38592/38592-h/38592-h.htm.

Barkhorn, Eleanor. 'Vote No on Women's Suffrage': Bizarre Reasons For Not Letting Women Vote." The Atlantic. Atlantic

Media Company, November 6, 2012.
https://www.theatlantic.com/sexes/archive/2012/11/vote-no-on-womens-suffrage-bizarre-reasons-for-not-letting-women-vote/264639/.

Bemis, Bethanee, "Mr. President, How Long Must Women Wait for Liberty?" Smithsonianmag.com January 12, 2017

Bort, Ina. Staff. "Suffrage on the Menu: The Marble House Conferences of 1909 and 1914." Behind The Scenes, April 21, 2017. http://behindthescenes.nyhistory.org/suffrage-menu-part-ii-marble-house-conferences/.

"Chronology of Woman Suffrage Movement Events." Scholastic. Accessed August 2, 2019. https://www.scholastic.com/teachers/articles/teaching-content/chronology-woman-suffrage-movement-events/.

Dolton, Tisha, Sally Lisk-Lewis, Tammy White, Caitlyn, Theresa Lanning, Joe DeFilippo, Tracey Tofield, and Denise. Woman Suffrage Memorabilia. Accessed September 22, 2019. http://womansuffragememorabilia.com/woman-suffrage-memorabilia/suffrage-journals/.

Harris & Ewing, Washington, D.C. Party Watchfires Burn Outside White House, Jan. United States Washington D.C, 1919. Jan. Photograph. https://www.loc.gov/item/mnwp000303/.

"History Bytes: Titanic Survivor in Newport." Newport Historical Society, September 21, 2011. https://newporthistory.org/history-bytes-titanic-survivor-in-newport/.

Korges, Wilson, "The Lasting Legacy of Suffragists at the Lorton Women's Workhouse." Smithsonian Magazine Online March 21, 2018.

"Lawshelf Educational Media." LawShelf Educational Media. Accessed September 2, 2019. https://lawshelf.com/courseware/entry/development-of-rights-of-women/.

Lunardini, C., & Knock, T. (1980). Woodrow Wilson and Woman Suffrage: A New Look. Political Science Quarterly, 95(4), 655-671. doi:10.2307/2150609

National American Woman Suffrage Association, "The Woman's Journal and Woman's Journal and Suffrage News", Boston : s.n., 1870-1917

National Endowment for the Humanities. "Chronicling America: Library of Congress." News about Chronicling America RSS. Accessed October 16, 2019. https://chroniclingamerica.loc.gov/newspapers/.

Rickard, J (21 August 2007), Champagne-Marne Offensive, 15-18 July 1918, http://www.historyofwar.org/articles/battles_champagne_marne.html

Robertson, Stephen. "Age of Consent Laws," in Children and Youth in History, Item #230, http://chnm.gmu.edu/cyh/items/show/230 (accessed October 4, 2019).

Salit, Richard. "TITANIC RHODE ISLAND TIES: Disaster's Ripples Still Felt by Passengers' Descendants." providencejournal.com. providencejournal.com, April 14, 2017. https://www.providencejournal.com/news/20170414/titanic-rhode-island-ties-disasters-ripples-still-felt-by-passengers-descendants.

Statewide Historical Preservation Report, N-N-1 and N-N-1; Rhode Island Historical Preservation Commission, March 1977

Suffragists Speak Timeline: 1918. Accessed August 16, 2019. http://groups.ischool.berkeley.edu/archive/suffragists/SuffragistsSpeak/1918timeline.html.

The Surprising German U-boat Visit to Newport, RI, During WWI. New England Historical Society https://www.newenglandhistoricalsociety.com/the-surprising-german-u-boat-visit-to-newport-ri-during-wwi/

Titanic Body Recovery • Titanic Facts https://titanicfacts.net/titanic-body-recovery/

The Speeches of Anna Howard Shaw, Ph.D. dissertation. University of Wisconsin, 1960, pp. 258-292 Woman's Journal. 1916. Schlesinger Library, Radcliffe Institute, Harvard University, Cambridge, Mass. http://nrs.harvard.edu/urn-3:RAD.SCHL:26209381

Tschirch, John. *Mapping the Newport Experience: A History of the City's Urban Development.* Newport Historical Society

Vitale, Tom. 'Armory Show' That Shocked America In 1913, Celebrates 100. February 17, 2013
https://www.npr.org/2013/02/17/172002686/armory-show-that-shocked-america-in-1913-celebrates-100

Weeks, Linton. "American Women who were Anti-Suffragettes."
https://www.npr.org/sections/npr-history-dept/2015/10/22/450221328/american-women-who-were-anti-suffragettes.

About the Author

Donna Russo Morin is the internationally bestselling author of eight multi-award-winning historical novels including *GILDED SUMMERS,* a Novel of Newport's Gilded Age, inspired by the city on the sea in her home state of Rhode Island.

Her other award-winning works include *PORTRAIT OF A CONSPIRACY: Da Vinci's Disciples Book One* (a finalist in *Foreword Reviews BEST BOOK OF THE YEAR,* hailed by Barnes and Noble as one of '*5 novels that get Leonardo da Vinci Right*'), and *THE COMPETITION: Da Vinci's Disciples Book Two* (EDITOR'S CHOICE, Historical Novel Society Review), and *THE FLAMES OF FLORENCE,* releasing as #1 in European History on Amazon.

Her other titles include *The King's Agent,* recipient of a starred review in *Publishers Weekly, The Courtier of Versailles* (originally released as *The Courtier's Secret*), *The Secret of the Glass,* and *To Serve a King.* She has also authored, *BIRTH: Once, Upon a Time Book Once,* a medieval fantasy and the first in a trilogy.

A twenty-five-year professional editor/story consultant, her work spans more than forty manuscripts. She holds two degrees from the University of Rhode Island and a Certificate of Completion from the National Writer's School. Donna teaches writing courses at her state's most prestigious adult learning center, online for Writer's Digest University, and has presented at national and academic conferences for more than twenty years. Her appearances include multiple HNS conferences, Writer's Digest Annual Conference, RT Booklovers Convention, the Ireland Writers Tour, and many more.

In addition to her writing, Donna has worked as a model and an actor with appearances in Showtime's *Brotherhood* and Martin Scorsese's *The Departed.*

Donna's creativity is currently undergoing a renaissance of sorts and she has discovered a passion – and talent – for painting. She is creating her first ten-piece collection, *Come with Me to the Trees*, which will be on exhibit starting June of 2020.

Her sons – Devon, an opera singer; and Dylan, a chef – are still, and always will be, her greatest works.

www.donnarussomorin.com

CPSIA information can be obtained
at www.ICGtesting.com
Printed in the USA
BVHW031309170921
616999BV00007B/37